THE MIND

BOOK TWO OF THE
DESCENDANTS OF EARTH

BY TARA JADE BROWN

BROWN DOVE
PUBLISHING

The Mind
Copyright © 2020 Tara Jade Brown
All rights reserved

Tara Jade Brown asserts the moral rights to be identified as the author of the work.

*All characters and events in this publication, other than those
clearly in the public domain, are fictitious, and any resemblance
to real persons, living or dead, is purely coincidental.*

No part of this publication may be reproduced, stored in a retrieval system,
or transmitted, in any form or by any means, without the prior permission in
writing by the author, nor be otherwise circulated in any form of binding or
cover other than that in which it is published and without a similar condition
including this condition being imposed on the subsequent purchaser.

ISBN: 978-3-9524946-3-9

Editors: Lisa Gilliam and Victory Editing
Cover designer: Deranged Doctor Design
Print formatting: Streetlight Graphics

BROWN DOVE
PUBLISHING

www.browndovepublishing.com

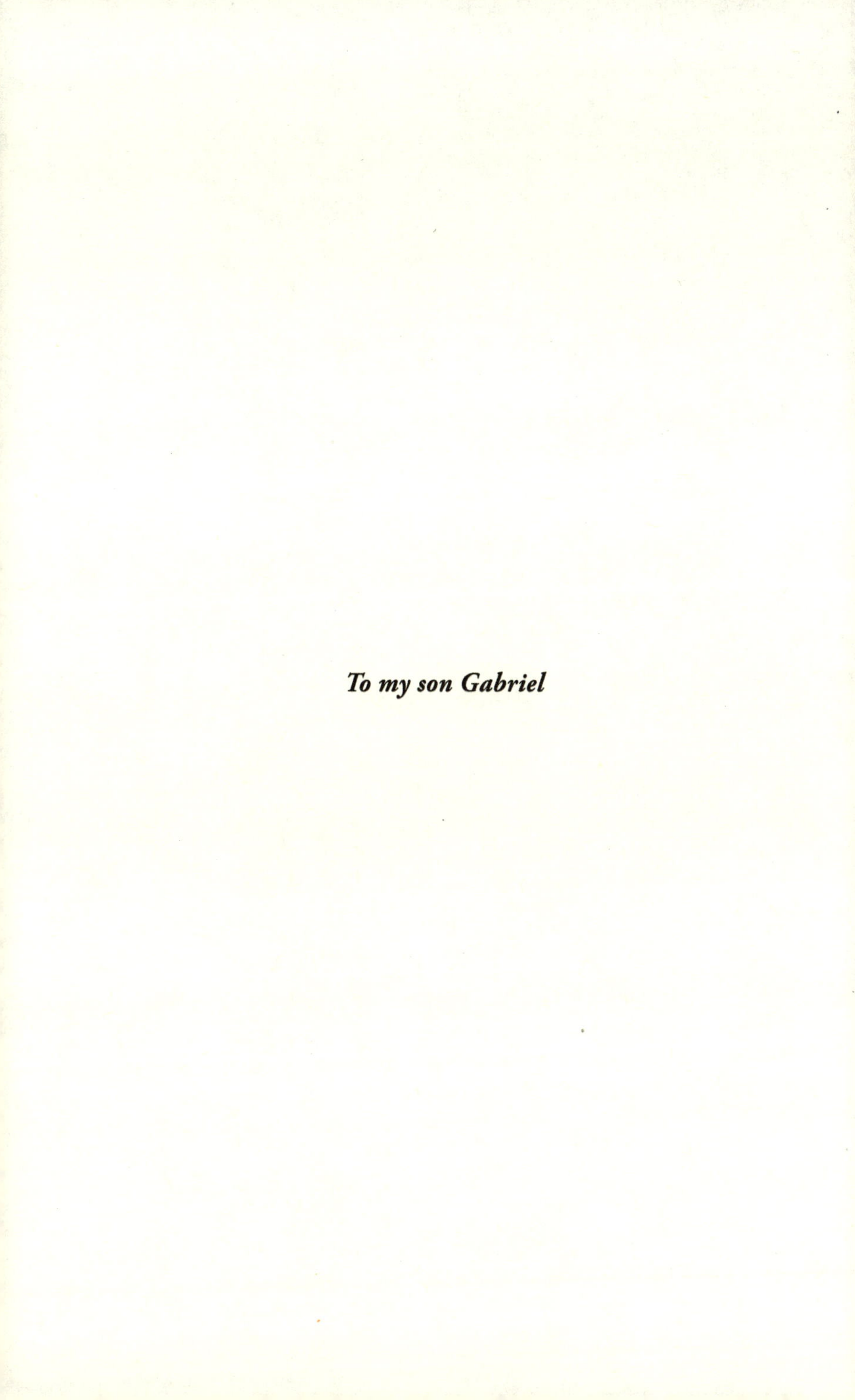

To my son Gabriel

A NOTE FROM THE AUTHOR

The Mind is the second book in the Descendants of Earth series, and it is tightly linked to the first book *The Senthien*.

If you haven't read the first book yet, I would strongly encourage you to read it before you dive into *The Mind*. Although you might enjoy *The Mind* on its own, you will have a greater entertainment experience if you are familiar with the story.

Enjoy!

CHAPTER 1

Earth

There is no choice but this.

I close my eyes.

There is no choice—but this.

I sit cross-legged on the small grass-covered hill. Buried underneath me lies an ancient portation chamber. I know what I need to do. But it's hard, so hard to leave the only place where I didn't need to hide. The only place—I press my lips together to stop them from trembling—I felt free. The only place where I felt at home.

The place where I fell in love with a Human.

It never should have happened. With all the rules governing the regulated Uni worlds, a Descendant should have never come in such close contact with a Human. And even when they did, they never should have fallen in love.

But it did happen.

And I knew it would before I even ported here, because I saw J in more Visions than I can count.

I loved him before I even met him.

I look down at the dusty ground, a few sprouts of grass, and I wonder.

Perhaps I could still stay?

Perhaps I will get used to seeing J and Monica together?

But the image of J hugging Monica appears in my mind, and it breaks me as it did when I first saw it. It crumbles me in a powder so fine even a light breeze can blow it away—and I'm gone.

I try to swallow the lump in my throat, but I can't.

I can't even take another breath.

And I cry once again, though I promised myself I wouldn't. I cry, silently, as the pain clenches my throat shut and the aching pressure squeezes my chest, crippling my soul.

There is no need to fear if there's only one choice to be made.

And there is no other choice but this.

I glance at my E-band, my vision blurred by the tears, and swipe commands to create a hyperspace-resonance field. The final command flashes on my screen.

I clench my jaws tight and tap to execute.

The bright light of day shifts into a purple hue as if dusk has swept in. The sounds of the forest change, the songs of the birds fade, and the wind in the high branches distorts into a moaning howl.

The relentless force of the hyperspace field starts to annihilate my reality, and as I gaze, at the place I decided to leave, the sorrow wrapping my heart in its claws, I can still see him. I can still see J reaching out to me as he stretches his arms forward in a long jump, trying to catch me.

The next moment, I am pulled back—with enormous speed and slow motion at the same time—seeing everything through a tiny hole, hearing his cry while he calls my name.

But I know it's all in my mind: my vanity wishing for the

impossible, wishing for J to have chosen me, to have picked me instead of going back to the old life he longed for.

Would I wish I never had this chance?

To love, to lust, to crave, to need—like I did here on Earth?

The answer comes before my question is done.

No. Never.

It was worth it.

Despite this pain that rips me open, despite a deep wound that will never heal, it was worth it.

And just before the port takes me, I manage to smile.

It was all *worth it.*

CHAPTER 2

Earth. Two days before.

Monica is leaning against the doorframe, her red curls trapped between her shoulder and the dark brown wood. She's gazing at a group of several women sitting in the cottage, some on large pillows, some on chairs, a few on beds. Two of them are talking to each other in soft, hushed voices, but the rest of them are quiet and focused.

Focused on something Monica always wanted but could never have. *Until now,* she thinks and smiles to herself. *Until now.*

All the women cradle their newborns, some of them only a few weeks old.

A scene like this would make her sad, maybe even cry, a few weeks ago. But now? It doesn't. Because this—this means something. Something special. And she will be a part of it too, very soon.

"Hey!" says J.

Monica turns around. "Hello, darling." She leans in for a kiss, but J shifts his face just slightly and the kiss lands on his cheek.

J looks down, leans on the other side of the door with his hands in his pockets, and peeks inside.

Monica glances at him for a moment, puzzled, confusion wrinkling the corners of her eyes, but then the next moment, she turns to look at the women again.

"Why are you doing this to yourself?" J asks quietly.

She presses her lips together, and her eyes fill with tears.

"Ah, Mon." J sighs and moves toward her and hugs her with one arm. "Let's go."

She shakes her head. "No. No, Jonathan," she whispers, not wanting to disturb the women. "Don't you see?" She wipes a tear from her face. "This is it."

"This is *what*?"

"That's what I need!" She is trying hard to keep her voice low, but it's difficult. She is too excited. "I mean, look at all those women. They all got pregnant!" She shakes her head in wonder. "There must be something here. Something magical to… to… enable them all to get pregnant. It must be *this*."

Monica turns away from the door and steps toward the fence, pointing toward the tree village and the forest. "This! The natural way of life. Good air, natural food, walking around instead of being driven around. No stress! No angry clients!

"No wonder we've had problems before. But now"—she smiles at him—"now things will work out, Jonathan. You will see."

J looks down at his feet.

Monica huffs and rolls her eyes. "What? I know that face."

"It…" He sighs again. "It might not be as easy as you think."

Her shoulders sag and she tilts her head sideways, still looking at J. "Why do you have to be such a killjoy? The birthrate here is incredibly high. *This* means something!"

J locks his breath for a moment.

"What?" Her voice is sharp now.

"The women there"—he nods to the cottage—"are all Jumpers."

Monica pauses for a second, then shakes her head. "So?"

"They were all pregnant when they teleported here, Monica. They didn't get pregnant on Earth."

Monica looks back at the cottage, narrowing her eyes.

"I am sorry," he says. "I really—"

"So what does that mean?" She shakes her head. "I need to port to get pregnant? I don't get it. Where is the trick?"

"There's no trick, Mon. They were already pregnant when they got here."

"So what, all the women who ported here were pregnant?"

J closes his eyes.

Dora…

"No. Not all women." And his thoughts drift away: Dora's long, dark gray hair, the green-within-green eyes, and the dark eyelashes framing them like a dazzling painting… the red lips and the way she bites them when she's unsure… the gentle, slim figure and the way she always straightens up whenever she brings out her Senthien. And the smile, broad and beautiful, that reshaped her face into joy itself.

"Jonathan?"

"I-I'm sorry. I was…"

"Yes, I can tell, somewhere else. So, what about her?"

"Who…?" J looks at her, startled.

"That woman, curly black hair? Her baby must be at least six months old."

J exhales. "That's Carmen. She was in her last trimester when she arrived." J sighs heavily, shaking his head. "We almost lost her. The only reason they both survived was because of—"

"And what about the others?"

"The others were very early. Most of them didn't even know."

"Didn't know what?"

"That they were expecting. They were too early into their pregnancies when they got here." J nods toward the cottage. "That's why the majority of the babies are being born now. And many of them—"

"Hold on! None of them knew they were pregnant?" She huffs a laugh. "Is there another way of *becoming* pregnant? Because I would certainly think they would remember the *event* that got them pregnant."

"Yes…" J rubs the base of his nose. "I think they—"

"J!"

J turns around to see Tania walking quickly toward him.

"Have you seen Dora?" Tania asks while catching her breath.

"No. Isn't she back yet?"

Tania shakes her head without saying anything, her face tense.

J's heartbeat speeds up a notch. He looks up at the sky, estimating the time of day. "Still a few more hours of daytime. She should be back within an hour or two. Latest."

Tania nods, distractedly rubbing her thin necklace pendant. "Oh, I feel like I've just gotten another child to worry about."

"She's a bit too old to be your child," J says, grinning.

"I know. I know. I just… worry about her. Everything is so new to her." Tania lets go of the pendant and tries to smile. "I wish we had a tracker like I did before cryo. I always knew where my kids were at any given time. Now look at me!"

"She'll be back within an hour. You'll see." J looks to the skies again, his frown returning. *She has to.*

"Yes… yes… She must have lost track of time… that's all," she says, her eyes unfocused on the floor for an instant. Then she looks at J. "Why don't you come for dinner at our place?" She glances at Monica. "Both of you, of course."

"Thanks, Tania, that would be nice," J says.

"Jonathan, darling, I don't think we can. Sandra invited us for dinner, remember?"

"I thought she invited *you*."

"Well, I… I assumed you would be joining me."

There is a stretch of uncomfortable silence, then Tania says, "Well, see what's best for you. Our doors are always open." She nods once and leaves.

"Darling, we *always* have dinner together."

J sighs, unsure whether to state the obvious.

"Whom was Tania talking about?" Monica asks. "Who is missing?"

For a moment the name is stuck in his throat. "Dora. She was talking about Dora."

"Who is Dora?"

"She's… she's the person who brought you back. She enabled de-cryo for the rest of the batches."

"Oh! I need to remember to thank her. If you see her before I do, please give her my thanks. It's great she got us all back. I never realized how many people went in the cryo. I wonder why it didn't work in the first place?"

"Yes, I will thank her. When she gets back."

"So, shall we go to Sandra's? She said early evening."

"Yeah, listen, um… Let me join you in half an hour. I need to do something before, okay?"

"Of course, darling!" And she smiles sweetly, the way she used to.

Normally, J would smile too. And he would also give her a kiss.

But not today.

He presses his lips together, then nods. "I'll see you later." And he turns around and leaves.

Monica's smile falters, worry bringing her eyebrows together in a frown. But then she shakes her head, dismissing the disturbing thought, and heads to Sandra's.

CHAPTER 3

Earth

J sits on the edge of the wooden chair in Dora's cottage, elbows propped on his knees, fingers threaded in his messy hair.

He's looking at the floor, wooden planks lined up next to each other. In between them, however, there are tiny cracks, gaps between planks, and he can see the ground underneath several feet below.

He runs his fingers through his hair, stands up, and walks to the window.

The sun has just set behind the horizon, but the sky is still bright, contrasting dark silhouettes of the treetops.

"Where *is* she?" he whispers to himself.

She should be back by now.

Then he hears footsteps on the bridge leading to the cottage. *Finally!*

He rushes to the door and opens the leaf curtain at the same time as Tania.

They look at each other, and for a moment no one speaks. Then J shakes his head to an unspoken question and steps away to let Tania through.

Tania looks around the room. The cupboard is half-open.

Dora's beige dress is neatly folded on her bed, the leather shoes at the base, one of which is flipped onto its side. On the table there is a clay bowl with a few spiky balls of lychee and dried figs.

She glances back at J looking out the window, his gaze intense, his body as still as a statue. His fingers are pressed hard onto his lips, laced together as if in prayer.

"J?" she says softly. "Dinner is ready."

"I need to stay here. She'll… She'll come back. She'll come home."

"J, did you eat anything today?"

J looks to the side, temporarily distracted, then focuses back on the window. "No, I was…"

"Busy?"

J sighs. "Yeah. You're right. I *am* actually hungry. I should join Monica at Sandra's though."

"Peter would like to see you."

J looks at her, then nods. "Perhaps that's better. I don't think I'm up for a chitchat right now."

Tania heads through the door, and J follows, but just before he steps through, he glances at the folded dress, then stops. The way Dora folded it, so impeccably, twists his stomach in knots.

"J, are you coming?"

J blocks his thoughts and steps outside.

The air is fresh. The first stars dot the evening sky. The sound of thousands of crickets spreads through the forest.

Before they reach the cottage, they can hear bantering and laughter coming from within. Tania swings the leaf curtain aside and they enter.

The table is full. Peter is already serving a second round for Lemony, Rick, and Melissa.

"Guys, there won't be anything left for your mom if you

continue like this!" jokes Patrick and winks at Tania as she sits at the table. Then he glances at the curtain closing behind J and frowns. "Where's Dora?"

"She didn't come back yet," says Tania.

Peter arches an eyebrow. "She's a wee bit late, aye?"

"A wee bit, yeah." J sits next to Tania.

"She must have done quite a hike," mumbles Rick, his mouth still full.

"Can you share your opinion *after* the food has left the playing field?" asks Tania.

"Sorry, Mom." Rick swallows, then continues. "She'll be hungry when she comes back!"

"Mom, is there more?" asks Melissa.

"Yes, I've put a portion aside for Dora."

Melissa gives her a thumbs-up and starts on her second serving.

"Where did Dora go?" asks Lemony, pushing her plate away.

"I'm not entirely sure," says Tania. "I think she wanted to collect some plant samples."

"Why?"

Tania glances at J and shrugs. "I… don't know."

"What if she gets lost? What if she can't come back?" Lemony reaches for her mother.

Tania smiles and pulls her daughter into a hug. "It's sweet you are worrying about her, but she'll be fine. She's got her E-band; she knows her way back."

"Could it be she went too far into the forest?" asks Melissa.

"Possible, I guess," answers Patrick. "If she went too far from the village, she might need to overnight outdoors. She'll be back in the morning."

"But it's too cold outside," Lemony says, her lips pulling down in a frown. "She'll get sick."

"She's got her skin suit, Lem. It will keep her warm. Don't worry." Rick gives Lemony an encouraging smile.

For a while no one talks, the only sounds are kitchen utensils scraping on the plates.

"Will Dora have to live with J and Monica now?" asks Lemony, looking at her mother.

J's spoon stops midway.

Time freezes in a silent breath as all eyes set on J.

For a long moment no one is moving. Then Tania gets up. "All right, guys, it's past your bedtime."

Rick frowns. "No, it's only—"

"Yes, it is. Let's go. Say good night to everyone."

Melissa gets up first, picking up her empty plate, Lemony and Rick a second after.

"Good night!"

Just before disappearing behind a door, Lemony turns to look at J. "I hope she comes back today still. It's not very nice to be all alone, on your own…" Then she leaves, following her siblings to a neighboring cottage.

A pressing silence covers the room like a heavy blanket, stretching uncomfortably from one person to another.

J's eyes are focused on an invisible dot on the table, right next to his bowl, his jaw muscles tight.

"Lemony is right," he says quietly.

"Lemony is just a child, J. She—"

"Yes. But she is right." He looks at Tania. "I don't think Dora wants to come back here."

"What are you saying, mate? There is nowhere else to go," says Patrick.

"Yes, there is." J looks up at them. "I think she wants to teleport back."

"Naw, she wouldna' do that!" says Peter.

"She barely escaped from there," adds Tania, then looks at Patrick. "Patrick, tell him!"

But Patrick is silent, his eyes on J. "I think J is right."

J stands up.

"And where are ye off to?"

"I need to stop her."

"Now?"

"Now. If she's not walking through the night, then I might catch up with her before she reaches the spot."

Patrick stands up as well. "I'll go with you."

"Thanks," J says and heads toward the door.

"J?"

J stops at the doorframe and looks back at Tania. "Yes?"

"What will you say to Monica?"

He sighs, his gaze at the floor.

"Search and rescue?" offers Patrick.

J glances at Patrick, then nods. "Yes. Search and rescue."

But Tania keeps her gaze on J. He knows what she's thinking, because he's thinking the same thing. *Monica needs to know.*

But not now. There's no time to explain.

He nods one more time, more for himself, then leaves.

CHAPTER 4

Earth

J lifts up his hand, ready to knock on the side of Tony's door, but then stops when he hears the laughter inside. He can't make out what Tony is saying, but it must be very funny since both Monica and Sandra laugh out loud.

He knocks, then moves the curtain away and steps inside.

"Did you hear me answer?" Tony turns, and both women burst into laughter once again. They are all sitting on the floor, drawings and blueprints scattered between them.

"Sorry. I thought it was okay." J takes a small step backward.

"Nah, just kidding you, buddy. Come in! Come in!"

"Where were you?" says Monica. "We already ate…"

"That's fine, I was—" He points his thumb backward, but then drops it. "Listen, do you have a minute? I need to talk to you."

Monica shakes her head disbelievingly as she stands up. "What kind of question is that? When would I not have time for you, Jonathan? Sometimes you behave like a total stranger!"

"Yep, that's what nine years does to you." Tony nods, looking down at the drawings.

Monica turns and stares back at Tony.

Realizing she didn't leave, Tony looks up. "You know that we've been alive for the past nine years, right?"

"Yes. I know it's been a few years."

"Tony," says Sandra, "why don't you give them some space?"

"Am I standing between them?" Tony shakes his head and looks down at the drawings again.

"Come," says J and nods toward the door.

The last streaks of daylight are gone, and the black night sky is sprinkled with stars, with no cloud in sight.

J leans on the fence, his arms rigid on the rope, his head bowed, eyes on the ground. Monica steps next to J, her body touching his arm.

"What is it? You look… uptight," she says, then strokes his hair.

For a moment J is silent.

"Jonathan, what is it?"

"There is a person missing. We think she went back to the teleportation location."

"Okay. So?"

J's hands still clutch the rope, as if he'd fall if he didn't hold on. "I need to fetch her. She can't port."

Monica's eyes narrow slightly. "Okay… why not?"

J sighs and runs his fingers through his hair. "Mon, it's Dora."

She shrugs. "Should I know—?"

"She's the person who brought you back." His voice is a bit harsher than he planned.

"Ah, yes. The Senthien." Monica nods. "Sorry! Too many names. But why shouldn't she teleport back? She's one of the Descendants, isn't she?"

"Yes?"

She tilts her head, a gentle look on her face. "Jonathan,

darling, she is going back home; she doesn't belong here. Why is that so surprising?"

J looks at her, unblinking, while she keeps smiling at him. Monica reaches to stroke his face, but he steps away.

"No." J's word seems final.

"I… I don't understand."

"Uni is not her home. This is." Then he takes her shoulders and leans in so that every word he's about to say strikes home. "Dora is half Human. And if she goes back, she will probably be killed."

Monica shrugs out of his arms. "Jeez, you have a dramatic way of explaining it. Fine. Fine. Go." And she heads for the door.

"I'll see you in a few days," J says.

Monica turns around. "You are leaving *now*?"

"Yes."

"In the middle of the night?"

"It's early evening, not the middle of the night. And this is good. If we leave now, we can still catch her before she jumps."

Monica sighs, then looks at him. "You're right. I'm sorry I'm being difficult. I would just like you to stay here, with me. I don't want you to leave.

"But I understand. I understand you need to go. If you really think her life is in danger if she does teleport, then by all means, you need to stop her." Monica pauses. "She saved my life. That's the least you can do for her."

Then she stands on her toes and kisses J's lips. "Can I do anything? Can I help in any way?"

J smiles, the tense lines on his face smoothing out. "Thanks, Mon. I think we're good." Then he turns around and leaves, his heavy steps shaking the bridge.

Monica hugs herself, sighing.

"Hey, you okay?"

Monica turns to see Sandra coming out of the cottage.

"The usual couple's struggle?"

"Struggle?" Monica deliberately relaxes her face and smiles broadly. "No, no, not at all. Jonathan is just helping out. As usual. That's just him."

Monica looks back in the direction J left, and her face clouds in doubts that make her stomach tighten. She doesn't understand it, and she certainly doesn't like it.

Then she plasters a confident smile on her face and turns back to Sandra. "So, tell me more about the ground expansion. Living twenty feet off the ground really gets to me! I'm really not a penthouse fan." She chuckles and hugs Sandra with one arm as she walks back into the cottage.

CHAPTER 5

Earth

"You know you're crazy for doing this," says Patrick, as he scoops up some biltong and pushes it in a leather bag, then ties the laces closed.

"Yes. I know. And you are crazy for joining me." J, crouching next to Patrick, pushes the rolled-up sleeping bag into a backpack.

"It's not going to be easy walking in the forest at night with just a torch."

"I've walked this path a thousand times. I could probably do it in complete darkness too." J takes a sip from his flask, then seals it and puts it in the side of the backpack.

"Oh, don't be so humble," says Patrick with a grin. "It's contagious." He swings a bag onto his shoulder, then grabs two torches and hands one to J. "Here! I also have two extra batteries, just in case."

J takes it and turns it on, the beam shining straight into Patrick's eyes.

Patrick shields his eyes with his arm. "Argh, it burns!"

J laughs. "Glad one of us didn't lose his sense of humor." And he changes the angle so the cone beam is now shining on the floor, making a large circle on the wooden planks.

J looks at it transfixed for a moment.

"What is it?" asks Patrick.

"I never thought we'd get access to torches again." His eyes are on the floor, but his gaze is far, far away.

Patrick nods. "Yes. You're right. A lot has changed since she came here."

J sighs deeply, then nods, picking up his backpack. "Let's go!"

Patrick looks back one more time, scanning the room to make sure nothing was left behind, then leaves as well.

The night is bright with moonlight, its white streaks passing through the dense crowns of the trees, leaving black-and-white patterns on the ground. The forest is quiet, but every now and then there is a sound: an eerie call of a bush baby or a nightjar, or soft footprints of a pangolin, or a polecat somewhere in the undergrowth.

J and Patrick walk one behind the other, their feet rustling the fallen leaves and dry twigs on the ground.

J turns his torch off.

"Good call," Patrick says, realizing the light of the moon is sufficient.

They walk a few more minutes in silence and then Patrick asks, "J, what happened?"

"What do you mean?"

"What happened with Dora? You're the one who saw her last before she left. What did she say?"

J pauses for a moment, then says, "She said she needed to get some samples. Vegetation samples. And she took some food with her. But only a little bit.

"I told her that her supplies will last only for a day. And… And she said she needs food only for one day." He shakes his head and breathes out. "I… believed her. I thought it was important for her to do this outing, and I thought that… that she would be back.

"I should have seen it right then. It was written all over her face. But I was… egoistic. I didn't see her." He stops and turns to Patrick, looking intently into his eyes. "I didn't *see* her. You understand? I should have heard—really heard—what she was saying." He sighs heavily then shakes his head. "But I didn't."

Patrick waits for J to continue, but when he doesn't, Patrick asks, "If she told you she wanted to port, if she didn't keep it a secret, what would you have said?"

"I'd tell her not to go. Of course."

"Why?"

"She can't go back to the Descendants. They'll… Well, I don't know what they'll do, but I know she ran away from there to save her life."

"Hmm." Patrick starts walking again, his dreads swinging side to side.

"What do you mean, hmm?"

"So, let's say that she told you she wanted to port, and you told her not to go, and she listened to you. Then what?"

"What do you mean then what? Then she is here, safe, on Earth."

"And you are here with Monica, a wonderful view for her to see."

J stops and closes his eyes for a moment. "Look, Patrick! I need time to figure things out, okay? Nothing is clear for me right now. I just… I just need time, all right?" Then he turns around and continues walking.

Patrick follows.

He doesn't say anything. He doesn't ask anything. He just waits.

He knows J well enough by now to know he'll talk again.

J shakes his head, answering an unspoken question in his head. "I remember how I felt when I woke up from cryo. I was desperate. I was crazy. I missed Monica so much. I-I wanted to kill myself."

Patrick nods. "Well, I think everyone in the first batch thought about that at some point in time."

"What I'm saying is that I *know* how Monica feels. I can feel it with her. I know what she's going through. And I just can't *leave* her. Not now. Not yet!"

"And you thought Dora would wait until you change your mind? Or *if* you change your mind?"

"Hey!" J stops in his tracks. "I thought you were on my side!"

Patrick looks at J seriously, his expression somber under the white moonlight. "J, I *am* on your side. That's why I'm telling you all this. That's why I am coming with you to get Dora. But when we reach her, you need to have your decision. And right now I'm trying to push you to make the right one."

"Patrick, you're only saying this because you don't know Monica, you only know Dora. You can't make an objective decision."

Patrick nods and starts walking again. "That might be true, but see, I have been watching you—no, we have *all* been watching you—for the past nine years."

"Who's we?"

"We. Tania, Peter, Simon, Noah—everyone! And we've noticed an enormous change in you since Dora came. And I mean, right from the beginning, J. It was so obvious you could see it with a blindfold on."

J doesn't respond.

"And then this morning, she leaves. And you turn into a mess. I've never seen you this"—Patrick scans him from head to toe—"miserable. And the moment you decided to go and get her back, life sparks back into you and you are full of energy. J, don't you see it?"

"Why don't you leave my life to me, all right? You don't know Monica. She is a wonderful, caring person. And she had my back when I needed it most."

"I'm sure she's caring. I'm sure she's wonderful too. But who gets your heart racing? That's what you should be thinking about now."

"Patrick, stop it! Now! Or otherwise, I'm continuing on my own."

Patrick sighs, lifts his hands and speeds up, not saying anything more.

J moves the burning coals and ashes around a small firepit with a milkwood branch, half drawing, half doodling random patterns in the ground to pass the time. They had been walking for many hours and decided to make a stop and get an hour of rest each before continuing on.

Patrick sleeps with his back toward the fire. His heavy breathing suddenly stops, and J turns to him, wondering if he has woken up. But then the snoring continues, so J turns back to the flames again.

He remembers the bonfire where he first saw Dora.

A few days before, a teleportation tube had been seen and

a group was assembled to fetch the new Jumpers, but J wasn't interested in joining. Not that time. He decided to help Jake and Noah on the north side of the village, pruning the fruit trees and vines, prepping them for the growing season.

And then evening came and he was on his way to the bonfire. They were always nice; a time for everyone to gather, a time for Old Mike to talk about the past, and sometimes the future if he felt inspired; a time to feel connected and remember they were a group and that they had survived. Survived and became something wonderful. Something stronger. Something better.

And after Mike's talk, there was always a long night of conversation, laughter, and sometimes dancing.

He saw Mike on the other side of the bonfire and headed toward the group.

But then, for no particular reason he can think of, he looked to the side at the group of people on his left and saw the most stunning green eyes in a delicate snow-white beautiful face, framed by thick, ash-gray hair falling down her shoulders all the way to her waist.

Wow...

J smiles to himself now. He remembers thinking exactly that: *Wow.*

The way she held herself, like a ballet dancer, so delicate and graceful one could almost mistake it for arrogance. But it wasn't. There was a soft, almost unnoticeable expression of kindness and empathy hidden in the corners of her lips, in the shade of her eyes.

She was breathtakingly arousing in her modest, completely unassuming way, with the supple softness of her feminine curves, sensuous lips, and long eyelashes shadowing her green-within-green eyes.

He asked Christoph who she was the moment he sat down.

"A new Jumper," he said.

"Well, what's her name?"

"How should I know?" Christoph shrugged, then turned away to continue his conversation.

And J?

J stared at the new Jumper, finding it impossible to resist.

He needed to talk to her—clearly—he needed to find out who she was, where she was from, what her name was, because… for the first time in so many years, there was *something*.

A quickening of his pulse, a tingling in the tips of his fingers, an extra sensitivity of his skin as the warmth of the fire on his bare chest suddenly became blazing hot, the blood rushing to the top layers of his skin.

The last time he felt like this was eons ago. And it was there, right there, from the beginning, from the very start.

J sighs heavily, drops the stick into the fire, and covers his face with his hands.

Patrick is right.

What am I going to do?

Mon is his best friend, she always supported him, she was the person he envisioned spending his life with. And he never doubted that. Even when she didn't wake up with him nine years ago. He never thought there would be someone else.

Until he met Dora.

And his world was turned upside down.

"Where are you?" asks Patrick, now sitting cross-legged facing the fire, watching J.

J peeks over his fingers. "With Dora."

Patrick nods and looks into the fire. "I thought so."

J hides behind his hands again.

"Time for your turn, mate. I'll wake you up in an hour, and we can continue."

But J pushes himself off the log and shakes his head. "No. I want to go now."

"J, you haven't slept at all. You can't go on through the night without a rest."

"You know, the more I think about it, the clearer everything gets. I need to stop her. She can't leave." He slides his foot through the sand, pushing it over the remains of the fire.

Patrick looks at him for a moment, then nods. "I understand." He gets up and stretches, then bends to pick up his backpack.

As soon as the fire dies, the darkness falls heavy on them, the moon hidden behind the horizon now.

Patrick takes out the torch from his backpack and turns it on. A circle of bright green undergrowth lights up, contrasting the colorless shadows of the night.

"Let's catch up to her!" J says and steps forward.

CHAPTER 6

Earth

Daylight starts breaking, a thin pale blue line appearing on the horizon under the dark blue sky. J is walking ahead of Patrick, his pace slow, his mind cloudy, the sleepless night slowly taking its toll on him. He's holding on to branches, moving them away, constantly being tortured by a buzz in his ear. He shakes his head trying to clear his mind. For an instant it works, but a few seconds later the buzzing returns.

He frowns and rubs his ears.

"Are you okay?"

"No, not really." J glances back at Patrick, shaking his head slightly.

Patrick frowns, looking at the dark circles under J's eyes. "You should have had a power nap earlier. You look like shit."

"Awesome, Patrick. Thanks. Just what I wanted to hear before I see Dora again."

After a few more minutes of walking, Patrick says, "Hold on a second. I have an idea."

J stops and turns around, making the whole forest spin. He reaches for a tree to stabilize himself. "A few thousand years ago, I could stay awake through the night with no problem. And work the next day! Look at me now." He blinks a few times and looks at the ground.

"Why don't you sit for a minute," Patrick says and crouches down. He takes a small leather bag from his backpack and digs in to grab something.

"Here!"

J reaches out, and Patrick drops a few hard grains in J's palm.

"Coffee beans?" Then he looks up at Patrick. "Where did you get coffee?"

"Noah found it while scavenging the Underground storage a few days ago. Most of it is in the ground now. It's the perfect time for seeding, or so he says, but he gave a sample, one bag, to Raf so he can roast it and we can look forward to what's coming. Now chew!"

J puts all the beans into his mouth at once, like an injured person swallowing pain medication dry, the beans crunching and cracking in his mouth.

J makes a face. "Ugh! It tastes better with cream."

Patrick laughs. "It's not meant to taste good. It's meant to wake you up."

"It was a good idea. Thanks!"

Patrick looks into his backpack again. "Shall we have something to eat quickly? I'm hungry."

J nods, still chewing on the dry beans. "Yes. I need to wash this taste away." Then he spits out the last bits still sticking to his tongue. "Argh!"

Patrick takes out a leather water bottle and a few slices of bread and dry meat wrapped in leaves.

As they eat, J looks east at the thin bright edge of the morning sky, the forest around them awakening with the first sounds of the birds. It is unusually special so early in the morning, and really beautiful.

I'm sure Dora noticed it. Perhaps she's listening to it right now?

Then he stops chewing and closes his eyes, fighting the emotions.

Why did she leave? Why didn't she give me more time?

"We'll find her, J."

Without opening his eyes, J nods, then swallows a half-chewed bite and says, "Yeah. Yeah, we will."

Only a few minutes later, both men stand up and stow the rest of the food in the backpacks, then continue, their pace fast again.

A few hours into the day, the air is unusually dry and warm. Several heavy drops of sweat trickle down between J's shoulder blades. He shifts his shirt, wiping them away. Then he drops his backpack, pulls the shirt off, and uses it to wipe his back.

With every step, his heart rate is a touch faster, his breathing ever so uneven.

Anticipation, joy, happiness burn inside his body. *I will see Dora again!*

But in the back of his mind, there is fear.

What will she say?

What will she do?

What will I do?

J clenches his fists and presses on.

The soil is getting darker, and the plants here are more compact, more stunted compared to the trees around the village. It means they are getting close.

I wonder if the teleportation affected the veget—

And then he hears a sound.

He stops. And listens.

"J? What's wrong?" Patrick stops behind him.

J lifts up an index finger and closes his eyes, focusing on the sound. Vague… deep… hollow sound of air distorting… as it shifts and moves for—

J opens his eyes. And then he starts to run.

Branches whip his body as he races through the thicket.

"J, wait!" He hears Patrick running behind him, but he's not stopping. He knows what the sound was.

As he runs, something catches his eye, a bright light.

He looks up.

Through the branches and the crowns of the trees, he can see a bright white pillar extending from the stratosphere to the unique spot on the earth's surface, a place where all the Jumpers land.

Oh no.

No!

J sprints, his muscles aching and burning as he pushes them to the limit, running toward the glowing column of white.

Next moment, the dense undergrowth opens up to a small clearing, and the glowing pillar touches the earth at the center of the glade.

And just there sits Dora. Her eyes are closed, her hands relaxed on her thighs as she kneels at the base of the teleportation tube.

"Dora!" he yells as he runs. "No!"

She is only ten meters away. Five.

He'll make it!

He stretches his arms and jumps forward.

Then Dora opens her eyes, and for the briefest of moments, their gazes meet.

But the next moment, she is gone, and the pillar retreats upward into the sky with enormous speed.

J's body slams flat on the ground, dust bursting around him.

He kneels hastily and reaches up with his hands. "Doraaaa!"

His voice echoes loudly over the treetops, but the sky is calm, clear, and blue, as if no porting pillar ever pierced it.

"No!" J clenches his fists, and bowing his whole chest forward, he slams them hard on the ground, pieces of earth and dust flying around the two dents like miniature explosions.

"No! No! No! No!" He keeps hitting the ground. His anger, his need, his love, all pour out, the physical outburst of a desperate man.

J hits the earth one more time and then collapses, his body bent forward, his forehead touching the ground, his arms dirty and flat against the dusty soil.

Silent and unmoving, he looks like the sculpture of a praying man.

Patrick stands behind him, silent, his gaze on the dirty ground at J's feet.

After a long while, J sits up and stares at the empty sky.

"Dora...," he begins, but his voice cracks and her name comes out only as a weak whisper, a question, for which the answer is already known. His head is slightly tilted, his arms resting dully on his side, as if his soul deserted the body, letting it hang lifelessly like a thin shirt on a metal hanger. Tears streak down his face, trails of sorrow, sliding down his cheeks, drawing clear lines on dust-covered skin.

Patrick sighs heavily, then slowly sits down next to J and puts an arm around his shoulders, without saying a word.

CHAPTER 7

Uni

THE AIR IS PULLED OUT OF MY LUNGS, MY ARMS HURT, MY LEGS HURT, MY HANDS ARE IN FISTS, PRESSING AGAINST THE PAIN. I LEAN MY HEAD BACK, TRYING TO RELEASE THE IMMENSE ACHE IN THE BACK OF MY SKULL.

AND SEE… PURPLE.

PURPLE EVERYWHERE.

EVEN WHEN MY EYES ARE CLOSED, I SEE IT. PURPLE AROUND ME, INSIDE ME, PRESSING INTO ME, TELLING ME…

TELLING ME WHAT?

I OPEN MY EYES DESPITE THE POUNDING PAIN.

I'M NOT ALONE.

THERE IS SOMETHING… NO—SOMEONE—WITH ME.

PURPLE.

THE PAIN INCREASES AND I CAN BARELY STAND IT.

WHO… ARE… YOU…?

I try to focus on the purple. Lines and lines of purple all around me. I keep turning around, but they are everywhere.

Where am I?

I don't understand.

Suddenly the pain is gone, vanished, as if it wasn't there at all to begin with. And then a warm breeze reaches me, hugging me in its embrace.

Who… are… you…? I try again.

The lines come close, and I realize these are not lines but rows and rows of purple slots aligned next to each other.

I need to touch them. I don't understand why, but I understand the need, the wish.

I reach out for the slot. I need to get it, but I'm too slow. No matter how hard I try, I can hardly move.

And then another need comes. Another craving.

Air.

I need to breathe.

But… I can't. Because I am not here, and this is not the air surrounding me.

It's Void.

I nevertheless try to fill my lungs with air.

I need air. I need to breathe!

My lungs are empty, and I can't seem to take another breath. I open my mouth so wide that it hurts, but I can't breathe.

Black dots appear on the inside of my closed eyelids and the world starts spinning.

Hypoxia, an automatic alert from my nanoprobes.

Yes, I know it's hypoxia. Just let me breathe!

And then, finally, my lungs open up and the air rushes in, making a long, high-pitched wheezing sound.

The inside of my chest burns, and I cry, tears streaming down my cheeks.

I take another wheezing breath, the pain radiating throughout my body.

I breathe and cry, breathe and cry.

I have no control over it.

With time, very slowly, the pain subsides. I roll onto my back, which triggers another sharp spike of pain in my lungs.

I am panting. My eyes are closed. My entire body feels broken.

After several minutes—or it might have been days—I try to open my eyes, but the bright light blinds me, and I close them again. I try to move my arms, my legs, but every movement hurts.

I try to swallow, but my dry throat doesn't let me, so I cough, and a crispy, dry air escapes my lungs.

With a lot of effort, I push myself up to a sitting position and look around, squinting.

White. Everywhere.

I know this... I have seen it... before.

But I can't think. Not yet.

I take another deep breath, and I feel I can hold it, the pain minuscule in comparison to before.

Not the Earth air. But still—air.

After another deep breath, I look around again.

I am only an IP away from the wall, and I slowly pull myself toward it so I can lean on it, my legs splayed on the floor as if I don't have any control over them.

And it dawns on me, the realization suddenly obvious.

Boolean Institute.

I close my eyes.

Not the best place to port.

But... better than Zlatharing.

I look down, turn my wrist slightly so that I can see my E-band.

The screen is blinking red: Portation time exceeded. Portation time exceeded.

I tap on it. The blinking disappears and then several numbers show up.

Most of them are my vital signs.

My heartbeat just lowered to one hundred and sixty-three. My blood pressure is still high. Nanoprobes are fully functional. Metabolism is on hold for another three passes. Temperature, one and a half degrees below average.

Under all the displays, at the very bottom of the screen, I see a number: the duration of the portation, but… I lift up my hand and look closer.

No. It can't possibly be.

Three?

Three passes?

No. It's impossible. No one has ever had such a long portation time.

All the ports, even those that span the opposite sides of Uni, last for no more than a few seconds. And most of them last only a few milliseconds.

But three passes?

I lean my head back and drop my arm to the floor.

I was out of body for three passes?

I close my eyes again.

Why did it take so long?

And then I remember the color… and the patterns… and the black-white shifts I could not understand.

What was that…? What did it mea—

The sound!

I open my eyes and look in that direction.

Voices, coming down the hall.

I take a deep, silent breath and bring myself to my feet. All my muscles hurt, my legs are shaking, and I am trying hard not to fall.

I'm leaning on the wall with one shoulder, limping along the hallway, away from the voices.

I keep glancing backward, hoping against all odds that I am faster. And then I shift sideways, into a recess.

I turn to look.

A door. Plain, white, with a small glass window at eye level. It's dark inside.

I try to push it open, but the door doesn't budge.

Of course not. They only open after a positive ID scan.

The voices are getting louder.

I glance down the hall again.

I can't see anyone yet, but they are closer. Two of them. Women.

I look down the other side of the corridor.

There are many doors, and all are scan protected. But I can't stay here, so I walk forward, dragging my feet, which seem to be made of Earth rock.

I'm hoping for a simple door. Or a side hallway I can escape into.

But there's nothing.

My feet feel heavy, and every step forward sends a thousand piercing needles through my muscles. I choke back my moan before it escapes.

I come to another door and press on it as well, but same as the previous one, it doesn't move.

The voices are close. I turn toward them and see a shadow on the opposite side of the wall as they make a turn.

I push hard on the door, trying to pry it open as my feet slip on the smooth, polished floor.

It is as impenetrable as all the others.

I turn around one more time and see them—the two women—wearing all white, their heads turned toward each other at an uncomfortable angle as they look straight into each other's eyes.

And I do the only thing I can think of.

I press my palm on the ID scanner, hoping for a miracle.

The door unlocks and swings open, and I fall flat on the floor.

The door silently closes again, as I scramble back toward it, pulling my legs up, hugging my knees so they can't see me if they look through the window.

I close my eyes, hold my breath, and wait.

Wait.

Wait.

After a while, I gather the courage to open my eyes again. The door hasn't budged. No one tried to get in. I slowly stand up and peek through the window. White, plain corridors and no person in sight.

I breathe a sigh of relief. For the first time ever, I am grateful for that eerie Boolean trait of looking sideways at each other. Had that not been the case, those TAs would have seen me for sure.

I place my palm on my chest, feeling my drumming heart. *That was close! I won't be able to rely on an ID system failure again, that is certain!*

I breathe out and look around.

Where am I?

The light is so dim that I can't see very far.

There is a faint light coming from a dozen long desks aligned parallel to each other. I hear buzzing, machines humming, metallic clanging, but all the sounds are inanimate. The room seems to be deserted.

Suddenly I hear a loud humming sound, and I press myself against the wall, my eyes wide open.

On the side of the desk in front of me, hovering on antigravitational tracks, appears an ellipsoid robot. It stops just a few IPs away.

Completely immobile and transfixed, I stare at the smooth, dark metal, its four mobile limbs with multiple joints in its protrusions making quick, jerky movements, manipulating something on the desk.

It's not turned toward me.

In fact, I don't think it's even aware that I am here.

And then, as fast as it came, it leaves, the faint humming sound disappearing along the tracks into the distance.

For an instant I stand still, too afraid to move. But my Senthien curiosity takes over, and I slowly walk toward the desk and bend down to look.

It's not really a desk, I realize, but a shallow laboratory bench, its workspace kept sterile under a glass cover, each side lit with a long LED tube. Inside I see many transparent boxes, tightly sealed, with a shallow layer of transparent pink liquid. Floating on top of the liquid are numerous thin gray leaflets, each smaller than the surface of one of my green nails.

What are these?

As I lean in to get a closer look, my breath makes a circle of condensation on the glass, and I can't see through.

I wipe the surface but then pull back my hand.

It's cold!

Minus twenty-two, an automatic response from my nanoprobes sounds in my ears.

I'm about to engage my optic nerve cam recording, but an increasing buzzing sound at the back of the room distracts me.

I look to my right.

More robots enter the hall and hover toward their work desks. One of them heads straight toward me. Fast. It keeps up its speed with no apparent intention to slow down.

I push away from the workbench, the robot just barely missing me as it swings past.

I'm staring at it as it abruptly stops a few IPs away and starts doing the quick movements on the workspace. The whole room is now filled with hectic robots.

I step farther toward the middle of the room, watchful I don't stand on any of the AG tracks, and glance at the other work areas.

In this section, a small conveyer belt keeps delivering small round samples. They are handled by metal pincers, then placed on a sharply inclined metal pedestal to which the sample is adhered. The pedestal tilts forward so it's right above the box with the pink liquid. Then it starts making quick minuscule movements, from side to side, repeating the action again and again.

I keep looking at it until I realize that the round sample stuck on the pedestal is getting slightly smaller with every movement. And then it becomes clear: the sample is being sliced into the transparent leaflets of tissue I saw before, floating in the pink liquid. I assume it's being done by a laser, but of course, I wouldn't be able to see it. All these thin leaflets fall on the pink surface of the liquid underneath and float aimlessly around.

Once twenty have been dropped, the transparent box is sealed and it moves farther along the distance of the lab table and a new box appears underneath the laser slicer and stops, ready to take the new samples.

I straighten up and continue walking, looking at the process on other workbenches.

Each has the same equipment doing exactly the same thing. And something about this whole setup makes me uncomfortable.

I don't know much about Boolean science. In fact, I probably know too little to make any kind of judgment, but…

I shiver involuntarily, my stomach crumpling up in a tiny ball. This just seems—*wrong*—somehow.

I close my eyes, trying to refocus. *I am not a Boolean. I am not educated or gen-modified for this work.*

I glance down again, watching another small sample being sliced.

This must be normal.

I swallow hard.

This is what Booleans do.

I breathe out loudly, then walk back toward the door I came through, avoiding the robots working at their stations.

Just… ignore it, Dora!

I stop at the door and glance through the small round window.

The only thing I need to worry about is how I will port out of this place. I don't even know where the portation chamber is. These hallways all look the same: every door identical to one another, all the hallways white and indistinguishable.

But perhaps if I find the library where I was the last time I visited Boolean Institute, I might be able to retrace my way back to the chamber. This seems like the best option.

I engage my tympanic audio enhancers, close my eyes, and listen.

I don't hear anything.

Then I look at the ID scanner again, take a deep breath, and press my palm on the cold surface.

The door silently unlocks and slides sideways.

I wait, completely focused on my TAE's input.

Nothing.

I take a deep breath and enter the bright hallway.

CHAPTER 8

Uni

I look left, then right. It all looks the same: white corridors stretching far in both directions. I have no idea where I should go.

I decide to turn left, my feet silent on the floor. I keep looking at the doors along the hall as I pass, their small round windows always dark.

I have no way of knowing how to reach the porting chamber. And even if I did, where would I go?

Senthia?

Senthia is not safe.

But where else? None of the Uni planets or moons are safe.

I slow down for a moment.

Maybe Fraya Spark, the sabbatical planet?

The accommodations there are barely controlled at all. I could hide there. I've done it before. That might work.

The only problem is the transport.

Porting onto Fraya is highly regulated. I'd need to take the place of someone else who is scheduled to go there, but I don't have the backup my parents had on Zema4.

I come to an intersection and slowly peek in both directions.

Brightly lit corridors exactly like the one I've been walking through for the past few passes.

It's like a maze. How do Booleans know where to go?

Unless—I engage the connection of my nanoprobes to the mainframe—*unless they follow a map.*

I give a silent command for the map search, then enter the Boolean Institute.

Ambitious, but it just might—

"Access denied."

My shoulders sag.

Yes, too ambitious.

I look once again, checking each corridor: long white hallways with an infinite number of unlabeled doors, all empty and deserted.

The few times I ported here before, I always found it strange: these long hallways with only me and the welcoming TA guiding me to the meeting room, with no one else in sight. Now, however, I welcome it. If it was any different, I wouldn't have been able to wander around as I'm doing now.

I turn right. Might as well. I'm about to take a step, but my ONC flashes a new notification.

"Access granted." The white path is now overlaid with green stripes, numbers and directions written on the side.

I hesitate.

I got access?

Why now and why not a moment ago?

I shake my head. What did J once say? *Beggars can't be choosers.* I smile despite myself. They do have funny little proverbs on Old Earth.

I initiate a search for the porting chamber, and the green stripe of the Direction Route Path heading forward lights up brighter. I pay attention to my TAEs once again, then after I'm sure I don't hear anyone, I head forward and follow the highlighted path. It takes several passes of meandering through the empty hallways until I make a turn in to a new hallway where the green path ends and a red dot pulsates on the floor next to a door.

This must be the porting chamber!

I jog toward it, already lifting my hand for a scan, but then I stop.

Through the small round window I see the brightly lit room inside.

My hand drops and I feel the anxious grip of fear.

Why did the DRP lead me here? This is not the porting chamber.

I need to get away. I need to escape!

I want to turn around, I want to continue searching, but the red dot slowly pulsing at the base of the door gives an audio signal as well.

I narrow my eyes. *That's unusual...*

I turn around and press my hand on the ID scanner, not really thinking it will work, but the door slides open. And I enter.

The room is filled with hundreds and hundreds of medical pods, all of them occupied. It's extremely cold, and my breath is making little clouds of condensation in front of my face.

I walk slowly toward the first pod.

It's covered with transparent synthetic material that makes a shield around the person inside.

I put my palm on the cover.

A Zema4 woman. She's dressed in a classic beige body suit, both her arms pierced with needles, the infusion tubes bringing liquid to her body.

She's lying there peacefully, not a fold or a wrinkle on her face, her breathing slow but steady.

I look up at the other pods. They all have Zema4 women inside.

Next to each pod is a display of several numbers. They are somewhat similar to the vital signs on E-bands, and they all seem regular. At the bottom is one number, more prominently displayed than all the others.

This display here shows fifty-six, cycle two.

It's a number of standard days.

I glance to the other pod. That one has forty-two, cycle one. The one behind her has sixty-eight, cycle three.

Sixty-eight days? Sixty-eight days of what? Or is it sixty-eight days until?

I can't tell. And nothing on the display gives me any clues.

I want to believe that they are here to recover, that they must be sick, because these are medical pods. *What else would they be here for?*

But I don't, because I am not at Anas. And this is not a medical center. I am in the institute where the Booleans perform experiments, and something in this room, something with these seemingly peaceful women, seems terribly wrong.

Right at that moment, an alarm signals in my peripheral view, and a DRP lights up bright green, leading back outside.

I need to leave!

I hurry toward the door but then turn around one more time, looking at the sea of med pods with hundreds of unconscious Zema4 women.

I clench my hands into fists, breathe out forcefully, and step outside.

Instantly my TAEs detect a rhythmic, heavy sound.

I pause. *What is that?*

I close my eyes and focus. *A group of people. Rubber soles, heavy weight. Running.*

I take a quick breath and turn in the opposite direction. The sound is getting louder, and I realize I know it from somewhere, I have heard it before, and it tells me—no, it's screaming at me—to run as fast as I can.

So I do. I run, full speed, ignoring all the pains I feel in my muscles, not caring if I'm making noise.

After two sharp turns, I finally reach the destination sign, but—it is in the middle of the hallway.

Moons of Senthia, this is not a porting chamber!

I stop at the pulsing red dot and look down, completely stunned.

No! No, it can't be!

I look back at the empty white corridor, hearing the steps approaching. *Oh no, they'll be here at any moment.*

I blink a few times, helplessly looking down.

I need a porting chamber!

Why didn't the DRP lead me to the porting chamber?

I look back, my eyes wide, my heart beating wildly in my chest, breaking out of my rib cage. Then all my strength leaves me at once and I kneel on the floor, feeling defeated.

I didn't want to go out. Not like this…

And my last thought… is of J.

CHAPTER 9

Earth

J has been sitting on his bed for the past hour, his head slightly bent, his gaze unfocused. The afternoon sunshine, golden bright on the wooden floor, fuses with the dancing shadows of the leaves, making intricate patterns shifting from light to dark and back again.

He has a small herbal bag in his hands. It's empty now, but it still holds the intense scent of comfrey. He brings it to his face and presses it to his nose, taking a long, deep breath.

He closes his eyes, pressing his jaw together tightly.

It's only been two days...

How am I ever going to handle a week?

A month?

A year?

He breathes out and drops his hand on his lap again, his life turning into a slow-motion, silent, black-and-white movie, making the passage of time even longer, even more desperate, even more futile.

"I simply can't believe this!" Monica walks in through the door, waving her arms. "I never—*ever*—had to share my bathroom!" She shakes her head. "You guys really need to improve things around here!"

Walking into the small kitchenette, she opens up a cupboard. "And this too. We don't have any bread." She slams the cupboard closed. "Why can't I have a nice iBoard on top of my cupboard—or a fridge, that would be even better—telling me, 'Monica, you are out of bread,' or 'You are out of butter,' or 'You are out of wine. Shall I put that on your shopping list?'"

She pulls the mane of her hair into a thick ponytail while walking to the table. "Yes, Mr. Cook, please put it on my shopping list, and please order the delivery for one thirty today, thank you.

"And this here." Monica collects her breakfast plate and puts it in a basket. "I mean, why can't I say 'Iris, collect the dishes and start the dishwasher, eco program'? Or, I don't know, something like 'Alexa, play Jason Knox'? Or 'Liberio, I want to continue reading my e-book. Please, open where I left off.'"

She huffs and sits on a wooden chair. "And these chairs! They are so hard. And even the beds. I mean, why isn't anything soft and comfortable in here?"

J is still sitting on his bed, staring at the floor, still touching the soft leather bag.

Comfrey. Simon used it when Dora was injured. But she probably didn't even need it. Her skin and muscles were sliced open, one-inch deep into the tissue. But then it all healed within two hours. It was incredible. She was—

"Jonathan! Are you even listening to me?"

He blinks once, then lifts his head. "I-I'm sorry, I was…" He takes a breath. "Distracted." He tries to smile. "What's bothering you?"

She smiles back. "If you weren't listening, how do you know something's bothering me?"

"You have this faint crease at the base of your nose. It means you've been frowning for a while."

"Ah..." She nods.

"So?"

"Ah, never mind. I'm just having a hard time coming to grips with this..." She waves her hand in the air.

"New world?"

"Lack of technology, really, more than anything else. I can't use e-Tracks, I have to walk everywhere. I mean, if I want to talk to Sandra, I need to *walk* to her. There's no FaceTime with Sandra or TouchIn with Tony. No! I actually need to go there! And if I want to meet a new friend, I can't! There are no CommonHangouts, or B2Fs either. I'm not able to meet people I have something in common with, for Christ's sake!"

J smiles weakly. "Well, it's healthier like this, more natural."

"Yeah, well, sure it's healthier, I mean"—she looks at J's chest muscles—"look at what this world did to you! You look like, I don't know, the latest Luc Aridierro CG model. I mean, wow, really. I wouldn't think you're real if I didn't see you in front of me."

J smiles. "Yeah, there are some bonuses that come with the new world."

Monica stands up and walks over to J, then sits next to him, putting an arm around his back. "I know. And I think your transformation is pretty astounding. Did you realize that you are now *my* age? And you look so much fitter than when I left you." Then she sighs. "But still... I miss our old lifestyle. Iris, Alexa, Gus? Gone! Neo. Voltan. Mr. Cook. I mean, I'm not even able to make a meal for us anymore. I can't drive anywhere anymore. Don't you miss that? At all?"

J looks at the herb bag, then he closes it in his fist and looks at her. "I did miss it. When I came out of cryo. But I missed you the most, and everything else that I might have missed faded in comparison."

Monica smiles at him softly and strokes his cheek. "Aww, that's so sweet of you to say. And I can only imagine. It must have been awful. Sandra told me about"—Monica looks down at the floor—"about the suicides."

J nods silently.

"Scary." Then she looks at him. "I'm so happy you were smart enough not to do something like that. I mean, I feel sorry for all who did, but"—she gets up and walks to the clothes cupboard—"it would have been an immature decision."

She opens up a cupboard and inspects the contents. "We need to get more clothing. I can't possibly have only four outfits, Jonathan. And the design! Oh!"

She turns to him. "Who makes them again? I need to talk to her. There needs to be some improvements. We can't continue walking around this world, wearing *this*." She shakes her body, pretending to shudder.

J takes a deep breath. "Mon, most of the women have only two outfits, not four. I asked for more because… because I know how much you like fashion."

She rolls her eyes. "This is not fashion, this is—" She shakes her head, searching for a word.

J stands up, putting the pouch into his pocket. "It's survival. And things are a lot better now than they were nine years ago."

She turns around, her shoulders sag, then she tilts her head to the side. "I'm sorry, darling. I know. It must have been terribly difficult. And this"—she turns halfway to the clothes cupboard—"is okay. For a start."

She smiles then. "I'm sure our designer just needs one or two inputs from her customers, and she'll make ravishing colorful outfits before you know it." She peeks into the cupboard again. "Instead of dyeing every piece of clothing beige. How boring!"

J scratches his stubble. "Well, first of all, our designer is a him, not a her. Second, we are not customers. We don't pay him anything. He makes clothes for us for free, just like I work in the fields, I hunt, I help build houses for free too. And third, the fabric is really difficult to make. Or at least it was up until now. We might get some automation, if there is something in the Underground, but no promises. And last, Mon. The clothes are not *dyed* beige. This is the linen's natural color."

"Oh… Okay… Well… Maybe there are some dyes in the Underground storage?"

He shrugs. "It's not something important for survival. But maybe things will become a bit different now that we have electricity and some of the old technology back." And his mind wanders to the person who made all this possible.

"Well, I certainly hope so. It will make our life *so much* better. Oh, maybe there is a stash of s-phones? Or s-watches, perhaps? Oh, that would be so good. We could upload all the necessary apps so we can—"

"Mon, sorry, I arranged to meet with Patrick, and I'm already late. I'll be back in a few hours."

"You're not running away from me, are you?" She lifts an eyebrow and smiles. "Say hi to Patrick, will you?"

"I will, thanks." J walks to the kitchenette and picks up a basket with dirty plates from this morning. "I'll take this down for washing as well."

Monica smiles. "No smart home to take care of that. But at least a smart man, right?" She winks at him.

"I'm afraid so. BravaCasa will have to wait a bit."

"Oh, I do miss her." She twirls on her heel and looks out the window.

"*She* was a computer."

Monica smiles mischievously, and in a high-pitched voice, she says, "*Have a nice day, Jonathan.*"

J laughs. "You sound just like her." Then he turns and heads for the door.

Just as he's about to exit, Monica says, "I'm sorry."

He turns around, frowning. "What for?"

"I realize I might seem a bit… spoiled."

He smiles sideways. "A bit."

"I just need to get used to… all this."

"I know, Mon. I know. And you will."

He turns to leave again.

"Jonathan?"

"Yes?"

"Aren't you going to kiss me?"

J swallows. Then he walks toward her slowly, his steps feeling strange and awkward.

He leans in and kisses her once, then pulls away, but Monica stops him. She slides her arms around his neck, pressing his body against her, and she kisses him, though this one is longer and deeper than before.

J doesn't resist.

It feels… familiar. He knows it. He knows it well. And it seems like he should want it too.

Yet—he doesn't.

Still, he tries to take it in, the warmth, the smell of her body, the shape he remembers, the feel of her tongue, the touch of her lips—

He pulls away. "I'm sorry. I really must go. I'll see you in the evening."

And he leaves without a backward glance.

CHAPTER 10

Earth

"Hey, J! Welcome to the party!" Patrick straightens up from a crouched position, then presses his hands on his waist and stretches backward even more, a few of his vertebrae cracking. "Oh boy, I'm not as young as I thought. I hate weeding!"

"Some party…" J wraps a flat bag with tools around his waist and bends down to start working.

"J?"

"Yeah?" J looks up at Patrick, but the sun blinds him, so he shields his eyes.

Patrick kneels next to him. "How are you?"

"I'm fine." J starts working.

"No, I mean, how *are* you?"

For a long time J doesn't respond, and Patrick doesn't push him. He waits.

"I am… I am lost, Patrick." He looks into Patrick's eyes. "I don't know how to feel. I remember how I was nine years ago," he continues. "I remember I was out of my mind with grief when I realized Monica wasn't here. And I remember I missed her, terribly, for such a long time. And now I have her back, but…

I can't… I can't bring my feelings back. I love her. I *do* love her and I always will. She is a part of my life, but…" He sighs deeply.

"But she is not the one." Patrick finishes his sentence. It's not a question.

J shakes his head slowly. "I don't know. I don't know. She was. I thought she was, for so long… But now I have this"—J presses his fingers into his chest—"emptiness." He looks at Patrick again. "No, not emptiness. Pain. In here. And this… is an answer in itself."

"What do you mean? I don't understand." Patrick sits on the ground.

"When I was working in therapy," J says with more energy, "before the Scramblers, when I worked on paraplegic patients or people who lost a limb in a drone crash, they often told me one peculiar thing. They said that they have this *pain* inside them, right here in the middle of the chest. Nothing I did relieved them of this particular pain. And I could never understand it. I always thought there had to be some nerve center, some junction, where the nerves from the lost leg or the lost arm connect with the solar plexus nerves and cause this phantom pain. But I realize now… that I was wrong."

"How's that?"

J looks at Patrick pointedly. "You see, all those people lost someone they loved in the accident that disabled them as well. I could not relieve their pain, because… the pain wasn't physical. It was grief. They all lost a part of themselves too."

Patrick takes a deep breath and looks away. "I see. And when Dora left, you lost part of yourself as well."

After a moment, J nods, more to himself, and looks down. "Yes…"

"I am sorry, J. I am really so sorry. I wish there was something

I could do to help you. But all I can do is fix computers. And weed the fields, apparently."

J smiles but it quickly fades away. Then he shakes his head, frowning.

"What?" asks Patrick.

"I just don't understand how she did it."

"You mean, how did she manage to teleport?"

"Yes." Then he looks at Patrick, his face emotionally contorted under his tanned skin and three-day-old stubble. "I…" He swallows. "I stayed there under the T-tube, hoping—wishing—it would teleport me as well…" He shakes his head slowly, his eyes unfocused in front of him. "And it didn't." He shrugs. "It just didn't. Why did it just work for her? Why not me, Patrick? Why not me?"

Patrick sighs deeply. "I don't know. Perhaps…"

"Yes?"

Patrick shrugs. "The only thing I can think of is that she used technology she had on her E-band. It must have connected to the teleportation channels. Somehow."

J pauses, then after a few moments, he nods. "Yeah… She mentioned something like that when we went to the city." J looks down at his bare forearm, the place where Descendants wear their E-bands. "No wonder it didn't work for me…"

"I'm sorry," Patrick says again. "If you need something, anything, just tell me, and I'll do it."

J smiles weakly at Patrick. "Thanks. I really do appreciate it."

"How about we both grow a long beard. In protest."

J's smile broadens.

"And shave off our heads bald!"

J laughs. "Like Jake in *Number Three*. I don't think so! People would freak out."

"Damn… You're right." Patrick looks into the distance for a moment. "But Jumpers wouldn't know. They'd be fine."

"Who knows? Maybe this horror story survived the apocalypse."

Patrick smiles broadly. "Maybe it did… Now, do some work, mate. You've been lazing around for ten minutes. Look at everyone else!" He points with his tool to the dozen other people around the field. "Everyone is working their ass off." He winks at J.

J shakes his head, smiling, and digs a spade into the ground, the smell of fresh soil hitting his nostrils.

Dora would love this smell.

Then his smile disappears and his shoulders sag once again.

Patrick immediately notices. He puts this hand on J's shoulder and says quietly, "It will work out. Somehow."

J doesn't respond.

The only future that would work out for him is simply impossible. Dora will not come back. *And he has no way of following her.*

CHAPTER 11

Uni

I'm kneeling on the floor, my heart raging in my chest, my heartbeat so loud it's blocking the sounds of the footsteps.

But then my E-band vibrates.

I glance down.

And the display on the screen is unmistakable.

The porting chamber! It's underneath me!

I swipe my E-band to initiate the port, glancing at the hallway at the same time.

Let's go, let's go, let's go!

I tap the last commands automatically, not looking at the screen, my gaze fixed at the end of the hallway.

And then, just before I see them, the white corridor dims into a purple hue, and I'm pulled away. Backward. Into nothingness.

I'm back.

Back in the Void.

But I don't see any purple. Or pink. Or flashes of black and white.

I turn around, or at least I want to. But it's black, all black, nothing around me.

No colors. Not even a sense of where colors might come from.

Simply nothing.

I want to take a breath, but I can't. Instead, I hear a wheezing sound.

Was that me?

Then a deep, rumbling sound overrides everything else.

A waterfall?

I keep trying to turn around, but I can't. I am not; there is nothing.

Except the sound.

Underneath the rumbling sound I can hear a song. Melancholic, despairing—and beautiful. I hear voices, many voices, and I've heard them before... But where?

The voices. The voices...

Ah yes, I remember now. I heard them... at the funeral.

Stevanion's funeral.

Someone died... A thought comes to me. But the thought is not mine.

Then the sound changes, grows, becomes so strong

THAT EVERYTHING INSIDE ME IS REVERBERATING TO THAT BEAT.

THUNDER.

JUST AN IP AWAY FROM ME.

I LISTEN TO THIS, AMAZED, MY BODY EMPATHIZING, VIBRATING WITH THE SOUND AROUND ME ON A SUBMOLECULAR LEVEL.

AND IT TAKES SO LONG. BUT I DON'T MIND. I WANT IT TO LAST. I WANT IT TO BE FOREVER, EVEN THOUGH I'M LACKING AIR, EVEN THOUGH I CAN'T BREATHE.

THE NEXT MOMENT, THE SCREAMS START. FROM A HUNDRED, THOUSAND, MILLION SOULS.

SCREAMS SO TERRIFYING THAT I'M FROZEN, FORGETTING THE URGE TO BREATHE.

IT'S A TERRIBLE, TERRIBLE SOUND, AN OUTCRY OF LOSS AND MISERY AND DEATH. A SHALLOW LIFE, A CRUMPLING SKIN ON AN EMPTY BODY, A SOULLESS EXISTENCE NEEDING TO END IT ALL.

I LISTEN, AND FEEL, AND SUFFER IN PAIN WITH THE CRIES AND SCREAMS, AND I KNOW IN ME, DEEP INSIDE, WHY. I KNOW THE CRIES. I UNDERSTAND. THESE ARE THE CRIES OF—

I slam hard on a cold floor. My whole body shudders, my lungs devoid of air.

I take an enormous breath, gasping for air, my lungs tearing in pain. But I have been through this before, so I take another breath, and another, even though I know how much it will burn.

With time, the pain subsides, and my breathing becomes even.

I open my eyes and look around.

I'm surrounded by rosenquartz tiles radiating the typical soft rose hue of a resting porting chamber.

I push myself off the floor and try to stand up, but I fall. My legs are too weak. I sigh. I've been through this before too. I know this. I clench my fists and try again. I lean on the wall and slowly walk to the door, holding on to the cold tiles.

As I approach, the door opens.

Outside, it's dim and I can hardly see anything. Nevertheless, I know exactly where I am.

I step out into the scarcely lit corridor, the illumination coming only from the faint green auxiliary tubes. There's no one around; the corridor is completely empty. I've walked this same path thousands of times before, yet I've never seen it like this, dark and quiet.

Could it be that it's night, so everyone is locked in their living quarters?

I glance at my E-band to check the time.

It's only 1700. The place should be full of people. But there's no one.

What is happening?

I head to the main square, passing the deserted Nature and E-fitness Halls.

The IC Hall, which is always full, is also completely empty, the transparent doors locked.

As I pass the closed doors of the DC Hall, I look up at the building, the several-stories-high construction of glass and metal. Normally, it's brightly lit and one can see people inside. Even the elevators and galleries are visible from the outside.

Now, however, the glass of the hall is black, reflecting only the contours of my body.

After several passes, I walk into a large square, over two hundred IPs in diameter.

The late afternoon light seeps through the transparent dome, radiating its white-blue light across the large tile-covered hexagonal area of the square.

I make a loop around the centrally located tree island, checking all the benches, chairs, Information Point Stations, and all twelve side tunnels leading in and out of the square.

And it's awfully, terribly, intimidatingly quiet.

I shiver, then head to the nearest Information Point Station and walk in as the door softly slides closed behind me.

Like a DC room, it's small, only one IP distance to the concave glass wall of the tube-shaped room. It's meant to be occupied by only one person.

I initiate the holo, and an AI voice, too loud for this quiet environment, greets me.

"Good day at Senthia, Tah Adnan Randstran. It is 1714. What would you like to do today? Please, choose from the menu."

I unconsciously take a step back, lightly banging into the glass wall.

I frown, narrowing my eyes.

Tah Adnan Randstran? Who is that?

I glance at the top right corner to check the profile image.

Pale face, thin purplish lips, short dark gray hair and green-within-green eyes. A typical Senthien.

I shake my head, confused. *There must be something wrong with the system.*

I tap on the blue button on the holo screen, and a new page with a full profile opens up in front of me.

Adnan is a male, 219 standard years old, with three rejuvenation cycles behind him, the fourth one due in twenty years. He has produced a series of Vision reports, with 72 percent accuracy. Three interactive couplings, no participation in the Office of Progeny as of yet.

And I have never met him before in my life. *So why does he appear as my profile?*

I take a shaky breath, then look around at the empty square.

Something really wrong is going on.

"Tah Adnan Randstran, please choose from the menu." I jump, the unexpected sound giving me a shock. I put a hand on my chest and breathe out, trying to calm myself.

I close the holo and walk out. My brain is buzzing. I close my eyes and focus, trying to find order in my chaotic thoughts. *There must be a logical explanation for—*

All of a sudden a hand grips mine and strongly pulls me down.

I drop on the floor.

"Shhh!" I hear next to my ear.

I look.

A Jacobson. She is hunched next to me, trying to stay under the wall behind the bench. Short platinum-blond hair frames her face, her gray eyes hiding underneath dark eyelashes. And like all other Jacobsons, she is extremely tall.

I realize at that moment that I have seen her before. She was the woman at the reception during my last DC Hall visit.

"What is happening?" I ask.

"Shhhh! They'll hear us!" she whispers urgently.

"Who will—?"

"They!"

I frown, then turn behind the bench wall to look. And then—I see them.

I hastily pull back, retreating behind the wall, my heart pumping wildly now.

Brookonians!

Oh, the Moons of Senthia! What are they *doing here?*

I feel a tug at my elbow.

"Follow me," she whispers, then crawls somewhat clumsily on all fours to the closest corridor leading out of the square.

Can I trust her?

She turns around and urgently waves at me.

I take a deep breath and follow her into the corridor.

For the next few passes, she leads me along the dim hallways, and I slowly feel the pressure of my genetically imposed Senthien who hates walking in uncharted territory with no adequate answers. Every Senthien, even a half-breed, desires correct information, needs to know where they are and where they are heading.

"Where are you taking me? Where is everyone? And what are Brookonians doing here?" I ask.

"I urge you to be quiet. They will hear us."

"Why are they here?" My voice is a tight whisper.

"We don't know for sure. But the probability is high that it is linked to you."

I blink in confusion. "But you don't even know who I am."

She smiles the broad Jacobson smile. "There were hundreds of Visions of you, Dora Dana Dasnan. By now most Senthiens, as well as many other Descendants living on Senthia, know who you are."

I stop walking.

No!

No, this is impossible!

Throughout the centuries I made certain to stay as inconspicuous as possible. My life depended on my ceaseless diligence. *How can this be?*

I realize the Jacobson is already several IPs away, so I snap out of my thoughts and jog to keep up with her.

"This—this must be a mistake," I say once I'm running at her side. "I do not hold any value to... anyone at Uni. I am certain of it."

She stops and looks at me, the obligatory gen-manipulated smile absent. "I'm not a Senthien, Dana, so I cannot tell you about all the Visions. You will find out more from your fellow Senthiens later. However, what I can tell you—and with a high degree of certainty—is that *you* might be the only person who can explain the strange course of events Uni has experienced in the past twenty-two days. Come now, Dora Dana Dasnan. We need to be swift. Our window is closing."

CHAPTER 12

Uni

I'm rushing after the Jacobson. Two more left turns, and then, in the middle of the corridor, she just stops. There's no porting chamber, no entry to a living quarter—in fact, no door whatsoever.

"Why did we stop here?" I whisper.

"We can't use the airing shaft from here," she says as if that would answer my question. "We are too far from our destination. We need to get to a Mag Rail Hub. And this is our best option."

She takes a low-intensity torch from her skinsuit side pocket and puts it in her mouth while she trails her fingers along the wall tiles.

I am now completely confused. *I've never used Mag Rail before, but I definitely thought that the entrance would look different.*

She's quick as she trails the tiles, but then she slows down, feeling something underneath her fingers. She takes a small flat tool from a chest pocket and uses it to detach a large carbon fiber plate off the wall, then silently puts it on the ground. The wall behind is black.

I don't understand what she is doing, and I'm completely

unable to foresee her plan. But then she lowers her head and aims, headfirst, into the black wall!

The black wall, I realize then, is not a wall at all but an empty space. It's a tunnel.

She looks down, then up, and pulls back again. "Good. You go first," she whispers, but there is an urgency in her tone.

"Is this a Mag Rail Hub?"

She pauses for a moment. "No, Dana. This is one of the laundry recycle tubes," she says. "We need to slide down and reach the Hub connecting to the Skinsuit Recycling Hall underneath us."

Obviously.

I look down the tube, seeing nothing but black. I swallow hard. *This just looks suicidal.*

"Dana, our window is closing in less than a pass. You need to go. *Now!*"

"Why aren't you going first?"

"I need to close the opening, otherwise the Brookonians will see the escape path we used. Now jump. And as soon as you land, roll to the side, all right?"

My heart is beating wildly, my palms sweating in the most Human way, my Senthien having no control anymore.

I press my lips together into a thin line. *I need more information. I can't simply jump. I don't know what's down there.* "There are too many missing variables in this situation. I can't foresee the outcome. I can't obey your request."

"The only thing I can tell you is that Adnan had a Vision—"

"Tah Adnan Randstran?"

"Yes. Tah Adnan Randstran. He had a Vision of meeting you. And many other fellow Senthiens had similar Visions as well. All of them were of you. Hence, it is highly important that we bring you to him."

"And… who is *we*?"

"We are the Seekers."

"I have never heard of Seekers. What do you seek?"

"The truth." She glances at her E-band. "This is your last chance. Go!"

I swallow dry. "Fine."

I sit on the rim and look down into darkness. Then I turn toward her. "What is your name?"

She smiles a broad Jacobson smile, and even though I know it's genetically predisposed, it looks genuine. "My name is Roana Lesya Anande. Go!"

There is no reason to fear… I close my eyes and push off the edge, holding my breath.

The tube is rectangular and slides at a steep angle. Then the angle changes sharply, and I bang against the metal, first with my behind and then with the back of my head. I don't even get to focus on the pain before the angle changes again into a vertical drop and I fall into an open space, landing on soft fabric and bouncing up and down a few more times.

I open my eyes and look around.

I'm sitting on a large mobile container holding a pile of skinsuits.

Then, remembering what she told me, I roll to the side—and just in time, because Lesya lands right next to me.

"Come this way!" Lesya rolls on the fabric to the edge, and while holding on to the metal edge of the container, she jumps down to the ground.

I do the same, realizing it is a touch higher for me than it was for her. I'm missing her height advantage.

The room is barely lit, but there is just enough light to see its size. It is very large, and it's filled with open containers like the one we just jumped from. I notice then that they have mag-tracks underneath, and just at that moment, the container we landed on moves away and a new one slides into its place. An empty one.

"I told you, you should hurry." She smiles, then heads forward.

The container hovers over the tracks. They don't make any sounds themselves, but the tracks hum loudly, and I raise my voice above the sound for Lesya to hear me. "Lesya, I have an inquiry." I jog behind her, trying to keep up with her long strides.

"I am listening."

"I am, or at least I was, linked to Adnan's profile."

"Yes, we know."

"Why was that?"

"Sinnya reprogrammed your profile so that the system isn't updated when and if at all you arrive back to Senthia."

"Why was that necessary?"

"We do not have a full understanding ourselves, but as I said, due to the number and the type of Visions the Senthiens in our group had, it is valid to assume it was necessary to avoid being captured by the Brookonians."

I shake my head, not understanding.

"It will be clearer for you, Dana, once you talk to Adnan. I am certain of it."

"I thank you," I say, but with all the background noise, I don't think she heard me.

The path we are taking is certainly not meant for people. The gaps between containers are very narrow, and they seem even narrower when the containers are moving.

"I've never been in here," I say. "How do you know where to go?"

She turns. "Can you please repeat, Dana? I did not hear you."

I try again, louder. "How do you know where to go?"

She smiles her broad gen-coded smile. "Data, transportation, and logistics. I *need* to know."

"Yes, I realize these are Jacobson traits"—apart from her broad smile—"but the Skinsuit Recycling Hall on Senthia? Why would you need to know that?"

"Skinsuit recycling, waste, food processor supplies, oxygen transport, data access and handling, water supplies, mag-tracks, electricity grid—it all needs to be handled and transported somehow within the planet itself. It's all logistics, one way or another.

"Hold." Lesya stops me going forward. I'm a bit puzzled until one of these large containers zooms in front of me, a lot faster than the others before.

"Oh!" I sway, putting a hand on my chest. "That was close!"

She looks at the hand on my chest, then at my face, then back at my chest again, a strange expression on her face.

Oh no! I didn't hide my emotional reactions at all. This is not the Senthien way. I want to say something, something that explains my actions, something to cover up the truth.

But I can't think of anything.

So I just drop my hand and look away.

"Come," she says and steps across the tracks.

I keep glancing around, afraid of the unexpected traffic, but I follow all the same.

We finally reach the back of the hall, and Lesya guides me along the dark gray wall with a rough texture that leaves light scratches on the back of my hand as I brush against it.

She walks quickly until we reach a door and pushes into it. It squeaks open.

We enter a small dark corridor, leaving the little light we had in the Skinsuit Recycling Hall behind, and when the door behind us closes, we are in the dark, the humming just a distant echo now.

Lesya turns on the torch, and we press forward.

Not long after, we exit the corridor and enter a room which, upon our arrival, lights up bright white. It is a small area that opens up on both sides to a large tube. At the bottom, there is a track, and it's humming faintly.

"Where are we?"

"This is one of the Mag Rail Hubs. It's mainly used for Belthomians. If anything breaks in underground systems—and I mean mechanically breaks, as opposed to electronics—then they use it to get here." She smiles at me, her teeth white. "In the past several hundred years, none of the machinery has broken down, so this path is seldom used. But I managed to arrange a pickup. With Sinnya's help. This is why we can use it virtually undetected."

A moment later, the humming gets even louder and then our transportation arrives. I have seen this vehicle before in general classes, but I never had to take one. It is oval-shaped. The smooth gray metal covers most of the construction. There is a little narrow window at the front.

The side of the Mag Rail facing us opens upward. There are two seats, one in the front and one in the back. Lesya heads toward it and sits on the first seat. "It takes a bit longer than the AirTran and it is not as comfortable"—she clips on her harness—"but it will get us where we want to go."

I sit in the back seat, into a fairly uncomfortable body-shaped transparent seat, which, of course, does not fit my body since it's made for Belthomians.

"Secure yourself, Dora Dana Dasnan."

I reach up and pull the harness over my head, the two metal poles crossing each other in front of my chest.

Lesya turns her head to the side. "It will take three hundred and twenty passes to reach our destination. Use your time to relax."

"What is our destination?"

"Sector D9."

D9. I've never been there before.

I lean back onto the backrest suddenly aware of my mental fatigue.

Three hundred and twenty passes might be just enough time for me to rec-hibe.

It's not without flaws though: a mind in rec-hibe is barely aware of its surroundings, and it's hard to wake it up. But I really need it. My mind has been exposed to too much data, and I doubt I will get a better chance than this one.

The door starts to close, and the lights outside automatically switch off.

It's very dark in the Mag Rail now, but I see some light coming from the front. I look, stretching my neck to see over Lesya's shoulder. The tracks in front of us are glowing soft blue. I sense the vehicle lifting up and then pushing forward, gradually at first but then speeding up rapidly. My back is pressed into the seat, and through the small frame in the front, the illuminated tracks looks like a thin blue triangle with its peak in the middle of the Mag Rail tube.

After only a few passes, my fatigue gets the better of me and I close my eyes, my eyelids shut as if glued together. My mind slowly sinks into the dark depths of theta waves as I lose myself in the step-by-step rec-hibe sleep.

CHAPTER 13

Earth

The night slowly settles in, and the nocturnal insects start their symphony under the light of the waning moon.

J walks down the hanging bridge to his cottage, looking ahead. The light coming from inside seems a lot brighter than usual, and it seeps through the curtains, painting thin, bright stripes on the wooden planks of the porch.

He steps into one of the stripes and looks down while rubbing the back of his neck. His neck, in fact his whole back, is sore from bending in the fields all afternoon. He stretches his shoulders, pulling his arms backward, his muscles hurting from the motion.

It's really the worst posture for working. And if anyone, I should know.

Didn't Walter mention he had found something useful in the Underground? It would be great to get some robotic assistance. The work would be done in half the time, and this utterly nonphysiological posture could be avoided.

He then turns around, looking at the bridge he just crossed with a new idea in mind. *Maybe I should visit him, see how this is going? Maybe he needs some help to make things move faster?*

But then he pauses, realizing he doesn't need to go to Walter's cottage right now… He just doesn't want to go into his own.

He sighs.

"Jonathan?"

He closes his eyes, then turns around and steps through the door, pulling the heavy leaf curtain away.

"Hi, Mon."

As soon as he enters, he notices a small tube-shaped light on the dining table. He walks over and touches the cool top of the tube. "Wow, Sol-LED. Where did you get that?"

"Rachel got it for us." Monica lifts up on her toes and kisses him. "You've been out for ages. Where have you been?"

"In the fields," he says and sits down on the bed. "We've been—"

"She also got us this." She turns on a different torch, a smaller one, and the light blinds J for an instant.

J squints. "That's useful."

"Useful? That's fantastic!" She moves the beam away. "Look, it can be hooked onto a belt, and I can use it when I need to go to the bathroom during the night," she says, tapping the cylinder fastened on her belt.

"And," she continues, "the light is not the *only* new thing we have around here." Monica smiles as she turns around. She takes something from a cupboard, and when she turns, she's holding two small shot glasses.

"Is that—*glass*?"

"No, it's whiskey, you funny boy!" She laughs and offers him one.

"Mon, I don't… I don't drink."

She blinks at him. "What do you mean you don't drink? Since when?"

"I haven't had a drink in nine years." He shakes his head. "I don't think I can handle it."

"Oh, for crying out loud! Where did my Jonathan go? You could take a dozen of those and stay sober. C'mon!" She pushes a glass to his chest, and he grabs it before she lets go.

"Wow, a real glass," he says, inspecting it closely.

"Why are you so surprised? What did you use before?"

"Wood… Metal…" He brings the cup closer to his face and sniffs it. Then makes a face. "Oh, it's strong!"

"Yes!" Monica says, delighted. "And there is more!"

"More?" J grins. "I'll be knocked out from drinking only *this*."

"Well, I think it's time to restart," Monica says, then clinks J's glass. "To a new future. And who knows, a new small life as well." Then she empties her shot in one go.

J is still looking at the glass.

"Jonathan? You need to drink it. The toast is for a new life, you know? It's for our baby."

J takes a deep breath.

He doesn't really want to drink. The smell is putting him off. *But Mon would be hurt if I didn't drink, especially now that she toasted it in such a way.*

He brings the glass closer to his mouth, blocks his nose, then tips the liquid into his mouth as fast as he can. And swallows.

Then shivers.

A moment later, his whole throat is on fire.

He coughs, almost choking.

"Argh!" He puts the glass on the table and coughs once more. "That would wake up the dead."

"Oh, come on! What happened to you?" Monica smiles, then turns around and refills both glasses, picks them up and hands one to J. "For the old-slash-new technologies. To make our life more livable." And she downs the second glass too.

J's brain feels foggy. He pauses for a moment, wondering suddenly if the wind had picked up enough to rock the whole tree house, because it seems to him that the cottage is not completely stable.

He closes his eyes for an instant, but that makes the room spin even more. *Ah, bad choice!*

He opens his eyes again.

Dora would hate this: losing her self-control. He smiles to himself. *Her impulsive Human would have no chance against her rational Senthien.*

Abruptly this thought makes him sad, so terribly sad that he can barely keep it together.

This is why she left. Her Human could not compete against her Senthien. So the Senthien won. And she's gone.

He looks at the glass, his throat tight.

Damn with everything!

Without a second thought, he downs the liquid, this one burning a little bit less.

"Jonathan, are you listening to me?"

J lifts his head. "I'm sorry. What were you saying?"

"My toast? For technologies?"

"Yes?" He sits down on his bed, his legs getting heavy.

"It's because Rachel… You know Rachel, the one who got us the light?"

"Yes, I know who Rachel is."

"Well, she said that there are many more things in the Underground storage, you know, techy things that we could use in our household. Though most of them are too large to bring up to the tree house." She tilts her head to the side. "So afterward, I was talking to Sandra, and I thought that we might, perhaps, you know, move into a house on the ground."

J looks at her, a frown on his face. He's not sure if he heard her correctly or if the alcohol is doing its deed. "But... we can't build on the ground because of the floods. Sandra must have told you about that, didn't she?"

"Yes, she did, but you see, now with all the stuff that they found in the Underground, they can construct better flood protection for when the water comes again. And"—Monica gestures behind her—"I would really like to have my own bathroom. I mean, this here, this is camping-style. And I'm not saying I don't like camping. I do. But this is something you do on vacation, not all the time!"

"We've been living like this for nine years."

"And what a great holiday that's been for you guys! Truly! A real adventure. But me?" She shakes her head while talking. "Walking out in the middle of the night when I need to tinkle. It's just not my style."

She sits on the bed next to J and swings her arm around his neck. "And a house on the ground would make me *really* happy."

The pressure of her arm makes his neck muscles hurt even more. He stretches his neck again. "Mon, I like living in the tree houses. It feels natural."

She shrugs and pulls her arm away. "Well, you've had your fun for nine years. Now it's time to take things more seriously. And also, when we have a baby, being so high off the ground is simply not an option. It's way too dangerous, and I will simply not allow it."

J's mind feels a bit sluggish, but he tries to reason with her. "Monica, we've had women with small children living here for years. We never had any accidents. Sandra and Tony made sure of that."

"Well, before there were no other options, I understand. But now it's different. And they are already building on the ground."

"But I like it like this." He stands up and looks around him. "It's natural, pure. We are one with nature."

Monica lifts an eyebrow. "*One with nature?* Well, tell that to someone who has a bacterial infection and can't get an antibiotic."

J looks away.

Maybe she's right. If Stevanion had proper medical care, if they weren't 'one with nature,' perhaps he would have survived.

"Besides," she continues, "you can be 'one with nature' on the ground too. Not much changes."

Monica stands up as well and comes closer to J. She wraps her arm around his waist, looking into his eyes and stroking his face gently.

This feels so familiar.

He closes his eyes.

Her hand, her touch, her body. This was his life for many years before cryo.

He knows it, it should feel intimate, it should feel special. But instead, it feels off.

Monica loops her hand behind his neck and slowly pulls him closer to her face.

J follows her pull, coming closer and closer to her lips. He feels he should resist. There is a reason, a good reason for resisting, but... he can't put his finger on it. So he keeps following her lead.

"It's been nine years since you've had me," Monica whispers. "Oh, I can only imagine how *hard* it must have been... Let me make it up to you..."

Her words float from her red lips, her face framed with large red curls.

It's what he used to like.

But does he now?

While his mind is struggling, his body is giving in. Monica presses her lips against his, breathing heavily. She wraps both her arms around his neck, pressing her body against him, feeling his body react. She slides her hand between his legs.

"Yes," she purrs, then she opens his lips with hers, searching for his tongue, and kisses him deeply.

And he kisses her back.

CHAPTER 14

Uni

A soft light on a wooden table illuminates the room, casting shadows on the floor.

I know this room well.

It's J's cottage.

J is standing next to the wooden table, slightly leaning on it, his fingers touching the surface as if he needs to steady himself. His eyes seem unfocused. And there is a slight frown on his face.

He glances down at the wooden table, looking at a small transparent cup, a golden liquid still swirling inside.

From the back of the room, Monica comes into view. She wraps her arms around his neck, bringing her face closer to him.

"It's been nine years since you've had me," she says, stretching her words. "I can only imagine how hard it must have been." Her voice is between a whisper and a song. "Let me make it up to you..."

Monica kisses him.

And he closes his eyes and kisses her back while she presses herself against his body.

"Yes," she whispers. "Yes..."

I snap out of my Vision, launching forward, but my seat belt holds me back, pressing tightly against my chest. My whole body is shaking, my chest squeezed under the heavy weight of pain. I can barely take a breath.

I close my eyes and swallow hard.

Why did I have to see that?

I take a shaky breath.

My throat is constricting into a knot, painful and sore, while I try to stop my lips from quivering.

I went away.

I went away!

I left him so he can have—another strained breath—*what he wanted.*

A sob escapes me. *Why did I need to see that?*

"Dana." Lesya turns her head sideways. "Are you all right?"

I can't answer. I need a moment.

As soon as my throat loosens its grip, I try to speak, hoping my voice will hold. "Yes, Lesya. Thank you for your concern."

"We will soon arrive." She looks back to the front. "Did you manage to get some sleep?"

"Yes, I did. I thank you," I say, this time with no delay.

"Did you have any Visions?"

I hesitate. "No."

You're back in Uni, Dora. Get used to being asked that. And get used to lying.

"Well," Lesya continues as if she didn't notice my pause,

"there will be a lot more information coming your way. You will have plenty of data to make new Visions."

The Mag Rail starts to decelerate, pushing me against the seat belt. Soon it comes to a complete stop and the door automatically opens upward.

Lesya unbuckles herself and steps out.

This room is brightly lit, just like the Mag Rail Hub before, and I hope my emotional torment is not showing on my face. But I can't stay in the shadows forever.

"Where are we?" I step out.

"I believe it will be obvious once you see it."

The exit platform is large and leads into an equally large corridor; this one is definitely made for several individuals and their IP requirements.

After several turns, she passes through a sliding gate, and we find ourselves in a large, extremely bright hall, the light reflecting off numerous layers above us.

I look up, and it is like looking into the pool bath back on Earth, the water refracting the bright green. Above me are multilayered sheets of shallow pools containing algae, each layer a living ecosystem of the oxygen-producing blankets of chlorophyll. *And it looks beautiful.*

"Do you now realize where we are?" Lesya asks.

"I do."

These are the 3D lakes where the majority of Senthia's oxygen is produced. This oxygen plant is connected to the whole of Senthia's inhabited domes and quarters, linked by an intricate airing system. But nowhere else are oxygen levels as high as right here in the production plant.

I take a deep breath.

It almost reminds me of Earth's rain forest.

Almost.

It also becomes clear to me why Lesya mentioned the airing system when we were escaping the Brookonians. If we were closer to the 3D lakes, we could have used airing shafts to reach this place. But using the Mag Rail turned out to be more advantageous, considering our distance.

"I have never been here before," I say, looking up into the pools.

"Not many have. Just like the Skinsuit Recycling Hall, access is restricted to Belthomians. And the workers."

"Which workers?"

"The Zema4s."

"Of course."

We have been walking for more than ten passes, all the while hooded by layers and layers of transparent green oxygen-creating sheets. I have seen pictures of the algae lakes on the holo screens several times, but seeing it with my own eyes, from under the sheets rather than from above, is simply unique.

At the place where one pool area above us ends and before the next one begins, a large gray cube on the floor blocks our path. Only once Lesya disappears behind the cube do I realize it's a staircase entry. I follow her down the stairs and enter a room not much bigger than my living quarters. Unlike my room though, which is fairly empty, this room is packed with fourteen beds. At the end of the room, there is a transparent cabin with a shower and a toilet.

A basin is placed next to it.

The room has no windows, no view to the green algae lakes, only the white artificial light coming from the ceiling.

"We are in the workers' quarters now," Lesya says.

I look around this uncomfortably packed room. *It figures. Fitting for the lower species.* I snort inwardly.

"Are you certain that no workers will find us here?"

"The 3D lakes have been expanded fairly recently, and there is a very high likelihood that it will not be revisited for several years. We have therefore chosen this particular venue to meet."

"The Seekers, you mean?"

"Yes." She looks at her E-band. "We still have several hours to wait before the lockdown ends. I will use the time to rest. I suggest you do the same. Perhaps this time you will be rewarded with a Vision."

I sit down on one of the beds. It feels hard and uncomfortable, but it reminds me of my bed back in my cottage on Earth, and with no warning, I suddenly get emotional. My eyes sting, and I lie down, turning away from Lesya as the tears silently slide down.

Though I know I won't be able to sleep, I still close my eyes, pretending to.

I hear a shuffling sound and I open my eyes again.

I turn to see Lesya sitting on one of the beds, her eyes on the staircase. Then she looks at me. "Good morning, Dana."

It seems I did fall asleep. "Good morning. Did you sleep well?"

"I slept. Not well. The mattress was too hard. How about you?"

"I slept… well. I guess I was overwhelmed with a set of recent events." I sit up.

"And there will be more." Lesya smiles. "The others are arriving in thirty-three passes." She looks back toward the staircase as if she didn't just tell me we need to wait a bit before they arrive.

"Lesya, what happened here? What happened to Senthia? Why are things so different?"

"Adnan will be able to give you a more accurate picture," she says, still looking at the staircase. "The only thing I can give you is my limited view."

"I would like to hear what you have to say. When I ported to Senthia, it was 1700, and yet everything was deserted. There was no one around. Except for Brookonians. What happened? Where are all the people?"

She stays silent.

I am starting to think she is not going to answer, but then she says, "The lockdown time was expanded. The living quarters and all the public areas open at 1100 morning time, and they close at 1500 afternoon time. This is why you haven't seen anyone."

"Why is that?"

"The war," she says flatly.

"Which war?"

"Against the Humans."

Humans? "Did Humans escape Zema4?"

"No. They are still there."

"But—how can there be a war if they are still stuck on that prison planet?" I know I should use "surveillance planet," the official terminology, but I don't care.

Lesya either doesn't notice it or doesn't react.

"A couple of weeks ago, Zlathars released the news. The Humans were tampering with the Mind and they sabotaged the ports. Zlathars pronounced a war."

"Humans don't have any means to tamper with the Mind. They don't have access to any computer systems at all."

"I too believe that this is very unlikely. But I don't know for certain. This is why I am here, with the Seekers, seeking to find the truth. Four weeks ago, I would have believed it, but in the past twenty-two days, a course of events changed my mind."

At that moment, I realize that she might have a different opinion of Humans than a typical Descendant. Perhaps not completely correct, but different from that blind spot Zlathars pushed us all into. Or at least they tried to. "I am listening."

"I worked at the main DC Hall, next to the square."

"Yes, I remember you."

"I had an overview of searches Senthiens were doing. Many of them used the same keywords, and I could only assume that this was because they all had repeating Visions of the same thing."

"What were they looking for?"

"They searched for Uni worlds with dense vegetation."

They must have seen Earth.

"They searched for data on Zema4."

They've seen Humans.

"And they searched for APC. The chip."

Just like me!

"And then"—she looks at me—"they searched for *you*."

"Me?"

"Yes. Your name: Dora. Dana. Dasnan."

I turn my head, looking at the room but not really seeing it, feeling a little sick to my stomach. *This is not good!*

My heartbeat speeds up and my palms start to sweat.

The secret that I tried to keep hidden is seeping through the gaps of a Senthien genetic supertrait. My carefully constructed protective shield is falling apart. I am no longer invisible.

"I would not have thought this unusual," she continues. "I have often seen several Senthiens looking for the same keywords because they get the same indication of a future event. But what happened next I would never have thought possible. On their way out of the DC Hall, each and every one of those Senthiens were arrested. By the Brookonians."

I take a quick breath. "They arrested Descendants?"

"Yes."

"But that's... impossible." My eyes are wide, my calm Senthien appearance gone.

Brookonians were made—genetically designed—for only one purpose. To fight Humans. *So how can this be possible?*

"A few days after," Lesya continues, "Adnan came to the DC Hall. He started querying the same keywords, asking the same questions, but I interrupted his protocol before he got too far. I sent him an internal DC message that he should come down to reception so I could transfer him to a new room.

"When he came down, I asked him to follow me, but of course I didn't lead him into a new DC room. Instead, I told him everything that I have seen, and I told him that should he continue his search, the likelihood was that he will get detained.

"I asked him then if he believed me, and he said, yes, of course he did. He had already heard me telling him all this once before. He had obviously seen me in his Vision, but he was just polite and waited for me to finish." She smiles a soft un-coded smile.

"He went back to a DC room then, and he continued his search but used different keywords, and those did not raise alarms at all. He was free to walk out without getting intercepted.

"Over the next few days, I stopped several more Senthiens from searching the critical keywords, and I have put all of them in contact with Adnan."

"Did you stop me?" I ask.

"I do not understand."

"When I searched for my keywords, I was stopped when I inquired about APC chips. Did you stop me continuing my search?"

"No, Dana. That was not me. If I remember correctly, it was a power outage."

"How many power outages did you experience in the DC Hall during your time?"

She pauses. "One. Yours."

"Do you still think it was a power outage?"

She looks away. "No."

A few moments pass before I continue. "So, did Adnan find this place to meet?"

"No. It was me. I have access to maps and blueprints, transport and logistics, as well as data on mechanical procedures and processes happening on Senthia. I knew this place would be safe."

"How many people are in the group?"

"It is small. Twenty-four. For now. But more people are coming every day. We are trying to instruct other Senthiens to keep their Visions hidden, to not report all of them to the Zlathar council. But it is difficult. They are used to reporting all Visions, and it is difficult to prevent them from doing something they've been doing for hundreds of years, especially for senior Senthiens whose ways are set."

I can understand why this might be challenging with older Senthiens. Instinctively, I think of Jodar. I wonder if he had revealing Visions of me too.

"So," I start, "would you by any chance know the Visions that drove them to these keywords?" I'm trying hard not to give my eagerness away, but I am extremely keen to find out what made them search for my name.

"I have heard some, but I would prefer if you…" Then she stops, lifting her gaze to the stairs. "Ask them yourself, Dana."

"Dora Dana Dasnan."

I turn to the voice.

At the base of the staircase, with more people behind him, stands a man with a pale face, piercing green eyes, thin lips, and short, dark gray hair. I've seen him already on my profile image.

He walks toward me and stops one IP away. "I am honored to meet you, Dana. Finally."

"Thank you, Tah Adnan Randstran. I am honored to meet you and your group of Seekers." I glance behind him and see that not all the Seekers are Senthiens.

As they enter the room, I see that one of them is an Ana. She is wearing a typical pale blue skinsuit, equipped with miniature diagnostic units and measuring devices. Next to her are two Jacobsons, both tall, with cropped platinum-blond hair and pleasant smiles.

On my left I see a Lorean, and next to him stands a Belthomian woman, taller than the Lorean, stronger as well, her skinsuit pale white and full of straps and pockets.

The others are all Senthiens: pale faces, with dark gray hair, purplish thin lips, and piercing green eyes.

"We are all extremely happy to see you."

I look back at Adnan. By Senthien standards his smile would be considered broad.

"And may I add," he continues, "one person in particular."

He moves sideways to make way for the person behind him.

The moment I see him, I smile—the most Human, carefree smile—as joy hugs my heart.

Father!

CHAPTER 15

Uni

"Father!" I gasp and want to run to him. But I stop. I don't know what the others know about us.

So I don't run toward him like I want to. I don't run toward him to almost knock him over. Instead, I tightly control my body movements. I slowly approach, careful to remain as steady and as emotionless as possible. I stop one IP away.

"Dana," he says, "it pleases me to see you."

"Likewise, Father," I answer, trying to stay calm and aloof. "I am glad you are among this gathering."

Then I turn toward Adnan. "The gathering I would like to hear more about. Adnan?"

He smiles, then motions with his hand toward a table behind one of the Senthiens. "Let us eat first, as some of us left for this meeting without an obligatory morning nutrition. Nadir has arranged food for us."

On the table lay many wrapped food bars, nutrition balls, and water bags.

"I thank you, Nadir," says Adnan and then turns to the rest. "Please, the intake of food is at your disposal."

A few people approach the table, but my father doesn't.

"Will you not take anything?" I ask him.

"No, my child, I have already eaten."

"Which food bar did you take?" I really don't care about his morning nutrition, but what I do need to find out is if he thinks we can talk freely here or not.

He smiles just slightly, a tiny motion at the side of his lips. "It was VRA-08."

I blink slower than usual, telling him that I understood him. VRA-08 means danger. It means the topic should not be discussed.

I realize, however, that I *am* hungry. I haven't eaten anything for more than a day.

I stand in line.

Once the two people in front of me move away, I step closer, then bow slightly to Nadir and thank him. I take a water bag and one of the food bars, then make space for the others. I hurriedly fold back the foil and bite into the food bar. Then I stop, my face locked in a twisted gesture. *Ewww! How am I ever going to get used to this again?*

"Dana, is everything all right?" Adnan asks.

I swallow the dry blob. "Yes, Adnan, of course. Is there a reason for such a question?"

"Your facial expression looked… uncomfortable."

Uncomfortable? I really need to get back into the game. I can't have all my thoughts on display like this! "I usually take VRA-07. I am not used to"—I quickly access my nanoprobes, checking the bar code printed on the foil with the knowledge database—"MMR5."

Adnan smiles slightly. "I understand, Dana. We are all victims of our habits, aren't we?"

"Indeed." *Phew!*

I continue chewing on the paste, hoping I can sufficiently control my facial muscles.

Several people around me are eating, but the majority aren't. Still, no one is saying a word. Everybody is waiting for those who are eating to finish. And though I thought this normal for most of my life, my few weeks on Earth—where people talked, laughed, and ate at the same time—changed that.

I do miss that. I sigh inwardly. *I miss that a lot.*

As soon as I push down the last dry bite, I glance at Adnan. He's sitting calmly in his dark olive-green skinsuit, the long coat folded over his legs, his eyes unfocused on the floor, completely still.

I, on the other hand, am extremely impatient, and I am very well aware that they will want to know things from me. And right now I am not sure if I can trust them.

I glance at my father and then make a quick decision.

"Adnan, while the others are still eating, I would like to converse with my father. We have not seen each other for some time, and I would like to exchange the latest news."

Adnan bows his head just slightly. "All right, Dana. But please remember not to take too long. We have limited time to converse, and we need to find out additional information, we need to know what is going on, to have a better chance of making accurate Visions."

"I understand. We won't take long."

My father and I climb up the stairs and start walking. I wait until we gain some distance from the room before I ask, "Do you trust Adnan?"

"Nothing in my Visions so far warned me that I should not. As I anticipated, he approached me on my way back to my living quarters. He said that he had Visions about you, and he asked me to meet him and the others here under the 3D lakes. So for the past three days, this is what I have been doing."

I stop walking, leaving only half an IP between us. "Do they know? About me? About my mother?" I whisper.

"I could not tell that, Dora. It doesn't look like they do."

"I see."

"But I don't think this is important for them."

"What do you mean?"

"I don't think it plays a role in what they are really interested in."

"So what *are* they interested in?"

"I don't know for sure, but I can tell you that something unusual is happening. It became clear to many Senthiens very early on, and this is why Zlathars had to react so strictly here on Senthia."

"What do you think will happen?"

"I don't know. I just know, from some of my Visions and from the others I've heard, it's something big. And Adnan..." He sighs.

"Yes?"

"Adnan seems to think that you have a major role in whatever is about to happen next. Which is why he—and everyone else too—wanted to meet you, to talk to you. They want access to your information." He takes a noticeable pause as he looks at me. "They want to know where you have been for the past twenty-two days. Because wherever it was that you went, it started an array of Visions."

Of course! As soon as I ported to Earth, I changed the course of probable events. There would have been a series of possible future probabilities, all culminating when I decided to port back to Uni. And Senthiens, gen-modified as they are, would have registered it. They would start getting appropriate Visions.

I sigh.

It all makes sense. Why hadn't I thought of that?

"Dora?"

I look up at my father.

"So? Where *have* you been?"

I look back at him, and for the first time since I returned to Uni, I smile.

"Earth. I went to Old Earth, Father."

CHAPTER 16

Uni

He takes a step back. "*Earth?*"

"Yes."

"What do you mean Earth?"

"I mean Earth. Our old planet." I'm still smiling broadly. *I couldn't have imagined how good it would feel to say this!*

"No. No, it can't be. Earth is dead."

"It's not dead, Father. There is life. A wonderful life." I take a breath. "And there are people there as well."

"People? Who?"

"Those who didn't leave during the Evacuation. Those that were left behind. The original Humans."

"Oh, the Moons of Senthia! The original Humans? They survived for five thousand years?"

"They were cryopreserved. They woke up just recently, only nine years ago."

"Astounding! What are they like, these original Humans?"

I had a lot of time to think about it, but still, I had no answer ready. "They are… more close to each other than Descendants ever were. They are a team. A tight, deeply connected team. And they are fighters, here, within," I say, pushing my hand to my chest.

"Fighters? Whom are they fighting against?"

I smile. "No, not a real fight. What I want to say is that they are survivors. They *fight* for their survival. And the land is beautiful, Father. It really is. But their life is not easy. They need to work hard to survive."

"Describe that, please. I do not comprehend."

"Well, to start, they need to grow their own food. A bit like Zema4, except that Zema4 Humans do get a lot of raw materials from Uni. The original Humans build their own houses. They hunt. And what I found most fascinating is their will to continue, after realizing what had happened, to push forward and live. To *not* give up."

My father looks down and nods. "I see what you mean. It is the same concept I found when I frequented Zema4 many years ago." Then he looks up at me. His voice is different, cautious. "How did they receive you?"

"They received me very well, Father. They didn't know about Uni and Descendants until recently, so they did not hold a grudge against me in any way. But Jumpers did though."

"Who are Jumpers?"

"Zema4 Humans. Women. Those that have been mis-ported."

"You mean, all the mistakes that the Mind made happened to Zema4 Humans?"

"I can't be sure. I lack the knowledge of all the mis-ports that happened. But what I do know is that no Descendants ported to Earth. Except me and—"

"And who?"

I lower my head. "When the port mistake happened, I

was not on my own. I traveled with another Senthien. Barka Stevanion Narth."

"Is he still there?"

"No. He died."

My father is very still, unresponsive, as if he didn't hear what I just said. I'm about to say it again, but then he shakes his head. "Descendants don't die. Did they…" He swallows hard. "Did they kill him?"

"Oh no! He died because he lacked the immune system to fight off a viral infection."

"I see." He nods slowly. "An undeserving loss." Then he looks up at me. "But you managed to fight it off, didn't you? Because of your mother?"

I nod and smile. "Yes, I did." Then I remember how quickly J figured it all out. How he saw me, completely and fully, as if the wall I built around myself was only air to him.

J. I close my eyes. *J…*

Then I look at my father. *I need to tell him about J.* I take a breath and start. "Father, while I was there, I—"

"Dana? Maswan?" We hear Adnan's voice from afar. We both turn.

"Could you please return to our premises? We are in need to hear your report before the lockdown time."

"Yes, of course." I glance at my father one more time. His gaze is intense. He's rooted to the ground, unmoving. He wants to know what I was about to tell him. I can sense it.

But I can't tell him now. Not when Adnan is near.

"Let's go," I say.

Almost unnoticeably, he nods, and we head back to the workers' room.

Inside, just as before, all is quiet. Some of the Senthiens are sitting on beds, some of them are standing, but they are all in the same position as when I left them.

"Dana, we are ready to hear your report," says Adnan.

I take a deep breath and glance once more over the group to which I will, in a few passes, reveal the most shocking information they have ever received in their life.

"Twenty-two days ago, I was given a task to report to Zlathars Council."

"In person?" asks Lesya.

"Yes."

All the people in the room look at each other.

They are shocked just as I was when I first learned it; meeting Zlathars in person is extremely unusual, and I suspect none of them have ever done it before.

"It means that the reason for the meeting must have been extremely important," says a Senthien woman, standing next to Lesya.

"Laveena is right." Adnan looks at her. "Could you share with us what the reasoning for your port was, Dana?"

"They wanted to know if I had any underlying Visions to explain the port mistakes the Mind had made."

Adnan nods, his gaze unfocused on the ground. "Yes, it is linked."

"Adnan?"

He looks up at me. "In the past twenty-two days, a lot has happened. On Senthia but also on other Uni worlds too. You have seen Brookonians, have you not?"

"Yes. Lesya and I managed to avoid them in the main square."

"Most of us have never seen Brookonians in real life before." Adnan glances at the other Seekers, and they all respond with a nod. "The fact that they are here, and on many other Descendant worlds as well, means that Zlathars are extremely concerned. And the porting mistakes are a very good reason for them to be concerned. However…" Adnan now looks at me. "I don't think they are here only because of porting mistakes."

His stare feels heavy. I refrain from swallowing a lump in my throat, feigning indifference as if the last comment Adnan made missed me.

"All of us"—he points to the other Senthiens—"have been seeing Visions of you, Dana. I believe that Brookonians are here because of *you*."

"I do not see the link, Adnan. Could you please elaborate?" I say flatly, confident my face does not show any of my emotions.

"You did something, changed something, started something, that triggered the amazing amount of informative Visions. For all of us. Some reported it and were taken away. Some of us realized it unwise," he says, giving a side glance to Lesya, "and we are still here. But we only have fragments, Dana. You need to tell us the rest."

I hope my uneven breathing, the heat I feel in my cheeks, stay hidden from Adnan and the other Seekers.

If I just knew what they had seen, I would be able to adapt my truth to them. Because—I sigh inwardly—I don't want to tell them about the original Humans. The Earth Humans are safe as long as no Descendant knows about them.

And… I don't want to tell them about J.

"What have you seen?" I ask, looking around at the rest of the Senthiens, hoping my assertiveness would work and they would talk first.

I expected a Senthien would volunteer, but when an Ana, a brown-haired woman with short, spikey hair, delicate skin, and small stature steps forward, I am taken by surprise.

"Dana, I am Tre Mada Paolo. Laveena is the one who saw me." Without pausing for Laveena to tell her Vision, Mada continues. "She saw me telling you something. Something important."

"Yes, Mada, please continue."

"I work at the Office of Progeny. I do not have a crucial role in the process, but I have information that links to mis-ports in a specific way. At the Office of Progeny, we receive many Zema4 inhabitants. Many Zema4 women."

I frown just slightly. *Humans in the Office of Progeny? I thought Anas treat only Descendants.*

"I cannot tell you why they were there. I assumed, until recently, that their health had been compromised and Senior Anas have been adjusting their bio-parameters to the optimal levels."

"Why do you say until recently? What changed?"

"In the past six months, we have been encountering an issue. When we ported these women to Boolean Institute—"

"I'm sorry, Mada. Did you say Boolean Institute?"

"Yes, Dana, that is correct."

The image of the hundreds of unconscious Zema4 women in med pods I saw on Boolea appears clear in my mind. "You were… going to say?"

"When we ported these women to Boolean Institute, sometimes their destination was unknown. First, it was very seldom. But with time, the ratio increased dramatically. These are the mis-portations Zlathars are so worried about."

"I see. Were these the only cases of mis-portation."

"To my knowledge, yes."

"Do you have a database of these ports?" I ask.

Mada lifts up her E-band and swipes a few commands. "When Laveena found me, she explained to me that I would be telling you exactly this. This is why I joined the Seekers. I thought this information might be useful for you, Dora Dana Dasnan."

My E-band sounds a signal and I glance at it. A new file has been received. "Thank you, Mada. Do you know why these women were sent to the Boolean Institute?"

"I am sorry. I am not authorized to have this information. I only control trespass of visitors to the Anas, that is all."

"Thank you. At this point, I do not perceive the urgency and importance of this information, but I trust Laveena's Vision that it will become important in the future." I nod to Laveena as well. "I do have additional information for you on the Zema4 mis-ports you have witnessed. I will talk about this in a moment. Anyone else?"

A woman on my left, a Senthien with long but fairly thin dark gray hair starts, "I have seen—green. Lots and lots of green. Really tall plants that I have never seen in real life before. Not even in the Nature Hall. And I have seen you, walking among this green."

I can explain that. "Yes, Senthien…"

"Goya. Lindar Goya May."

"Yes, Senthien Goya, what you saw is true. I will explain. Did anyone else have a similar Vision?"

"Yes, I had the same Vision."

"Mine was very similar too."

"Here as well."

But then I hear something different. "I saw you with different individuals."

Oh the Moons of Senthia! Original Humans!

I look at her. She is standing next to Laveena, one IP away.

"And it seemed that—"

Oh no! What did she see?

"—that you broke the IP border with them."

I swallow, my heart sinking. *Did she see me with J?* "Broke how?" I ask with a steady voice.

"You were just close to some people. There was a big group where all were standing too close to each other, almost leaning on each other, looking at a… bright flashing light."

She saw Stevanion's funeral. "Yes, your Vision is also true. I will tell more. Anyone else?" I keep hoping that my praise for their accuracy will trigger others to talk.

And it does.

Some of them saw the wooden cottages that float in the air, some saw large image walls showing scenes they could not explain and long fields where golden plants grew in matrix-type arrangements.

"Mine," says a woman standing next to Adnan. "Mine was different."

"This is Drina Kata Ras," Adnan explains. "My Vision was to bring her here."

"Yes, Kata," I say. "Please, tell me your Vision."

She glances around once, somewhat nervously, then starts. "It wasn't this new place that everyone had a Vision of. Mine was of Sinnya." She looks at the Lorean standing an IP from her. Sinnya has a smooth hairless head, his skin warm brown, and he is wearing a typical dark blue skinsuit. A distinct earring follows the shape of his earlobe. This is not jewelry. It's a statement: he works on the Mind and he excels at his work.

"I saw Sinnya giving you something," Kata continues. "Something he found at Lorea. I didn't know what it was, but in my Vision, it was clear to me that it was very important. When I first joined the Seekers eleven days ago, he was already here, thanks to Adnan. I described my Vision to Sinnya in great detail." She glances at him again. "Once he knew what he was looking for, he ported to Lorea and found the item."

I look at Sinnya.

"It's a guidance chip," he says, answering my unspoken question. "It is used to control and guide robotic machinery, planetary transportation, and to access chip-controlled sectors. You can use it for all these tasks, but"—he glances at Kata while taking a small chip out of his chest pocket—"based on Kata's Vision, it is highly likely you will be needing this one to control a BD series robot."

"I don't know much about them, Sinnya."

"The BD series performs a range of tasks from continuous maintenance of server towers, design and manufacture of computing hardware, to general support tasks, RT Mind assistance, up to supporting Brookonians in combative actions." He lifts up his E-band, his fingers gently tapping a few commands. "I'm sending you all the data now."

My E-band alerts me that the new data has arrived, but I don't look at it. "Thank you, Sinnya. Do you know which BD this is meant for?"

"I do not," he says and hands it to me. "But I don't think it matters. It will work on any. All I know"—he glances one more time at Kata—"is that it is vital that you have it."

I store the chip in the thin pocket behind my belt, then gaze at the rest of the Senthiens. "Did anyone have a Vision that is related to Kata's Vision?"

When no one answers, Adnan turns to me. "I am sorry, Dana, it seems we have not had any useful Visions for your particular query. However, I am certain we will have many new Visions if you could please share with us your recent past events. You said you were about to port to Zlathars…"

"Yes, Adnan, I was. And as I will be reporting now, you will see where and when your Visions came to be."

Adnan adjusts in his seat.

"The port I was telling you about did not lead me to Zlatharing. The Mind made a mistake, and I was ported to a new destination."

"Where did you port, Dana?" asks a Senthien standing next to Lesya.

I pause, clenching my hands into fists. *I have to tell them. They need to know.* For no other reason than to enable them to *see*, to provide them with a possibility for the most accurate Visions.

But… I am afraid.

I glance at my father.

I'm afraid that at some point, one of them will be able to solve it. One of them will figure out why I was the only Descendant to have been mis-ported, while all other Jumpers were Zema4 Humans.

My chest feels the tightness of dread as I intentionally and deliberately break my code of self-preservation.

I look up at them.

They deserve to know.

"I ported to Old Earth."

Silence.

They keep looking at me, unmoving. No surprise breaths, no wide-open eyes, just silence.

They are as close to shock as a group of Descendants can be.

And I do understand them. What I'm saying right now contradicts five thousand years of their beliefs.

No.

Not beliefs.

Knowledge.

They *know* that Old Earth is dead.

And they wouldn't believe me either had they not seen parts of it themselves.

"The land was green, covered with dense vegetation."

"Green," says Goya. "I have seen it."

"I thought it was barren and lifeless. This was the last image of Earth before the Seedships left the solar system," says a Senthien man, sitting behind Goya.

"I only saw one small part of the planet. It is possible that the rest of the planet is different. I cannot tell at this point in time."

"What about the people that we saw?" asks the Senthien who reported seeing people in her Visions.

The Humans.

My Humans.

I can't tell them about my Humans. They are not ready.

"Who are they?" she asks again.

"They were—" *Should I tell them the truth?* My heart is racing now. I know I have to tell them the truth if they are to predict the future, but… I dare not. "They were Zema4 Humans that mis-ported to Earth."

And then, without any order, questions pile up.

"What does that mean?"

"Did they cause the mis-portation?"

"Could it be that Zlathars were right?"

"Were they violent?"

"Did the Zema4s inflict any pain?"

"How did you escape?"

I look at them, shifting my gaze from one pair of eyes to another.

Seekers.

Yes, seeking the truth but still afraid of the one race they were taught to despise. *They will not get very far in their search if they do not open their minds.*

"No. Zema4 inhabitants did not show any violent behavior. And they did not have any influence on the portation at all. They were mis-ported the same as I was."

"But how is it possible to port to Earth in the first place?" asks Laveena. "There are no porting chambers."

"How did you get back?" Sinnya asks.

"Were there other Descendants being mis-ported?"

Oh no, not that one…

But the questions continue, without me being able to answer any.

"Where are the Zema4 Humans now?"

"Did they port here with you?"

The last question has a slight degree of panic in its tone. They are afraid. Still.

How did Zlathars manage to accomplish that?

Glad I can pick a question to answer, I say, "I can't tell you how the portation to Earth is possible and if it can be controlled at all. My return to Senthia was another mis-portation."

They don't need to know I chose to leave Earth. And they certainly don't need to know the reason. "None of the Zema4 Humans came with me. As far as I know, they all remained on Earth."

"What about—"

The sentence, however, is interrupted by a faint beeping sound on everyone's E-bands, except mine.

Adnan glances at his, then switches it off. "We have about one hundred more passes before the next lockdown. We need to go back to our base location before our disappearance causes any concern. If there are more questions, please note them and place them to Dana tomorrow."

Unlike Humans, my fellow Descendants don't argue. They each bow to me slightly and head for the stairs. I return a bow to each of them until only Adnan and my father remain.

"Let us meet again tomorrow at the same time to discuss our new Visions. I am confident that after today's conversation, there will be plenty," he says. "Fenea Maswan Denk, do you have a safe premises for Dana, or shall I arrange a sanctuary?"

"Thank you, Adnan. We will be safe until our meeting tomorrow. I appreciate your concern."

"Good. May Torquemada Joseph Na—" He stops in the middle.

I know where his thoughts are going. Descendants have been using this parting greeting for millennia. But now, for the first time, Adnan is placing everything in question. Even the high Zlathar priest, it seems.

"Be safe," I say. "Until our communication tomorrow."

He nods, then turns swiftly and leaves, his dark green robes swishing as he climbs the stairs.

I sigh audibly, lower my head, and slump on the hard bed. My shoulders sag as I visibly relax.

"This was not an easy ordeal, Dora. You performed well."

"I thank you for your remark." I look at the floor, my gaze unfocused. "It is difficult to carve a path when mine is not clear to me."

My father sits next to me, close, almost touching me. I

expect him to put an arm around my shoulders, but he refrains. He's cautious, just as I would be. We are still in a public place.

"It is a difficult path to walk, like a tightrope with several hundred empty IPs beneath you. You do not know how long the rope is or how far it is to safety.

"But for all creatures of the universe, even us Senthiens, who see glimpses of probabilities, the true future is unknown. The only thing we can do—the only thing anyone can really do—is to choose what to do in this present time. In your *now*."

I look into his green-within-green eyes, and I feel he is talking about something else. Not the Senthiens or Zema4s, the mis-portations and Brookonians, the Zlathars, or even my impure bloodline.

It is something else. And he can see it because… he had felt it himself too. He lost someone before too.

And he can recognize it.

I feel the tears pricking, so I look back to the floor, avoiding his gaze.

I know what he's really saying. He's telling me to live in the present, in the now, independent of what happened or what will happen.

But how can I continue living when the best part of my life is behind me?

"One pass at a time, Dora," he says, as if reading my thoughts. "One pass at a time."

CHAPTER 17

Uni

It's early morning, and the forest is bright, the sun stretching its rays in between the dense foliage, saturating my eyes with vivid shade of green. The air is fresh, intoxicatingly seductive, and I want to keep on inhaling, again and again, without ever needing to exhale.

I know this forest. It's only several hundred IPs away from the tree village.

I smile within and keep on walking, my feet bare on the soft ground as the breeze moves the dress around my legs.

I hope I will see J in this dream. Just for a moment.

But then suddenly I feel a pressure in my chest, and I stop.

As soon as I do, I notice something strange, and I wonder why I didn't realize it before.

The forest is silent. No birds, no sound of the breeze moving through the foliage, no sound of my footsteps.

The pressure inside my chest gets even stronger, as if trapped in a barbed wire cage.

Then I look up. And see J, resting on the ground.

There is an instant moment of happiness, joy, and I wave to him.

But then I realize he's asleep.

I approach him slowly, too slowly, when I notice that he is lying in a pool of opaque brown water.

Or is it mud?

I can't tell.

But the scary thing is that he is sinking! The brown liquid covers one side of his face now, his body half submerged.

"J!" I shout.

His eyes are closed.

I shout again, as loud as I can, while fighting against my rigid muscles to get closer to him.

He opens one eye, slightly above the murky water.

"J, wake up!"

He frowns and tries to push himself up, and then—he disappears, disintegrating into a white smoke.

My muscles release and I spring forward from all the pressure I was putting into them, then stumble and fall on my knees, just at the edge of the dirty water.

I reach with my hand, but instead of dipping my fingers into it, I touch hard brown soil.

And I exhale.

I wake up. The bright lights turn on, blinding me though my eyes are still closed. I cover them with the back of my hand and sigh.

"Are you all right, Dora?" My father is sitting at the small table next to me, his back straight.

I sit up. "Yes, Father, I thank you for your concern."

The walls of this small area are pressing on us. We are not in my father's living quarters. Nor are we in my own.

Both of those would be unsafe.

We are in my father's private research center. Despite the name, there is not much to it: a small room with DC access, a seating area, and a food processor. Senior Senthiens with a high degree of Vision accuracy get access to these rooms so that they can do their own research without needing to go to DC Halls.

"I have ordered two portions of the VRA-08," he says. "A *real* VRA-08." He smiles and pushes the plate toward me.

I grin as well. *No code, just simple food.*

I take a spoon and scoop up the dense whitish liquid, determined to ignore the taste. Or the lack of it.

"Did you have a revealing Vision?"

"I am afraid it wasn't a Vision. Not this time."

"Are you sure?"

"I am sure. There was no logic to the sequence of events."

He puts the spoon next to his plate and pushes it away, then asks, "When you left Earth, was it truly a mis-portation? Was it truly a mistake?"

I stop, my spoon halfway between the plate and my mouth. I lick my lips and put the spoon back down. "No. I chose to leave."

"Why?" Behind a well-trained, aloof tone, I sense something else. Disappointment? Sadness? *Anger?*

I look up at him.

"What happened on Earth?" he asks.

"While I was on Earth, I... I met a man. And he was, I believe, what my mother was to you."

My father's gaze on me is deep and serious. Then he looks down. "I see."

After a long while, he asks, still not looking at me, "Why did you decide to come back?"

I understood at this moment his disappointment, his sadness, his anger. He thought I would be safe there. He would have wanted me to stay. And he would be right.

"I'm sorry, Father, but... it was not meant to be." Tears gather at the rim of my eyes. "It wasn't meant to be. Let's just leave it at that."

"I am sorry for this loss you feel. It will abate with time, but..."

"But...?" I ask.

"But it will never go away."

I look down again, feeling the sorrow crawling back, wrapping up my heart.

"I am sorry," he says again.

"I know."

Then he reaches out across the table with his hand, and I lift up mine so that he can touch them.

"Remember what we did when you were small?" he asks. "When we got back to Uni without... without your mother, when you felt sad? Remember that?"

I nod.

"Let's do that again, shall we?" And he has the softest smile, just like when I was small.

I nod and force a smile as well. "Thank you, Father!" *For everything.*

And we both close our eyes, while our fingertips still touch.

I relax my muscles, starting from the toes, up the calves and quadriceps, relaxing all the muscles of my torso, leaning onto the backrest while I lose direct contact with my father's fingertips. I loosen the muscles in my neck and face, the tiny almost unconsciously tensed muscles behind my ears.

And despite the terrible sorrow bringing back the images of J in front of my closed eyes, I focus on my breathing, forcing myself to be calm, quiet, and detached. And with time—I am.

At 1100, we are ready to go. We are both wearing the same skinsuits as yesterday, waiting at the front door until the lockdown phase allows us to leave.

Five passes later, we are walking down the road leading to the main square of D7. There are many other people around, in fact a lot more than is usual for Senthia at this time of the day. This is expected. The free-roaming time has been reduced dramatically, so everyone tries to use the time available to them.

We both try to keep a normal Senthien gait, paying close attention that we are not too fast, and that we keep the IP distance. We exchange random sentences as if engaged in a discussion, but we are both scanning the area to catch anything out of the ordinary.

To avoid a group of Brookonians, we use a different path than planned to reach the 3D lakes, and we arrive later than we would have wanted.

We enter the large 3D algae lake hall from the other side,

and it takes us longer to walk to the workers' room, but just like yesterday, I still find it breathtaking. I look up into several layers of transparent green sheets above me, seeing the light refracting off the white floor.

"It's beautiful, isn't it?" my father says.

"Yes." I want to elaborate, but something as special as this cannot easily be expressed in words, so I just add, "Yes, it is."

Then I remember something. "I haven't asked you about your Visions, Father. Did you have any last night?"

"I am not sure, Dora. I saw something that… that I don't really understand. I have never seen it before, and I can't grasp what it really means."

"Could you describe it for me?"

"Everything was bathed in blue light. And there was a ball, or an oval maybe, that was being cut into thin slices, which dropped like thin leaflets and fell down on the floor, only it wasn't the floor, it was a pool of liquid of some kind."

I slow down. This very much reminds me of something I have seen myself, for real. "Could you tell how big this oval was?"

"I cannot tell you. There was nothing around it that I could use for scale. It could have been as big as Scapia or as small as my—"

"Nail."

He stops and looks at me. "Does this mean something to you?"

"Maybe," I say and glance at the entry of the staircase. "Maybe now is not the best time, but I think I might have seen that."

"Where?"

"I will tell you later," I say in a lower voice. "I didn't know at the time that it was important, but now I am certain it is, because you have seen it in your Vision. Shall we talk about it later?"

"Yes, I am in agreement with you." So he continues toward the staircase.

I start to follow but abruptly stop.

"Dora, what is it?"

I look back at him, but my range of sight seems narrow, blurred.

"Are you all right?" He comes closer.

I haven't told him about my awake Visions yet.

I smile. "Yes, I am all right, Father. Just another thing I need to tell you about."

"Let's go to the Seekers, and you can sit down."

I nod and start walking again, but the next moment I don't see anything anymore. My sight is blurred to unrecognizable blots and splotches, and above it I see, very clearly, the room we are heading to.

All the Seekers are there. They are all still, looking at someone in front of them.

I pass between them, trying to see who it is. Someone is clearly holding their attention, but no matter where I move, I cannot get a good look.

"Dora!"

I snap out.

"Dora, what is happening?"

I'm kneeling on the floor. My father is holding my shoulders, his face as expressive as I have ever seen it. He is looking at me intently, trying to see if there is any obvious damage.

I have to smile within. "I am all right, Father." I get up. "I…"

"Yes?"

"I had a Vision."

He looks at me bluntly. "Vision? *Right now?*"

"Yes. Sometimes I have Visions in real time, while awake. I discovered that while I was on Earth."

He slowly shakes his head, but his face softens from worry to relief. "You don't cease to amaze me. Come, let's sit down and you can tell me more."

We climb down the stairs, our footsteps soft on the floor, but then a tight sensation grips at my heart, and I stop.

"Father?" I whisper.

But he continues and enters the room.

A feeling of dread rises up my back, increasing my heartbeat. *Something is wrong.*

I swallow.

I don't want to climb down. I don't want to go into that room. I want to turn around and run.

But... I can't leave my father.

So I continue, one slow step after another, while thin strings of anxiety enclose me in a crushing embrace.

CHAPTER 18

Uni

They are here.

The Seekers.

All of them.

They are looking at the front of the room. Something—or somebody—is holding their attention.

The room is quite a lot dimmer than it was yesterday, and on some subconscious level, it raises my vigilance even more, though I can't quite grasp why.

I step behind a person in a last row just next to my dad, who is now also standing still, looking at the front. He must see it as well. I stretch my neck, trying to see, but there are too many people and I can't.

I want to whisper to him, I want to ask him what it is that he is seeing, but then I realize—that I can't.

No voice comes out.

I want to turn my head toward him, and I see—I can't do that either.

I want to step forward, but instead I stand still.

In an instant, panic seeps in and waves of heat sweep over me, as I begin to realize what might be happening.

I then try to move my arms, my fingers, my toes, anything! But I can't.

I am frozen to the floor.

At the corner of my vision, I see movement. I have an instinct to turn my head to the side, but again—I can't. The only thing I can do is focus on the periphery of my vision as best I can.

Through the gaps between the Seekers, I get a glimpse of a person appearing from my left. The figure slowly moves toward me in a most unusual way.

It glides.

The hairs on my back stand up.

There is only one Descendant species that moves like that. And my bones become ice-cold.

The figure appears in front of me. Tall, thin, in a long, dark hooded robe, its face in deep shadows.

My heartbeat accelerates tremendously.

Zlathar.

"I hope you don't mind the dim light, Dana." The voice is soft, smooth, young.

Of course, I can't answer him. Or is it her? I can't tell.

"We are not used to the bright light. But you would know that, wouldn't you?"

I stay silent. Even though it's soft and gentle, his voice gives me shivers.

"You can talk, you know," he says smoothly.

I can? "Why are you here?" My voice is rough, as if I haven't used it in days.

"Is that the very first question you have for me? Nothing more ambitious? Just, why am I here?" He makes a sound. I think it's a chuckle, but it doesn't sound like it. "Let me tell you the answer to the *real* question you should have asked, Dana. Nanoprobes."

I don't understand. I want to frown, but I can't.

He turns around and glides away but makes sure I can still see him.

"The first question should have been, how do you do this? How do you control twenty-six fellow Descendants?".

Then he turns toward me, his robes swirling around him. The shadow under his hood seems even darker than before. "*Nanoprobes.*"

Nanoprobes! He can control the nanoprobes! This is why none of us can move.

Another sound under the hood. A soft, airy sound. Smug.

"Now that we have that cleared up," he says, moving to the side so I can't see him anymore, "let's talk about something far more fascinating. You might recall not so long ago you were invited to join the High Council."

He slowly, very slowly, glides forward. The approach is so unnatural it makes my skin crawl.

"But you did not come." He seems hurt, his voice an octave higher.

"It was not my choice—"

Darkan Ramsimir Far, my nanoprobes signal automatically.

"—noble Councilor Far. I was mis-ported."

"Ah, yes…" A slow murmur under the hood. "Indeed, so you were."

There is a moment of silence, and for some reason this scares me even more.

"As you might or might not know, the porting mistakes happened to Zema4 inhabitants. To Humans."

He swings back to me. His voice, two octaves deeper now, reverberates somewhere deep in his throat. "*Only* to Humans.

"You can imagine our surprise"—his voice is cheerful once more—"to find out that two of our Senthiens went missing to an un-coded territory.

"We were extremely intrigued by how this might have happened. We made a full inquiry of all the data we had on Barka Stevanion Narth. We found nothing. But you? You turned out to be quite a surprise for us." With the last of his words, another deeper rumbling sound almost growls at me. "It was superbly done, escaping all our high-level checks. A worthy plan, I have to admit."

From the corner of my eye, I see another movement.

"Don't strain, Dana. You can't see him, but don't worry. He will soon be here."

And then my father steps right in front of me.

"Father…," I whisper.

He is standing so I can see his profile, but he doesn't turn toward me. He just stops midmotion between the Zlathar and me.

"He was such an important individual in our Senthien community."

A sharp sting pierces my heart. "Was?"

"Ah." He rolls a sound that doesn't exist in *ah*. "You picked it up, didn't you? *Was.* As brilliant as Maswan is, he is a traitor. And we don't tolerate traitors."

I ignore the growling sound behind his words. "You can't do anything to him. He's not a Human. He's a Senthien, a Descendant. He is protected," I say with as much force as I can.

"No?" he says cheerfully as he tilts his head to one side.

And the very next moment, my father drops to the floor like an empty piece of clothing.

I yelp, looking down, though my head is fixed straight. I want to kneel next to him, grab him, pick him up. But all I can do is look down, my body frozen, unresponsive to my wants and needs.

My throat collapses, and sobs that can't be formed push their way out of my lungs. And I cry, without tears, as I look at my father crumpled on the floor.

"Father?" My voice is broken and rough. "Father…"

"Oh… I'm sorry, was there still something you wanted to say to him?" He sighs. "I will keep that thought for the next time. It didn't—it didn't cross my mind."

I look into the dark shadows underneath the hood. Cold, moist air drifts toward me. And I'm nauseated. By his words, by his smell, by his act.

"You. Can't!" I say through my teeth.

For a moment he doesn't move, as if he's under the spell of one of his nanoprobes. Suddenly all twenty-four people in the room fall on the ground, as if invisible strings holding them up just got cut.

My mouth is open but I can't breathe in.

"I can," he whispers. "And I did."

Inside, I'm shaking. "No… No… No…"

"Oh Dana…" His voice changes once again. It's soft and gentle and in such discord with his deed. "If anyone, you would know best. They have heard too much. They know too much. And this can't spread. It would bring out a whole new set of Visions. We simply can't have that."

I look down, still shaking, but despite the quiver, my voice is strong. "It will happen, Zlathar. Senthiens *will* see it."

"Oh, so innocent." Chirpy tone, almost like a child. "Yes, of course they will. But we will erase it. No one will remember any Vision they shouldn't."

I turn to him, my face contorted. "You tried it before. And it didn't work. The Seekers still happened. And they will form again. You failed."

The laughter that comes next is so high-pitched it hurts my ears. Then abruptly it stops.

"We failed on purpose. We needed the Visions. We needed to find out what was happening to our yield. We *needed* the Seekers. And they did exactly what we wanted them to do. They brought us to you."

"I won't tell you a thing."

"You won't have to." A shadowy whisper over his chirpy voice. "Your nanoprobes will.

"Monsignor Nadraque will see you shortly," he says more swiftly, as two Brookonians appear next to me. "Since we can't afford to port you—who knows where you would end up next time—our beloved High Ruler will come to us.

"I am sure he will be extremely pleased with the progress we have made." His voices are mixed with one another—the chirpy, the airy, and the rumbling one—like a group of conspirators huddled together, whispering to each other in secret.

"How many of you are in there?" I can't help but ask.

His head snaps up amazingly fast, and he's still, unmoving, as I stare at the blackness under the hood.

The next moment, a deep, dull ache in my skull makes my eyes roll backward.

I fall on the floor and all goes black.

CHAPTER 19

Earth

J is sitting at the table, hunched, his hands resting lifelessly against his thighs. He is looking at his plate still full of food, now cold. His thoughts are a jumbled mess, each corner of his mind speaking several languages at once, and he can't understand any of the dialects.

His body feels weak, but at the same time, it is tight, as if all his muscles are working, twitching constantly, with no proper rest.

"Darling, what is it?" Monica comes from behind and slides her fingers through J's ruffled hair, then sits down next to him, pulling his plate closer to him. "You need to eat. You haven't had a proper meal in days. You will vanish!"

J is looking at the food, his gaze unfocused, completely still.

She leans a bit forward and looks at him, scanning him so that he can clearly see it. "It's such a waste, you know." She smiles sideways, raising one of her eyebrows. "I mean, look at this body. We don't want to lose that, do we?" She winks at him. "I, for sure, don't! Come. Eat, darling."

But J sits still.

Monica puts her hand on top of his thigh, lacing her

fingers with his, even though there is no tension in his palm. "I understand, or at least I think I understand, how it must have been for you the past nine years."

J is rooted to his chair, frozen.

"Sandra… told me some things."

Now finally J looks at her.

"She told me how hard it was for you. She said everyone could see it… And I'm sorry. I'm sorry that I wasn't there."

J takes a deep breath and turns his head away to look through the window, into the gray distance where the thick steel-blue clouds completely block the sun, threatening rain.

Monica hugs him with one arm and leans on his shoulder. "But I am here now." She looks at him, and J finally meets her gaze. "Come back to me."

Her words burn in J's mind, tightening his throat, and he returns her hug. "I know," he whispers. "I'm sorry."

Resting her chin on his shoulder, Monica sighs. "We'll have what we had soon enough, darling. It just needs time."

J's throat closes shut. *Time. That's what Dora said. That I need time.*

She gave me time. She gave me lots of time. But what I needed, what I really wanted, was for her to stay here, on Earth.

And now this *time* has lost its importance, because Dora is gone.

J closes his eyes, fighting the tears, willing them away.

But one of them escapes.

And slides down his cheek.

J quickly wipes it away with the back of his hand, then stands up. "I…," he starts, staring at the floor. "I need to be on my own for a moment."

Monica is staring at him, speechless.

"Things are—" His breath gets locked in. "Things are just different."

Monica looks down, her eyes searching for some pattern on the wooden planks, something to make things clear and right. "Okay, different. But…" She looks up at him. "But we are still *we*, aren't we?"

And his heart breaks in half.

He sighs heavily. "I don't know, Mon. I don't know."

And he turns quickly and walks out the door, leaving Monica staring helplessly behind him.

He bumps into Simon on the way out of his cottage.

"Hey, I was just about—"

But J swings past him. "Not now!"

"Oh, okay… Are you all right?" he calls after him.

"No!"

And J starts to run across the tree village, over the bridges, around the houses, toward the nearest exit tree.

Once he reaches it, he climbs down so fast that he misses some of the protrusions, and he scrapes the skin on his shins and forearms. He drops on the ground, still muddy from last night's shower. His feet are bare, and the brown muddy slush pushes between his toes. Then he starts to run, leaves, small stones and branches sharp against his feet.

He runs fast, his muscles burning, but J pushes them more, sweat breaking on his skin, his heartbeat loud in his ears, drumming behind his breastbone, about to explode.

He speeds up even more.

The air burns as it passes down his throat, his chest

constricting as the pain gets stronger, gripping his heart in its fangs.

Yes! Faster…Faster… Faster! So fast it can't take it anymore. So fast—it stops!

And at that thought, he abruptly halts.

Until my heart stops.

The thought is there again.

He leans with one hand on a large tree, blood flow buzzing in his ears, blocking all the sounds of the forest, his heart still drumming crazily, trying to recover, his chest heaving uncontrollably.

After a long while, his heartbeat slows back to normal, his breathing even again.

He pushes himself away from the tree and in that moment, the tree catches his attention. A thick, tall, strong tree, with brown crusty bark, reaching far up into the sky; and elegantly wrapped around it, embracing it in the body of arms and legs of smooth light green bark, lives another tree.

J steps forward and slowly, very slowly, puts his hand on the green tree, folding his palm over the smooth, concave branch.

And, unavoidably, he thinks of Dora.

Dora's green eyes, her soft, pale skin, her delicate hands with green-tinted nails, and he realizes that the color of this hugging tree is exactly the same shade as Dora has in her eyes.

He knew where the color had come from, but it wasn't the color that drew him. It was the depth he saw in them, like a forest lake he could dive into and stay in forever, not wishing—not needing—any air.

Then he wraps both his arms around the large brown trunk, hugging the green tree as well, leaning his cheek on the smooth vine.

He closes his eyes, but the tears find their way. And he cries without a sound, hugging this tree, embracing his Dora.

Gone.

Gone.

She's gone.

Then he drops to the ground, his knees on muddy soil, and buries his face in his hands, the tears finding cracks between his fingers, falling uncontrollably.

He can't make them stop.

I let her go.

Oh my God, I let her go…

And he sobs, his throat dry and broken.

I wish… Oh, I so wish there was a way for her to come back.

His breath hitches between sobs.

She needs to know.

She needs to feel it.

She needs to understand that… I can't be without her…

She needs to come back.

And he cries again, because he knows it will never be. She will never come back.

And the thought breaks him, suffocates him, blinds him.

Kills him.

He bows his head down to the ground, his forehead touching the dirty mud, and then, like a wild animal that just received a deadly bullet, dignified yet agonizingly tragic, he falls on his side.

His eyes are open, but he's not seeing anything. He's listening, but he's not hearing anything.

The dark slowly covers the forest, and the cloudy night sky breaks into a loud thunder as the first raindrops start to fall.

One lands on the puddle before him, making a tiny splash of dirty water on his cheek. Then another one drops on his neck, finding its way to the ground through the pattern of sweat and dirt covering his skin.

And then the rain truly starts, heavy and deafening.

The water bouncing off the puddles splatters into his eyes. It stings, but he still keeps them open. He watches the puddles growing larger, as darkness falls on the South African forest.

It feels cold. It feels good.

I'll... stay here... for a moment.

So he closes his eyes and lets the night embrace him in its darkness.

CHAPTER 20

Uni

I wake up, sitting on the floor, twisted and awkward, stiff and sore all over my body. I've been lying here for a very long time.

I'm in a narrow glass tube, diameter less than one IP.

An Access Point station.

It is narrower than the Data Center room I used many times before, but it has a similar interface. I glance at the dark holo screen. This one is not functional.

The glass tube is open at the top, and a strong light shines into the cell. It's too bright and I need to squint.

Outside it's dark, and all I can see on the concave glass wall are the hard shadows that the bright beam of light drops on my face.

I sit up straighter, trying to release the cramps in my back muscles. But then I collapse again in a small ball, hugging my knees and burying my face between my arms. My lips are trembling, my eyes stinging, and I try to fight back. I try to stay strong. But I can't.

I hide my face in my palms and I cry, sobbing hard, the sound echoing in the empty dark room around me.

The grief of losing my mother so long ago comes back,

mixed and mingled and multiplied many times over with this new, raw pain.

I cry for a long, long time, empty of thoughts, with only images of me and my father, me and my mother, me and J, flashing behind my closed eyelids. And with enormous pressure squeezing my heart I realize that I will never, ever have another memory like those again.

My throat constricts and I cannot take another breath.

The world crumbles inside me, and the only things that remain are ashes and dust.

After a long time, my tears run dry. I'm staring emptily at the contorted reflection of my face, white powdery streaks on my cheeks, my eyes swollen and red.

It's uncomfortable, lying like this, cramped and twisted, but I don't care.

It doesn't matter.

Nothing does.

I close my eyes, and my eyelids feel scratchy, collapsing over my dry eyes.

It feels good to have them closed. To keep them closed. And never open them again.

My mind is full of thoughts, bright flashes in a dark room, appearing without any order. But at the same time, my mind is silent. And empty. And hollow.

I am just a shell, reliving the past, the flashes that come and go as they please.

Then I hear something. Two birds fluttering from one side of the room to another. I automatically look up.

But there is nothing here, of course. There are no birds on

Senthia. It is only the sound of a recording I made on Earth that flashed as one of my many uncontrolled thoughts.

I sigh and then decide to let it play.

I play everything that I have saved.

The bonfire threading its sparkly brilliant waves into the dark sky.

The breathtaking dark blue liquid eternity with white waves galloping over its surface.

The thunderous sound as gallons of water crashing over black stone and falling into the deep pool with a brilliant bow of colors glittering above it.

And I remember…

I remember touching the ferns with my fingertips.

I remember the moss on the bark of the trees, the fabric of the dress floating and dancing around me in the breeze.

I remember Tania's voice and Stevanion's last words.

I remember J's messy brown hair and sun-bathed skin. Rough palms and his large hands.

The warm skin tensed over tight muscles.

Small dimples in his cheeks, whenever he smiled.

The kiss.

The cave.

Us. In the cave.

Feeling him with all of my body as he brings me to the most sensual inner place I have ever been.

And for a moment I feel it, the inner earthquake, the distortion of reality, that two people—two Humans—can share.

And the love that makes it all possible.

I had it.

I did.

The love.

The love of a mother. The love of a father.

The love of J.

I had it all.

I sigh, deeply and contently.

I *had* the best time of my life.

And now it's behind me.

There's a strange type of comfort in this notion, almost transcendental, because there is nothing ahead.

My life has already happened. And there is nothing to fear any longer.

Freedom and a strange, bizarre contentment are woven through my sorrow and grief now.

I lean back on the cold glass wall and look at my reflection, shadows of black and white.

Despite my new inner peace, my body feels weak. Drained. Flat. And I can see it in my reflection.

The grief, no matter how mental it is, has real physical consequences.

Then, without warning, thoughts of my father dropping down on the floor right in front of me come up again, and I clench my jaw muscles, fighting the inner anguish.

But then I deliberately and intentionally, just as I learned many centuries ago, relax all my muscles as best as possible in this confined space, and I erase all my thoughts.

I send them away. Far, far away.

And I breathe, focusing on the rhythm of my breaths.

They are slowing down.

Slower… and slower… and slower…

Until… I don't hear them anymore.

CHAPTER 21

Earth

It is a bright, sunny day. Midmorning. The leaves dance in the sunshine, casting dashing shadows on the ground.

It is one of those wonderful days that J always likes, except that… there is something missing.

He takes a breath and looks to the crowns of the trees, swinging in the wind.

And then he realizes. It is quiet.

There is no sound of the wind blowing through the branches, whizzing as it cuts down through each and every leaf's edge.

There are no bird songs.

No insects buzz.

Just silence.

Quite suddenly Dora appears. She's here, only a few feet away.

She's wearing the sleeveless top and long beige cotton skirt. The slow breeze on the ground is lifting the fabric away from her bare feet.

Her ankles show, and with certain gusts of wind, so do her calves.

She's walking toward him, slowly, almost seductively, smiling at him.

He smiles back.

The breeze seems to slow down her every move, the fabric gently moving around her legs, her footsteps slow as she walks toward him.

Dora... So graceful...

He gazes dreamily at her.

A part of him is afraid. Afraid to move because he thinks if he does, she would surely disappear.

So he stays still. And continues looking at her, enchanted.

She's next to him, a deep frown on her face.

Why is she frowning?

She kneels next to him.

"J!" she shouts.

He moans.

"J! Wake up!"

J opens his eyes. And then coughs hard, spitting out the dirty water collected in his throat. He keeps coughing, trying to expel the water, and once there's no more air in his lungs, he takes a long, wheezing breath, and this again causes another fit of coughing.

After several minutes, the coughing finally stops.

He leans with his hand in the puddle next to him and looks down at it, crossly.

Stupid.

He pushes himself off the ground and coughs once more, then looks around.

It is dark and wet, and he can hardly see anything.

His left eye is burning, so he rubs it with the back of his hand, but that makes it even worse.

He ignores the itchy eye, ignores the throat that screams for another round of coughing, and tries to orient himself.

He looks up, squinting.

The rain is falling hard. It's dark and he can't see much, except faint lights on his right.

He's about to turn to walk toward the lights, but just before he sets off, he glances at the tree next to him, the dark brown wrapped in a green passionate embrace, almost invisible in this darkness. He touches it, his rough palm on the smooth green branch, then a moment later he lets go and sets off toward the village.

His bare feet stamp on the wet ground, beige trousers now completely brown, heavy and wet, sticking to his skin. Two bright tubes of LED torches are moving in midair, but it's too bright for him to see the people carrying them.

Soon he hears his name.

"J!"

It's Patrick.

"J, for crying out loud, man! What are you doing?" Patrick stabs the torch in the ground, and now J can see them both. Peter is here too.

"Are ye off yer mind, boy?" Peter grabs him by his shoulders.

J coughs once. "I'm… I'm okay."

"No, yer not! Look at ye! C'mere!" Peter pushes J forward, then says, a bit more softly this time, "Yer sanity teleported away the same time as Dora."

Patrick puts an arm around J's shoulder and walks in rhythm with his pace. "You've been gone for more than six hours."

Six hours?

"What happened?" The heavy rain almost drowns Patrick's words.

"I… I have been thinking."

"Yev been thinkin'?" shouts Peter. "*Yev been thinkin'?* In the middle of the night? Durin' the downpour? Seriously?"

J smiles at Peter, his voice loud over the rain. "It wasn't dark when I left. And it wasn't raining either."

Peter shakes his head, an exaggerated motion to make a point.

After several minutes they reach the entry tree of the village.

"J, can ye please head to our place? Tania saved some dinner for ye," says Peter, then he turns to Patrick. "I'll tell the others we found 'im." He sets off in the opposite direction to find the other search parties.

Love, Peter thinks. *Can make yer life miserable, yet ye can't live without it.*

CHAPTER 22

Earth

The cottage is quiet.

The LED torches are all off, but the place is lit by three candles shining a soft orange light around the room.

J is sitting on a wooden bench next to the table, cupping a steaming metal mug between his hands. He's wrapped up in a blanket, and there is a small puddle underneath his seat.

Patrick is leaning on the windowsill, looking at the stormy, dark weather outside.

On the other side of the table sit Tania and Peter, looking at J like a defused bomb, wondering if there is a second fuse somewhere they didn't think to check.

J blows on his tea and takes a sip, the hot liquid burning the tip of his tongue. He's focused on the small ripples on the surface of the liquid, but from the corner of his eyes he can still see them staring.

"Can you please stop looking at me like that?" he says.

"Aye. When ye finally tell us what ye were doin' outside in this crazy weather."

J bows his head, then puts the cup on the floor between his feet. "I was…" He shrugs. "I needed space."

"From Monica?" asks Tania.

J nods, but after a moment he adds, "From everybody, I guess."

"Well, it wasna' the best o' timing, yer know?"

After a while, J says, "I don't care."

"J, I understand what you feel, but…" Tania sighs. "This wasn't all that clever."

J doesn't react.

"J? It wasn't your fault." She tries again, trying to bring more authority into her voice. "It wasn't your fault she left. It was her decision and she—"

"This is where you are wrong, Tania. I *chased* her away."

"She didn't really give you a lot of time to digest everything. And there was a lot to digest, that's clear for everyone!"

"She could've given ye a wee bit of time, ye know?"

J smiles emptily. "Guys, I know you're all trying to make me feel better. But…" His voice dies out as he looks down at the floor again.

After a long while Patrick says, while still looking into the night, "I was still hoping she wouldn't manage."

Tania turns to him. "What do you mean?"

"I thought the teleportation wouldn't work." Patrick looks back. "I was certain we would see her at the drop point, and"— he shrugs—"we'd just take her back home."

Patrick shakes his head, deep in his thoughts. "And we saw her. She was just sitting there, and I thought, it's gonna be fine… I thought we'd—" He glances at J and then stops talking.

J's face is an array of agonizing contortions. He is trying to hide it, but he fails. He bows his head low and presses his thumb and index finger firmly on his eyes, his elbow resting on his knee.

"I'm sorry, J," Patrick whispers. "I didn't mean to… I'm sorry." And he turns away again.

And the silence covers them again, thick and heavy, for several long minutes.

"I knew the beam would pick her up. Even before we saw her," J says quietly, almost to himself.

"How?"

"The sound. It changes in the most unusual way. I just thought…" He swallows hard now. "I thought I could jump in and it would catch me as well."

There is the cry of a jackal far in the forest, and the moon finds a gap between a few of the clouds, shining white silvery threads into the cottage, mingling the cold colors on the wooden floor with the soft yellow of the candlelight.

"Well, she should have stayed," Tania says and stands to pick up the plates from the table. "Just to give you a bit of time to think about it. That's what I would have done."

"You are a hundred percent Human," Patrick says.

"What does that mean?" Tania stops cleaning up.

"It means that her decision was made by her Senthien," he responds and pushes away from the windowsill.

"And why wouldna' she listen to her Human?" asks Peter.

"Because it was her Human that got hurt, and she didn't trust it any longer," says J with finality.

Patrick reaches for the piled-up plates. "Let me take that, Tania."

"Thanks." And she sits down, then glances at the still-full plate in front of J. "Aren't you going to eat something?"

"I'm sorry, Tania. I just don't feel like it right now."

"You haven't been feeling like it for the past five days."

Patrick waits for a moment to see if Tania's comment changes

J's mind, but when he sees that it hasn't, he piles J's plate up on top and takes it away.

"Ye know," Peter says. "We might need to feed him intravenously before he *fades* away."

Patrick laughs from the kitchen, and J's lips, for the first time in days, spread into a smile. He nods. "You might actually be right."

"As brilliant as this idea is," says Patrick, coming back to the table, "I highly doubt we'll find a functional IV set somewhere in the Underground."

"Aye, ba' perhaps we don' need it," says Peter with a grin. "Maybe we can use Stevanion's E-band. There might be some hidden integrated med kit we don' know about. And then we can intravenously feed J for the rest of his days." Peter winks at J.

But J's smile disappears.

Peter turns serious as well. "Um… sorry, J! I was just—"

"No!" J lifts up his hand, his eyes open wide. "You said Stevanion's E-band!"

Peter shrugs. "Aye. So?"

"I don't think there is a med kit anywhere on Ste—" Patrick starts.

"Do we still have it?" J interrupts. "The E-band?"

"Yes… we do. Why?" Tania is wary, her eyes narrowing as she looks at J.

Then, out of nowhere, J starts to laugh so hard it shakes the table.

Peter turns his head to Tania, though still looking at J. "I think we've just lost 'im."

J keeps laughing for almost a minute, tears running down his cheeks, while the rest of the company waits, frozen and unsure.

He wipes the tears from his cheeks but can't stop laughing.

Then Patrick smacks his forehead. "Oh, of course! Why didn't I think of that?"

"Er…" Peter glances at J, then at Patrick, then back at J. "What are ye talkin' about?"

Patrick is smiling broadly now as well. "If you stand at the drop point, at the base of the teleportation tube, it doesn't just automatically teleport you. You need to have something to enable it."

"And what would that be?" asks Tania.

"An E-band," J says and stands up from the table.

"Oy, where are ye off to?"

J smiles broadly. "I am going after her."

CHAPTER 23

Uni

J is sitting on the side of a bed. Monica seems to have just woken up, her curly hair wild around her face.

They are talking about something.

Monica puts a palm on J's face, stroking it gently. "Doesn't it matter to you what I think? What I want?"

J hesitates a bit, then he takes her hand into his, lacing their fingers together. "I think Dora deserves to be saved. She is the one who lifted this village out of the Stone Age. She is the person who stopped the cryo for your batch, Mon. She is the one who brought you back. You wouldn't be here if it wasn't for her. Don't you think she deserves saving?"

"Yes, Jonathan, but why you? Why can't anyone else go? I mean, we are together, finally, and we need time with each other, now more than ever."

She lowers her gaze. "Maybe—maybe Patrick can go?" She looks up at J. "Patrick could go. Or Simon. Or... or... Timothy. Well, anyone. Anyone else. Why do you need to go to Uni?"

I suck in a wheezy, long breath, pulling in the air as if I just emerged out of water. Holding my hands against the glass wall, I hyperventilate, trying to come to grips with what I just saw.

Uni?

He wants to go to Uni?

No! This… can't be real. He wouldn't do something like that, would he?

But the Vision was vivid and clear, as all my true Visions are.

He would.

And he will.

Oh, for the Moons of Senthia, how could he even think about something like that?

I bang my fist on the glass.

Stupid!

This is *so* stupid of him!

If he comes to Uni, he will be in danger, even greater danger than I am now. He will be labeled as a Human. He will be captured—I swallow hard—and most likely killed. And it will happen no matter which planet he lands on.

Oh, this is such a badly substantiated decision, J. Why would you do something like that?

But, of course, I know why. He said it himself: he owes it to me. I am the person who saved his wife. And now I am in danger. He feels obliged to try to save me.

It is as clear as that.

Stupid, but clear.

I cover my face with my hands. *What am I going to do?*

I look up the tube.

I need to get out.

I need to find him before anyone else does.

I look up, judging the height of the cell's edge, then push myself off the ground.

I could try to climb over, but it seems too high.

I glance to my right.

The silent holo interface is smooth, but its dent might give me leverage to climb up.

I look at the glass, though I can't see through. A Brookonian might be standing right in front of this tube and I wouldn't be able to see him.

Still, it doesn't change a thing.

There is no need to fear, if there's only one choice to be made.

I lift my leg as high as I can and hook the tip of my boot at the top edge of the interface, then press my palms flat on the concave glass and push as hard as I can off the floor.

But my boot slips and I fall, the sound reverberating off the glass in the dark room. The fall pushes the air out of my lungs, and I need a moment before I can catch another breath.

I look up again, press my lips in a stubborn line, then position my boot sideways on the dent and try again.

The foot holds and I manage to grab the top edge of the glass tube. With all my might, I pull myself up, the muscles in my arms burning from the exertion. But I don't let go. I can't. I need to hold on.

I pull up to my chest, my muscles quivering, and I'm afraid they will just let go. Then I manage to swing my elbow over the edge and pull myself up even more.

The room outside is small with three other Access Point rooms like mine. The place is empty.

Still holding on with one of my feet on the wall, I swing the other leg across the edge and move myself to the other side. The edge of the glass, though not sharp, feels very uncomfortable as it scrapes against my belly.

As soon as I feel the balance is shifting to the other side, I change my grip so that both hands hold on to the outer side. Then the complete weight switch comes faster than I anticipated, and my fingers, unused to this load, release. I fall on the other side.

Ignoring the pain, I stand up and turn around to face the exit.

Thankfully Senthia does not have classic containment cells, otherwise my escape would not have been so easy.

I walk to the exit, giving my E-band a command to open it, but the sliding door remains sealed.

'Inaccessible' blinks on my E-band.

Oh, the Moons of Senthia! How am I going to get out now?

Panic rises inside me as a steady breeze from the airing system cools the beads of sweat on my forehead.

There's an ID scanner next to the door. If I try to open it, it might alert them that I've escaped. But if this is the only way for me to get out—I raise my hand to the scanner—so be it.

I place my palm on the cold ID scanner. It blinks red and the doors stay closed.

I drop my hand.

Argh, the Moons of Senthia! I need to get out! I need to leave this place.

Leaning on the door with my shoulder, I try to slide it sideways, pushing with my hands as well.

My heart's drumming wildly, every beat heavier than the one before, enhanced by the adrenaline surge.

Come on!

I need to find J before anyone else does!

I need to save him!

I need a way out!

I'm almost screaming these words in my mind, banging my hand on the rigid door.

Let me out!

I turn, looking around, more panic settling in and making my arms sweat, my body shake, my breath quivering so much it's making me dizzy.

There has to be something.

I keep turning, scanning the room. There is nothing I could use to pry the door open. I start walking to the other two APs while wiping sweat off my forehead.

Think, Dora, think! I pace around the small room.

Then a thought comes, and I stop.

It sounds crazy, but I might as well try.

Holding my breath, I command my nanoprobes to find the closest porting chamber, and then within a micro-pass, the green direction path lights up.

From my standpoint, the DRP leads to the door, but then it does not disappear behind it; rather, it slides up the gray door and ends on the ceiling.

I slowly approach and look up, only to see the grid of the airing system: the intricate connection of tubes transporting oxygen from the 3D lakes to all the domes, living quarters, and—porting chambers.

I realize Zlathars control the nanoprobes, and I know I just might be walking into a trap, but this has helped me once before. And right now it's my best option.

I retreat a few steps, then run and spring upward, grabbing the grid. If I hadn't had Earth's gravity to train me in the past twenty days, I might not have been able to do this, but now I manage to hook my fingers in.

Under my weight, the grid detaches from the ceiling and I land on the floor, the grid banging loudly as it hits the ground.

I grab it again and position it vertically so it gives me more elevation, then stand with my foot on the edge and push myself upward off the balancing grid. I pull the top of my body above the shaft, and the grid falls loudly on the floor again once my feet let go. I pull the rest of my body into the airing tubes, the breeze feeling invigorating on my skin.

I silence my E-band so I'm not traceable, then look around. The DR lights a path on the metal floor of the airing shaft, and without thinking, I follow, crawling on all fours as fast as I can.

CHAPTER 24

Uni

I follow the green track, changing directions every so often. Some tubes are larger and I can kneel and move around. But some are very narrow and small, and I need to lie on my belly and slowly push myself forward.

As I'm following this path, one thought becomes completely clear. This is not a map that I'm reading from. The official maps cover streets and paths of the Uni planets and moons. *Not the airing shafts.*

I squeeze through a particularly narrow corridor.

Definitely not the airing shafts.

This DRP has been made for me. And although I don't know the source, I have to trust it because it hasn't failed me yet—and this is the only option I have.

After more than thirty passes, I need to rest. I lean my head on my crossed hands while relaxing and extending my sore neck muscles.

I tilt my head left and right, and just before I'm about to continue, I hear something.

I look up.

I don't see anything yet, but I hear it. A swishing sound, regular, circular—and coming closer.

I enhance my TAEs and listen more closely. *Where is it coming from?*

Could it be the corridors underneath me?

I close my eyes and focus even more.

No!

It's in the airing shaft, right behind me.

I start crawling fast, looking back every second or two.

I don't know what this is, but I need to be faster. I need to get to the porting chamber before it reaches me.

I push myself forward with all my effort, ignoring the strain in my muscles.

And then, from one moment to the next, the sound changes from medium to loud.

I look backward and see it.

It's a maintenance robot, a half-sphere dark gray metal capsule, quarter of an IP in diameter, here to clean the airing channels. It is not very large, but it moves a lot faster than I am, and when it gets here, there won't be enough space for both of us in this narrow tunnel.

I look to the front, quickly checking left and right, trying to see if there is a side turn I could sneak into.

But several dozen IPs ahead, I see none. Only one straight tube.

I glance backward. It's only ten IPs behind me and advancing quickly.

I straighten my legs and prepare for impact.

It hits my feet first, my boots giving me solid protection from the clash with the metal. It pushes me one IP forward, then stops, my weight too heavy for it to continue. It starts getting louder, putting more pressure on my feet. I won't be able to keep my legs straight for much longer.

Using my arms, I push myself to the side and exhale all the air in my lungs, making myself as thin as possible as I try to blend in with the metal wall.

The robot is released, and it pushes its way next to my belly, my chest, scraping its metallic brushes along my skinsuit. But the fabric resists. If I was wearing any other skinsuit than this one, it would have been shredded to pieces, together with the skin underneath. But not this one.

The sound gets terribly loud as it approaches my ears. I turn my head and bury my face in my shoulder, closing my eyes.

Please let it be enough… Let it be enough…

And—it pushes past me, a few of the metallic brushes scraping my right cheek.

It's over.

The robot continues while I'm still plastered to the side of the wall, trembling as my muscles loosen from the high exertion.

I take a deep breath and then roll flat on the floor.

The scrapes on my cheek burn.

I touch them with my finger and realize they're bleeding profusely, and it hurts a lot more than I'd expect.

I wipe my fingers on my skinsuit trousers, dismissing the thought. It should heal quickly.

And I continue, my eyes on the green path.

After a long while I finally come to the DRP's blinking red end point.

I crawl to the shaft and peek through.

The opening is just above the porting chamber entrance, a few dozen IPs from the corridor gate.

Perfect!

I check my TAEs, making sure there is no sound, then sit on the edge and slam my foot into the grid.

With almost no effort, the grid lets loose and falls on the ground.

Loudly.

I need to be fast; this will draw attention.

But where should I port?

Where would J go?

No. That's the wrong question.

Where would the Mind *send him?*

And then it dawns on me. The only way to find out is to go to the place where the database for all the porting trajectories are kept.

Lorea.

I push myself off the edge and jump into the pre-port room while engaging my ONCs to give me just enough light to see something in this darkness. I set my TAEs to the highest sensitivity level, making sure I'll hear if anyone approaches.

I turn toward the porting chamber door, and I'm hoping that if I just step toward it, it will open.

But it doesn't.

I glance at the ID scanner on my right and roll my hands into a ball.

I'll need to ID…

I look down, my brain buzzing with possible options. I turn, looking back at the long corridor leading to the entry gate.

I won't get a better option than this, if I'm to escape Senthia.

I turn back and then press my hand on the cold panel.

I can only hope that the port is faster and I am gone before the Brookonians get here.

The door in front of me slides open, but at the same time

the lights start flashing red. An alarm starts a penetrating wailing sound, and it pierces my ears. My TAEs are screaming.

I run into the porting chamber, decreasing the volume of the TAEs to almost the minimum, and the only thing I hear now is my heavy breathing. I swipe new commands to direct my port.

"The port number 452-79-898-01 to porting gate 7251'21'13 will start in one pass," says a pleasant AI voice, muffled because of my decreased TAEs.

The porting door slides closed and I exhale, the whole of my body relaxing to such an extent that I almost sit down with the lack of the body tonus.

I'll be fine.

I take another deep breath and look around. It's a large porting chamber, easily for fifty people or more.

But then I hear something.

My body tenses again as I increase the sensitivity of my TAEs and hear the running footsteps of a group of Brookonians from the porting corridor. They are running toward this chamber.

"I'll be fine. I'll be fine," I whisper as I stare at the closed porting gate. "I'll be fine."

"The port will commence in three—" a calm AI voice announces, an ironic comparison to the dread I feel inside.

I'll be fine. They cannot open the gate if the porting had already sta—

The gate slides open.

No! No, it can't!

I take a few steps backward and touch the back wall of the porting chamber, my eyes frozen on the first Brookonian soldier as he passes through the porting gate, with many more behind him.

The moment he sees me, he runs toward me, reaching out with both his arms.

"Two—"

His hand grabs my throat and he squeezes tightly, the pressure on both my carotid arteries blocking the blood flow to my brain, and my vision blurs with a million black dots. I can't take another breath.

"One."

The purple wave washes over me, heavy on my body, pressing me from all sides while I'm still yearning for air, my throat squeezed shut by the heavy gloved hand.

Next moment, everything around me is gone. And I'm back in nothing.

CHAPTER 25

Earth

The first rays of sunshine seep over the tree village.

All is quiet. The sounds of nocturnal creatures fade as the night disappears, but the chirpy sounds of the dawn birds haven't yet started, and all the villagers are still asleep.

Except J and Patrick.

They are packing their load for the trip: several days' worth of food, extra clothes should it rain during the hike, a torch, and some medical herbs.

Without looking at J, Patrick says, "I can't go with you to Uni."

"I know."

Patrick stops packing and looks at J. "I wish I could."

J stops now as well.

"I wish," continues Patrick, "I wish I could give you some backup so that you're not on your own, you know. It might not be… Well, it *isn't* a good place for a Human in Uni, we know that, right? I mean, you are aware of that, right?"

J smiles warmly and puts a hand on Patrick's shoulder, with an encouraging squeeze. "Yes, I am aware. And thank you for your support in everything, Patrick. I really do appreciate it."

"Of course. Always." Patrick takes a deep breath, then stuffs the last bit of items into the backpack and closes it. "J?"

"Yes?"

"How are you going to come back?" Patrick avoids J's eyes.

J stands up and looks through the window at the breaking dawn. "I don't know. I don't know. The only thing I do know is that I need to go after her." Then he turns to look at Patrick and smiles, softly and peacefully, as if this is the only possible reality. "I have never been so certain about anything as I am about this."

Patrick nods. "I understand…"

"I need to talk to Monica." J heads for the door. "Give me a few minutes, will you?"

Patrick looks up at him. "Good luck."

J steps to the door, about to lift the leaf curtain to enter, but then stops, the tips of his fingers touching the long, heavy strips. His mind is suddenly blank.

He was so thrilled, so ecstatic to find even the slightest possible way of finding Dora that, until a moment ago, he hadn't properly thought how to explain all this to Monica.

He rubs his hands over his face, trying to focus.

I need to tell her. I need to be honest.

But I also need to be gentle.

She has been through so much.

He takes a deep breath and walks in.

Monica is in bed, still sleeping, her curly red hair sprayed around her head like a wild halo. He used to like seeing her like this.

He still does.

There is a part of him, a big part, that loves her, that cares for her. Which makes this next step even more difficult to do.

He sits at the edge of the bed and strokes her hair away from her face. Monica sighs, smiles and moves toward him, leaning her head on his lap.

"Hello," she says in a sleepy voice.

"Hello."

"I was waiting for you last night, but then I fell asleep. Sorry. When did you come?"

J is silent for a moment. "Now."

Monica tries to open her eyes more. "Now?" Then she glances at the window. "But… It's already morning. Where have you been?"

"In the Underground storage. I needed to charge the E-band, and that took some time."

Monica blinks a few times and rubs her eyes with the back of her fingers. "Charging what? Why?"

J ignores the question and says, "Mon, I'll need to leave for a while."

She lifts herself off the bed to a sitting position, wide-awake, her eyes fixed on J. "Where are you going?"

"To Uni."

"What?" Her eyes get even wider. "You can't be serious! Why?"

"I need to save Dora."

"Dora? The alien?"

J clenches his jaws for a moment. "She is not an alien, she's a—"

"Jonathan, I don't care what she is, you are not going! You must be out of your mind. I talked to Julie. I know how it is for Humans in Uni. You will not survive there! You can't go. You simply can't. I will not let you!" She crosses her arms on her chest.

J closes his eyes for a moment, then looks at her. His face bears traces of fatigue, but his expression is calm and resolute. "I didn't come here to ask for permission, Mon. I came here to tell you so that you know where I am. I *am* going."

Her arms drop. "Doesn't it matter to you what I think? Don't you care how I feel? What I want? What happened to us?"

After a moment of hesitation, J takes her hand in his. "I think Dora deserves to be saved. She is the one who lifted this village out of the Stone Age. She is the person who stopped the cryo for your batch. She is the one who brought you back. You wouldn't be here if it wasn't for her. Don't you think she deserves saving?"

"Yes, but why you? Why can't anyone else go? I mean, we are together, finally, and we need time with each other, now more than ever." She looks around the cottage, thinking. "Maybe— maybe Patrick can go?" She looks up at him. "Patrick could go. Or, Simon. Or… or… Timothy. Well, anyone. Anyone else. Why do you need to go to Uni?"

J holds her gaze, anguish threatening to squeeze his throat so he won't be able to speak. He swallows, looking down at their hands. "It has to be me." He looks up into her eyes. "Because I love her."

For a moment everything is frozen. Monica doesn't move. She's not even blinking.

J sighs heavily. "I'm sorry, Mon. It hurts me to say it to you, but you deserve to know the truth."

Monica shakes her head silently, then lets go of his hands and stands up. "I don't believe it!"

She turns around. "I *don't* believe it. I never—ever—thought you would cheat on me!" She's loud, and her voice carries across the sleeping village.

J stands up. "I'm not going to justify myself. I was a widower for nine years. And I mourned for nine years. And it was terrible. And horrifying. Inside, I was dead. But then something—no, someone—happened. And she made me feel alive again." J squares his shoulders. "So I'm going after her."

There is a pause, when they look at each other, when a million things still need to be said, yet no words come out.

Monica takes a breath. "Fine. Leave. I don't care." She turns her back on him.

At the door, J stops. "I am sorry. I'm sorry for hurting you… I hope… you will find a way to understand."

He leaves, his steps heavy on the hanging bridges.

Monica turns around, her lips trembling. She covers her face with her palms and cries.

CHAPTER 26

Earth

The path is canopied with the crowns of trees, leaving sunshine patterns on the ground. J looks up ahead, narrowing his eyes to see farther. This must be the last part, a slight uphill slope just before the teleportation drop point.

"We're almost there," says Patrick behind him. "How are you doing?"

J stops and turns to wait for Patrick, his face a strange blend of determination, anxiety, and joy. "I'm just… unsure."

"About what?"

J shrugs. "Everything, I guess."

For a few more moments neither of them speak. The birds are loud above them, twigs and dried leaves crunching under their feet.

Then Patrick says, "You know, it might not work. The teleportation."

The blend of emotions on J's face changes dramatically. "Yes. I know that's a possibility…"

"But it might." Patrick grins and taps J on the shoulder.

Five hundred meters later, Patrick drops his backpack on the ground. "All right, we're here."

J does the same, the layer of dry earth and dust stir around the bag. He squats next to the backpack and takes out Stevanion's E-band. He looks at the black screen for a moment, then ties it around his forearm.

"Go on! Turn it on!"

But J waits. "I'm afraid. I'm afraid it won't work. And if it does, I'm afraid I won't find her. I don't even know where to start looking."

"I know," Patrick says with a sigh. There is nothing else he can say. J is right. The chances of finding her are minuscule. "But, as you said yourself, there is no other way."

J takes a breath and swipes the screen, bringing it out of standby.

Patrick squats next to him, then taps on the few indicators, following the instructions. "Self-explanatory," Patrick says and stands up.

"Well, maybe to you. I wouldn't know what to do."

The hint of a content smile appears on Patrick's face. Then the screen dims with one single command line. "That's it, J, you're good to go."

"What if we are here at the wrong time?" J looks up at Patrick. "What if there are special times when the connection is open?"

Patrick shrugs. "Possible. But you won't know anything until you try."

J clenches his fists and swallows but still doesn't move.

"J." Patrick kneels next to him. "I know you're afraid. I'm afraid too. I'm afraid…" He sighs heavily. "I'm afraid that this is the last time I will see you. I'm afraid you won't be able to come back. And… I don't want this, J. I don't! I actually want you to stay, where I know you're safe.

"But here's the thing, man. I know you. And I know what

will make you happy." He shrugs, a half grin on his face. "So, I do think this is the only way. But, J? Do your best to come back, will you?" Patrick arches his eyebrow, looking into J's eyes.

"Thanks. I will give it all I got."

Patrick smiles at him, then stands and moves backward a few steps. "Safe travels!"

"I will see you later." J says this more like a prayer than a goodbye. He looks at the screen one more time, takes a deep breath, and swipes for the initiation.

And then—

Nothing.

J breathes out, looking at the band, and grunts annoyingly.

Damn it!

It didn't work!

He looks at Patrick to comment, but Patrick is not next to him anymore.

In fact, he's at least a hundred feet away.

What the—?

And then it starts. The sounds change into a wailing cry, the trees' rustling becomes a howl, the green around him becomes a purple hollow, reshaping itself again and again, and the air moves into him, pressures him from all sides as if he's submerged under the water.

And then—everything is gone.

Black.

Nothing.

There is nothing.

He is nothing.

Except a sound?

No… Something else.

And even though there is nothing, it still feels cold. Not skin cold, but bone cold. Deep and infinite.

Between the cells, between the atoms, between the single levels of vibration.

There is nothing in there.

Empty.

Space.

And he knows this… from somewhere.

He had seen it… somewhere.

It is a—

He slams hard on the firm dusty soil.

Then he spits; his mouth is full of sand.

He cracks his eyes open and wipes his lips with the back of his hand.

And then, in front of him, he sees—boots. Large, dust-covered, skinsuit boots.

He looks up, the bright sun blinding his eyes, and he shields it with his hand.

Two large men are standing next to him, their silhouettes black with the sun behind them.

He sighs within.

This is, most likely, the wrong place to start looking.

CHAPTER 27

Uni

I'm choking. I cannot take another breath. I can still feel the hand on my throat, squeezing, endlessly. But the hand does not exist in here because I do not exist. Traversed into the purple vacuum of nothingness, I am not here. But I am not there either.

I am... remembered... and reshaped... and remade...

But I can still feel.

I feel I'm missing air.

I feel fear. I do not understand it, I cannot decipher it, but it creeps up my back, freezing my heart.

I feel pain. And it's excruciating.

The feeling of muscles cramping and spasming so that every fiber breaks and tears, ripping away from the tendons.

I am falling apart and it's terrifying.

HOW CAN THIS BE? I DO NOT EXIST IN HERE, SO WHY DO I FEEL ANYTHING?

AND THEN INTO THIS PAIN FLOWS... PEACE.

THE PAIN IS GONE, THE MUSCLES RELAX, AND I FEEL LIKE I'M FLOATING ON THE SURFACE OF A LIQUID THE SAME DENSITY AS ME. IT'S DARK AND COMFORTABLE.

AND I WANT TO BREATHE OUT IN RELIEF. BUT I CAN'T.

BECAUSE I AM NOT. I EXIST NOT IN THIS PLACE.

AND THEN THIS FEELING SUBSIDES AND TURNS INTO A DEEP, SORROWFUL PRESSURE IN THE MIDDLE OF MY CHEST, PRESSING MY HEART, CLOSING MY THROAT, PUSHING OUT TEARS THAT FLOW IN STREAMS AND RIVERS.

I SOB. I WAIL PAINFULLY.

WHY CAN'T ANYONE HEAR ME?

THIS IS THE DEEPEST SORROW I HAVE EVER KNOWN.

IT IS SO TERRIBLY, TERRIBLY SAD. AND NO ONE EVEN KNOWS IT. IT STAYED HIDDEN FOR MILLENNIA.

AND THEN THE FEELING CHANGES. A NEW ONE APPEARS. IT'S FOCUSED, STRONG, AND POWERFUL. AND—IT'S NOT MINE. THE STORM OF EMOTIONS WHIRLING THROUGH ME BELONG TO SOMEONE ELSE.

NO, NOT SOMEONE, BUT MANY, MANY, MANY OF THEM.

A REALIZATION HITS ME: I FEEL WHAT THEY FEEL.

WHO ARE YOU? WHY DO YOU FEEL LIKE THIS?

There is no answer, but the feeling persists. And I obey the new sensations.

My heart is pumping, my muscles are fully engaged, I clench my fists.

I am ready.

It's time.

To fight.

I fall hard, the sudden crush of my body against the metal surface squeezing the air out of my lungs. I can't seem to take another breath. My eyes tear, the pain in every muscle piercing and agonizing.

With my eyes still closed, I push myself to a sitting position. I keep wanting to take a breath. My mouth is wide open, but I can't.

I manage to open my eyes.

It's dark around me. But I am not in the Void anymore. I am somewhere real. I should be able to breathe.

But...

The dark surroundings get even dimmer as thousands of black spots dot my vision.

What is happening?

I reach to my throat and feel—something.

What is tha—?

And then, in a hundredth of a second, I understand: the gloved metal hand is still squeezing tightly on my throat.

I grab its fingers and claw it away with all the power that I've got.

The tight fingers release, and the body part falls on the floor.

I awkwardly crawl backward and stop only when I hit a wall, wheezing as I look back.

On the floor, only two IPs away, lies a Brookonian arm, the cut above the elbow sharp and smooth. It looks almost like a highly realistic medical model showing the cross section of bones and muscles. But the reality sets in a moment after, when I see a thick puddle of blood collecting on the metal floor, and in my next breath, I smell the meat, metallic, acidic, raw.

I press both my palms on my mouth and shut my eyes, trying hard not to vomit.

With my eyes closed, I crawl several dozen IPs to the side. I lean back onto the cold metal wall and take a small breath.

I don't... smell it... here.

I open my eyes, carefully avoiding the disembodied arm.

I remember that my TAEs are lowered to the minimum, so I bring them back, and right away the room is full of soft clicking and beeping, the sounds echoing around me.

I look up.

Although it's dim, I can tell the ceiling is extremely high. I enhance my ONCs and look around.

The hall is large, filled with tall metal towers, each row filled with green blinking lights.

I glance at my E-band and swipe the screen to check the data.

Lorea.

I take another deep breath, then stand up, straightening my back against the wall. I'm still very aware of the dismembered limb on the floor, but I force myself to ignore it.

I look in the other direction as the tall blinking pillars tower over me.

I need to find an Access Point station to find out where J went. But where to start?

I glance at my E-band. I won't be able to access any blueprints like I did on Senthia. All the data on Loreans is strictly confidential.

But—I can't help but smile within—*I might be able to get a guide.*

I touch the thin pocket on the inside of my belt, as the small coin-shaped chip gives resistance to my fingers.

Let's find a BD.

CHAPTER 28

Uni

I head left, and the pain from porting vanishes quickly as I hurry along the corridor, leaving the dismembered arm behind me. It will raise an alarm for sure. I just hope I'll port out before anyone notices.

My footsteps are soft on the floor while I check left and right between racks to find the robot Sinnya said I should use, but all the rows are empty, no BDs or any other robots seem to be around.

Then I hear a sound. A low-volume, buzzing, metallic noise. It's coming from the inter-rack corridor a few rows ahead. And it's getting closer.

I squeeze between two tall server racks, hiding myself from the corridor view, and wait.

I hear metal clinking.

The electronic buzz of a small motor.

A rubber squeak of the wheel track on the metal floor.

And then I see it.

I quickly search the data Sinnya sent me.

It's a BD75. It's one of the smallest versions, but for my purposes, it will do just fine.

The BD75 has six metal wheels that run over a rubber track, and at every turn, it emits a high-pitched squeaking noise against the smooth metal floor. It rolls in my direction, and just in front of me, it turns with its back toward me and lowers itself, as if crouching, then moves one of its upper limbs to access a rack in front of it.

Its large torso's back plate is concealing the view, so I can't see what it is doing, but I hear clicks and slides and buzzes in a quick successive order. I assume it's working on a server tower.

I don't know how long it's going to stay here, but if I'm to gain it as a tool to guide me to an AP station, I need to act quickly.

The back of its metal torso has several chip slots. Six are occupied but all others are free, glowing light blue. I pinch the chip between two of my fingers and slide it out of the pocket, my eyes still fixed on the BD75.

I'm about to squeeze out of the tight fissure between the towers, but then the BD75 shoots up into a straight position, pivots to turn to the direction it came from, then rolls back, the rips of the rubber track making soft but steady beats as it swiftly retreats.

Oh, the Moons of Senthia, I need to catch it!

It takes me a few moments to pull out, and then I run. The BD75 turns right and I lose sight of it. I speed up, but as soon as I make the turn, I bump into something, my forehead banging loudly on a cold metal surface.

I almost drop the chip—more from shock than pain—and look up, instinctively pressing a hand on my forehead.

Oh no!

I take a step back. I don't even need to search my nanoprobes for this one.

It's a BD308, much larger than the 75 and a whole different set of tasks too.

Quite unfortunate…

Its head, a long dark gray tube with a ring of blue LED bulbs and a crimson sensor plate as its iris, rotates half a circle and focuses on me.

This type of BD is not meant for any kind of communication, I know that.

I can try to run away.

Or…

I can try to use it.

At its shoulder, a metallic extension protrudes out of the frame.

I don't wait to see what that is.

I duck under the extended limb, then loop around the machine to get behind its back, hoping at least one of the chip slots is empty.

I'm quick, but the BD308 is faster. Without moving its body, it turns its head to focus on me again. With another multijointed arm, it reaches in my direction, the tip of it bright with an electric current.

I manage to avoid it just barely, the sparks passing less than a tenth of an IP, burning a few of my hairs.

Close!

Next time, it will manage.

I only have one chance.

I spot the array of slots on its back.

Most are full. But two are light blue.

As fast as I can, I stretch my arm, aiming for the space. At the same time, another extension arm reaches out and grabs my upper arm in two of its claws and starts squeezing.

The pressure hurts tremendously, but my skinsuit protects me just enough to slip the chip into a slot.

It clicks in, and the next moment, the increasing pressure stops but the claws are still tightly secured around my arm, the pain radiating from my bone.

"Release," I mutter through my teeth.

Immediately the claw lets go and the extension retreats back to its socket, the tube head repositioning into a vertical standby.

My heartbeat is loud in my ears, my breaths heavy as I rub my injured arm.

Then, a bit shakily, I take a look. The BD308 didn't manage to tear the fabric of my skinsuit, but my arm still hurts.

I groan and close my eyes. *The pain will subside quickly as soon as the nano-repair starts.*

Then I look up at 308 and between breaths, I say, "BD308… guide me… to the closest Access Point."

The BD pivots and starts rolling away. Quickly.

I kick into a jog, ignoring the pain in my arm, to catch up to it.

CHAPTER 29

Uni

The server hall turns out to be even larger than I expected.

I keep running after the 308, but after several hundred IPs, I am exhausted. Just when I think I won't be able to keep up, the 308 stops in front of an exit gate. It extends one of its multijointed limbs and plugs it in next to the door.

The door slides open, and a gush of warm air flows in from the hall. Somehow it feels familiar, comfortable, as if I've sensed it before. But I couldn't have. I've never ported to Lorea before.

The 308 enters and I follow, but then a moment later I halt in my tracks; this hall is packed full of BDs.

BD75s, BD80s, some BD88s.

These aren't Access Point stations! Why did the 308 take me here?

I take a step back and glance at the 308. I want to repeat my command from before, but I'm afraid it might raise the attention of the other BDs.

But the 308 is not going anywhere. It just stands still, its blue LED iris focused on the many BD machines working on large dark gray panels filled with thousands of luminescent rose lines, giving the whole room a pulsing rose hue.

And then—I remember something. And slowly, very slowly, it starts to sink in.

The room is warm. A soft breeze is finding its way around the purple towers, and I realize that the rose lines are not lines at all but closely aligned luminescent chips.

I have *felt* this before.

I have *seen* this before, too.

It was in the Void while I ported.

I remember what I did in the Void, so I do the same thing now.

I walk toward the tower glowing purple with thousands of tiny slots and stand between two BDs that buzz around me as their limb extensions work on the chips.

I glance back one more time to the completely immobile 308.

Then I take a deep breath, look at the glowing tower, and pull one purple chip out, just as I did in the Void.

I place it flat on my palm.

The APC chip.

It's warm and small. But it feels very robust as well.

The buzz behind me tells me the 308 is in motion. I turn to look and see it's moving away.

I slide the chip in my belt pocket and then run after it.

We exit the warm purple hall and enter an uncomfortably cold corridor. The 308 turns left, and I am ready for another session of sprinting, but it stops only a dozen IPs farther in front of the large metal doors of an elevator. There's no ID panel at the side, which means it's not meant for personnel, only for robots.

We enter the elevator and the heavy metal door slides closed. The very next moment it ascends at full speed, with virtually no initial acceleration. My knees give in, half from surprise, half from thrust, and I fall. I simply sit on the floor.

The 308 doesn't make a single movement, its head tube pointing to the door.

The moment I push myself off the floor to stand up, the elevator stops—no deceleration either—and I fly upward, just barely missing the ceiling.

I can't help but moan.

The cargo elevator. Definitely not meant for living passengers.

The door slides open, but the 308 extends two limbs to stop me from going forward.

At first instance I'm confused, but then I hear sounds.

As soon as I recognize them, I retreat backward, hiding behind the smooth metallic back of the 308. Within a quarter of a pass, a group of six Loreans pass right in front of us. I can see them through the small gaps between the BD's extensions. They are so deeply engaged in discussion that they just pass us by, not even glancing at the BD standing in the elevator door. As soon as they turn the corner, the 308 rolls out and I follow.

I jog after it along the intricate network of corridors for several more passes until it stops at a dark glass door and enters.

The room is large and concave with twelve transparent tubes.

The Access Point stations! Finally!

The BD308 rolls to the first one, and unfolding another of its limbs, it slides it into a lock. The AP wall, turning on its axis, slides open for me.

I take a quick breath and squeeze past the robot. I engage my E-band for connection with the AP console, hoping this will get me access to a porting database.

An empty holo screen appears in front of me, ready for queries.

So far so good.

I initiate a trace of all porting reports in the past five days.

The next moment, the holo screen starts listing pages and pages of responses, one on top of the other. It keeps coming, new pages flashing in front of my eyes.

Then it stops.

All ports in the past five days should be here. Good!

Now, let me think. *I need to exclude the Descendants and... I need to exclude women as well...* I swipe the commands on my E-band, giving directions to the AP computer. *I also need to cancel all who started at Zema4 and—*

But then I stop, my fingers only lightly touching the surface of my E-band screen.

The E-band...

The E-band!

I look at the ceiling, taking a deep breath.

Stupid! Why didn't I think of this before?

The only way J could have ported was to initiate the porting field resonator, and *that* he could have done only with an E-band, the only one he still has available on Earth.

Stevanion's E-band.

I place new search criteria, looking for a mis-portation twenty-seven days prior.

As expected, I get a single page with only two passenger IDs.

One is mine. The other is Stevanion's.

I copy his ID and then search for porting destinations over the past week. Inside I am hoping I won't get anything. I'm hoping that the Vision didn't come to be and he didn't manage to port.

I'm hoping he is still on Earth.

But the result appears before I even manage to move my fingers away from the console.

A single line of porting coordinate numbers appears.

I take a shaky breath while holding on to whatever is next to me for support.

Oh no! He managed.

He's in Uni!

Another heaved breath.

He ported yesterday.

Then I realize I'm holding on to the metal front shield of the 308 and I let go, straightening myself up.

All right, let's focus!

My breaths are still shaky, and my heart is pounding as I copy the destination coordinates.

I don't know where that is. But this is where I'm going.

At the same time, I copy the coordinates of the original porting station too. *The Earth.*

If I find him—No! *When* I find him—I'll send him back.

I transfer the data to my E-band and walk out of the AP station. "BD308, guide me to the closest porting chamber."

CHAPTER 30

Uni

The 308 detaches the connection to the panel, folding it to fit its socket, then rolls past me, out of the AP room. I'm quick on my feet, my jog turning into a sprint as the BD increases speed. For several more passes as we run though this lengthy corridor, we don't see anyone. I don't know if this is coincidence or—I glance at the BD as I run next to it—it might just have something to do with my new assistant. In either case, I'm glad.

We finally reach the end of the corridor and stop in front of what I think is another cargo elevator. The metal door opens as soon as the BD connects to it, and we enter.

This time I reach out and grab one of the many extensions on the BD's body that protrudes outward, preparing to ascend.

The door closes, but instead of going up, the elevator drops, my stomach rising upward too much for my comfort. I lose my footing but keep holding on to the BD while I shut my eyes, trying hard to focus.

The ride, however, is finished before I manage to form a proper thought, and I end up half crouching when the elevator stops.

The hall we enter is cold. My breaths make semitransparent bubbles of condensed air almost invisible in the dark. I enhance my ONCs but then stop. Around me, aligned row by row, are hundreds and hundreds of BD robots, a lot larger and taller than my robotic guide. They are all powered down, their tube heads bent low, their irises dark.

I shiver.

As I follow my 308, I do a quick search of the data that Sinnya sent me. These are all 500, designed for combat and joint work with Brookonians.

Lovely, I think as I look around. *Just a perfect place for me to be right now.*

At the end of the hall, the BD stops. We are standing in front of a large shining metal wall, and only once it starts moving upward do I realize that this is a gate.

As it opens, a soft rose light starts filling the dark hall, rising up my legs and ascending up my body. When it reaches my eyes, I realize that the floor, the walls, and the ceiling are all covered in rosenquartz tiles, a soft rose hue pulsing through them like waves on the water.

Ah, the porting chamber!

My muscles, tensed a moment before, now relax, and I visibly slouch in relief. This place feels more like home than anywhere else I've been in the past several days. I take a deep breath, my shoulders unknotting from their cramped position, and enter.

This chamber is one of the largest I have seen, and I assume the reason is that it is meant for porting of a large number of robots.

I turn around to the 308 standing in front of the gate. It's not entering the porting chamber.

"Aren't you coming with me?" It's a stupid thing to ask, I realize at that moment. BDs are not meant to communicate.

But then I get a beeping signal on my E-band.

I lift up my arm and see one line. 'Negative.'

I breathe in quickly. *It* can *communicate!*

"Why not?"

The 308 pivots its body to face the hall, but its head stays fixed, the blue iris still looking at me.

'Take. Guiding. Chip. Now.'

"Your guiding chip? Why?"

'Take. Chip. Now. They. Are. Arriving.'

"Who is—?"

The elevator door on the other side of the hall opens, and a troop of Brookonian soldiers run out, zigzagging between BDs, heading toward us, their weapons aiming red laser lights, which crisscross against the dark background.

Incredibly fast, the BD308 rotates its tube head toward them, then raises the top of its body, almost reaching the ceiling of the chamber, and entangles dozen of its multijointed limbs, extending them in all directions, making a metal shield in front of me, completely covering the entrance.

"BD, come inside!" I yell over the loud drumming of the soldiers, hoping it will react to a command tone.

My E-band beeps. 'Take. Chip.'

I clench my fists and step toward it, but at that moment, I hear a whizzing sound and see a bright yellow flash above the BD's right shoulder. One of the BD's extensions rips off, flying into the porting chamber, banging on the back wall and making a sharp clanging sound, a strange combination of glass and metal colliding.

I crouch and cover my ears with my hands, looking at it,

stunned. The ripped edges of the metal extension are white, pulsing with heat, then a moment later it loses the brightness and becomes a deep red.

Then a series of whizzing sounds starts, and it reverberates around the large metal hall. It's excruciatingly loud! So loud that my TAEs automatically adjust, lowering the sensitivity to the minimum.

And then all becomes silent.

In this terrible vacuum of silence, yellow flashes surround the 308, its limb extensions pulled out of its corpus, ripped away by the lasers, some parts flying sideways into the hall, others landing in the porting chamber next to me.

Sparks fly as metal hits the walls, filling the room with a heavy burnt smell, dense and suffocating, raising the gray smoke off the ground.

It's overwhelming.

I can't form a proper thought.

I can't grasp what is happening.

The rose hue of the rosenquartz tiles changes, and in that moment, I realize the port is starting.

Oh no! The chip!

I stand up and stumble toward the BD while the metal pieces break around it. I squint, raising my arm above my head to protect myself as I advance.

I can feel it: the heavy bones, the rigid muscles.

No, not yet! I need to get the chip!

With the last bit of my failing power, I manage to grab the green chip and slide it out of the slot. At the same time, the BD's tube head rips out of the torso and flies over my head, it's blue iris still bright as it hits the back wall.

Next moment, I disappear into a purple hue, away from the BD308, away from the attacking Brookonians, away from Lorea. Back into nothing.

THE VOID.

THE EMPTY FIELD.

I. AM. NOT. IN. HERE.

AND THIS TIME THERE ARE NO COLORS...

NO SOUNDS...

NO SENSATIONS...

BUT SOMETHING ELSE.

WHAT IS IT?

IT KEEPS REPEATING.

I CAN'T HEAR IT, I CAN'T SEE IT, BUT I KNOW IT.

WHAT?

IS?

IT?

ZERO...

AND ONE...

AND ANOTHER ONE...

ZERO, ONE ONE, ZERO ZERO, ONE ZERO.

ZERO ZERO, ONE, ZERO, ONE ONE, ZERO, ONE ONE ONE ONE, ZERO, ONE, ZERO ZERO ZERO...

It keeps repeating, incredibly fast.

I know it's impossible, but I still have to try. I give a command to my nanoprobes to store it, to remember it.

My nanoprobes are not here, because I am not here. But I do it all the same.

...One zero, one one one one, zero one zero, zero...

I don't know what it is, but I need to remember it. I know it's important. It's invaluable!

...Zero zero, one, zero zero zero...

...Zero, one one one, zero, one one, zero zero, one, zero zero zero...

And then it's gone.

I fall on a hard, sandy surface, my lungs empty of air.
I take my first painful breath, then spit sand out of my mouth.
And then I hear someone shout. "Get her! Now!"

CHAPTER 31

Uni

I want to look up, but it's so bright I need to close my eyes again. I focus on my other senses as I try to stand, still weak and tired from the port.

I hear many feet running toward me, and as they reach me, they slide to a stop, blowing sand into my face. I close my eyes tighter and turn my head away.

Then the extreme brightness is gone and I'm sitting in the shadow of the people circling me. I look up, blinking, trying to clear my eyes, but I can't see them properly; their contours are black against the sun.

Where am I? Who are these people?

Two men lean down and grab my arms, then lift me up like I weigh nothing at all, my toes barely touching the ground.

"A Descendant!" says a male voice in front of me, a nasty tone rumbling through the word. "Blind her!"

A black linen bag lands on my head, and I can only see a small section of the ground.

"Take her to the Stadtrat house."

The two people holding me start walking, my feet dragging

on the sandy ground as my head dangles in the rhythm of their steps.

I hear many voices now as people gather around us.

Under the bag, I can only see their beige-colored boots, with beige coats fluttering around them.

I sigh inwardly.

There is only one place with this particular color of skinsuit. Also the only place where the word *Descendant* would be used in such a derogatory tone.

I am on Zema4.

However—a twinkle of hope rises in me—if J did manage to port here, this would be the best place in the whole of Uni for him to be. I need find that out. Somehow.

After several passes of walking in the bright sunshine, we walk into the shadow of a building. The two men bring me up a couple of stairs, my toes banging on the edges as they drag me over them.

A sliding door hisses, and we enter a cooler and darker hallway.

"Take her to the holding cell," someone says. "Matt, Josh, you stay at the door. I don't want any soldiers to find her. She might be our best bargaining chip in this mess."

"When do we question her?" one of the two men asks.

"We have to do it in the evening. I want Farrell to talk to her too. He might get better info, considering what he's been through."

As he leaves through the main door, I can hear a crowd of people gathering outside, shouting their questions.

"Who is she?"

"Why did she also land outside of the chamber?"

"What does it mean?"

"We don't know who she is yet," the man says. "But we know that she is a Descendant. We will get more—"

The door closes and I can't hear them anymore.

The two men left with me guide me forward, still holding my upper arms tightly as if I could escape them. Under the blindfold, I can see the gray floor and the wall to my right.

When we stop, they maneuver me so I'm facing the door.

There is a clanging metal sound somewhere near the wall, followed by a few clicks. I can't decipher either of them. I've never heard them before, nor are they saved on my nanoprobes. The door opens. I'm dragged inside and pushed down on a hard wooden chair.

One of the men binds my wrists together behind my back.

Then they take my blindfold off.

They are both very tall. The one on my right has long blond hair, deep-set blue eyes, and the majority of his face is covered with a beard. The other one, standing to my left, has short, dark hair, a very symmetrical face, and brown eyes.

I look at one, then the other. One of them should be Matt and the other Josh.

They both look at me with the same intensity as I them.

"Josh, I think we've got ourselves a Senthien," says Matt, the dark-haired man.

"I've never seen one so close before," Josh replies.

"Me neither."

"Amazing eyes," Josh continues, narrowing his eyes and leaning in a bit closer.

I frown just slightly. *They are talking as if I'm some exotic animal and can't understand them.*

"Who is Farrell?"

They are slightly taken aback.

Yes, the animal can talk.

Matt lifts up his chin. "None of your concern."

I glance at both of them again, then decide to play the ruler card. I stand tall, pushing the chair away as the wooden legs scrape the floor behind me. "You just captured a Descendant. You know what the punishment for that is. You'd better release me now. Or suffer the consequences."

Matt pushes me back down on the chair. "It can't be worse than it already is, Descendant! We are *already* suffering the consequences."

What does he mean?

I still give it another try. "You need to release me, or the Brookonians will sweep the entire Zema4 planet to find me."

"They are everywhere already," says Josh.

"They are?" My Descendant authority is gone.

"We've got thousands of them in the past two weeks," Matt continues. "How many more do you want to bring?"

I look at the floor. *Thousands? In the past two weeks?* "Why?"

They look at each other, then back at me. "Don't you know?"

"I… I have been absent for my project. What is going on?"

Matt looks at Josh. "I think she's lying."

But Josh doesn't seem convinced. He looks at me. "What do you know about the current situation in Uni?"

Not enough. "I know that Zlathars are watchful."

"Why's that?"

"I… I don't know."

Matt nods to me. "Aren't you guys supposed to see *the future*?"

"It's not the future," I say, reciting my father's mantra. "It's the most probable course—"

"The most probable course of events, yes, yes, we've heard that." They both say that in unison.

I frown. "Where did you hear that?"

Matt leans into me. "You're not the one asking questions here, Senthien. We are."

Josh, who seems a lot more amicable, asks, "Why are you here, Senthien?"

I take a deep breath and try to straighten myself. "I need to find a particular Human."

Matt laughs, somewhat forcefully. "Forget it, Senthien! It's not happening."

"This Human is in danger!" My emotional voice breaks through. "The data I have point out—"

"I. Don't. Care." Matt leans over me.

"Matt, perhaps she has—"

"No!" Matt slices the air with his hand. "She's trying to Descendant on us now. No. Not this time. Now she is *our* prisoner, not the other way around." Then he heads to the door. "Come, Josh! Let's go."

Josh stays for a moment longer, his eyes on me as if trying to see more, trying to see deeper than the obvious, but then he turns around and follows Matt out.

The large wooden door squeaks as they close it. The metal clanging sounds twice from inside the door, and then all is silent again.

As soon as I have a moment by myself, my mind goes back to my last porting experience. This time so different: No colors, no sounds, no senses. Just zeros.

And ones.

What was that? *Why* was that?

Zeros and ones…

Zeros and ones…

I close my eyes, trying to decipher it. It reminds me of black-and-white flashes I've seen in my port to Boolea.

Black and white.

Zeros and—

I take a sharp breath. *Oh, the Moons of Senthia, it's a sequence! A binary sequence.*

It's a message! It has to be!

I engage my nanoprobes, send a command for translation, and wait a few moments until the sequence is decoded. As soon as it is, I let it play.

What comes out, however, are not words, as I expected, but a moving picture, as if I am watching a high-quality holo program. Snippets, short little sequences, folding and molding from one moving image to the other.

Trees.

Wind blowing the leaves.

The fire. Large, sparkling, and magical.

Many people around me. Close to me.

And then the eyes. The eyes I will never forget.

J.

But no, wait!

It's not J. It's a—I blink—a boy.

Big dark eyes, dark curly hair, dressed as any child in the tree village. But I'm certain I haven't seen him before. Who is he?

Then he smiles at me.

And I simply have to smile back. I know it's a replay of the binary sequence I recorded, and the boy cannot see me, but I just have to. I can't not respond.

He lifts up his hand and waves, and I want to lift up mine, I want to wave back. But my arms are tied down and I can't. Then the moving picture stops, and the boy is gone. The end of the binary code message.

I open my eyes, my gaze on the floor, unfocused. *Who is he? What does this mean?*

I grunt involuntarily, my Senthien curious and eager to find out more, but it's clear that the only way to do that is the next portation. Before that, however, I need to find J, which means I need to escape. Somehow.

I look around, scanning my surroundings. Apart from this wooden chair I'm sitting on, the room is completely empty. There is nothing here I can use to escape.

Even the doors. It's such old technology that even my E-band can't hack it.

The Moons of Senthia, I am wasting my time here!

I need to get out!

I need to find J!

I need to—

Stop.

I close my eyes, then intentionally and deliberately, using a specific trained sequence, I calm myself down.

Panicking won't get me anywhere.

It takes me just a few moments to recalculate all the different probabilities to escape.

Then I move my gaze back at the door. The best way, and the only realistic way for me to escape, is the next time someone comes in.

CHAPTER 32

Uni

I make slow, focused movements, trying to pry my wrists free of the rope. I am tempted to try to pull them apart by force, but I know that won't work. The rope is too strong. The only way is to slowly, very slowly, loosen it.

Then, quite unexpectedly, my stomach growls.

I stop wiggling my arms, close my eyes, and listen.

Another growl.

I think I'm... hungry.

Another growl, this one with an uncomfortable twist in my stomach. One thing is for sure: I'm not getting any food as long as I'm detained here.

I try to picture the knots and imagine the way my hands are tied together. Once I see the picture in my mind, I close my eyes and start to wiggle my hands again.

But then I hear voices outside in the corridor.

I enhance my TAEs and listen.

"Michelle, I don't think this is the best idea." I hear Matt's voice.

"Why not?" a woman answers.

"She's a Senthien. She might, I don't know, do something

to you." He's whispering this to her now, but I have no problem hearing him.

"Like what? Pierce me with her laser-green eyes?"

"I don't know what they can do. Do you?"

"I will know more if you let me in, that's for sure!"

After a moment's pause, Matt says, "Fine. But I'll be with you, just in case."

"Sure, Matt, if that makes you feel calmer," I hear her say, then very loud in my ears, I hear the same metallic clinking sound of the lock, and the door squeaks open.

I reduce my TAEs to adjust to the sound.

A woman comes in wrapped in beige clothes. As she lowers her hood, a few grains of sand collected in the grooves fall on the floor. She is quite small, even smaller than me. White highlights in her dark hair, intense dark eyes, and olive-colored skin. Her expression is pleasant, a soft smile on her lips, a malleable posture, but at the same time her calm demeanor commands authority as well.

"Oh, poor thing! She's all skin and bones, look at her," she says and rushes toward me.

Matt rolls his eyes. "Maybe she's designed like that?"

"Nonsense. I know what Senthiens look like."

"Is that so?"

Michelle turns around. "Yes, Matthew Pester—"

"Lester."

"—it is so. There is more to the truth than you think!"

She turns to me, and Matt, glancing at Josh, wiggles his index finger around his temple. I don't know what it means, but I doubt it's well intended.

"Give it a break, Matt!" says Josh, shaking his head.

Ignoring them both, Michelle swings a sheet of her clothing

behind her, and I see she's carrying a cube-shaped bag. She puts it down on the floor.

"You must be hungry," she says as she unzips it.

Inside is a deep bowl with an opaque green liquid. She takes it out and puts it on my thighs, and with her other hand, she gives me a spoon.

But I don't move.

For one, I can't, my arms are still strapped behind my back. And second, I'm too astonished to respond. I certainly did not expect someone would come to bring me food.

After a moment of confusion, she widens her eyes and says, "Oh, you're not sure if it's safe! Well..." She takes the spoon, dips it in the liquid and brings it to her mouth, blows on it, then slurps it in one go.

"You see!" She smiles, then wipes the spoon with a tissue next to the bag, and offers it to me again.

She frowns when I don't take it. "What is it? Aren't you hungry?"

As an automatic response, my stomach growls. "I am currently unable to hold the spoon," I say.

She tips her head back. "Currently unable? I... I don't understand."

I glance at my arms. "My arms are tied behind my back, so I—"

She leans on her knee to stand up and then loops around me. "Oh, for goodness' sake!" she says, and I can feel her untying the ropes.

"Michelle, I don't think that's a good idea!" says Matt.

"I was told she should be restrained at all times," Josh admits.

The scratchy feeling on my wrists disappears, and Michelle

stands up behind me. "What am I supposed to do then? Feed her like a baby?"

She sits in front of me and once again offers me the spoon.

I move my arms forward, the shifting causing some discomfort in both my shoulders. Then I take the spoon and with the other hand bring the bowl closer to me so it doesn't spill.

"It's not the tastiest," Michelle says, "but it has a lot of healthy herbs. It's perfect for recovery." With that she looks at the scarring on my cheek.

The soup is very warm and it tastes—delicious. *Finally, proper food.*

I grab another spoonful, then another, and another, without stopping until I take the very last one.

Michelle keeps looking at me with eyes wide open.

When I finally lower my bowl, she bursts out laughing.

"Oh shame, you poor thing. You really *were* hungry."

Then she turns to the two men. "And shame on you two! How can you let the girl go hungry?"

"She's not a girl! She's a Senthien, for crying out loud! She's probably hundreds of years old!" shouts Matt.

Michelle stands up and points a finger at him. "A Senthien had a life here once, remember? A Senthien loved one of our own, and she loved him back. Remember that?"

"No, as a matter of fact, I don't remember," he says. "It was way before my time, and it's probably not even true. It's just a story to make our miserable Human lives more decent." He turns around and walks out the door, saying in a squeamish voice. "*A Senthien and a Human.*" Then back to his own deep voice. "My ass!"

"Farrell says—" Michelle starts.

"I don't give a fuck what he says!" And he walks out.

"I'm sorry, Michelle," says Josh after a while. "The past few weeks are really getting to him…"

She shakes her head. "I understand." Then she turns to me and smiles, seeing the empty bowl. "Do you want more, dear?"

I shake my head, wiping my lips with my arm. "No. This will suffice. I thank you."

She nods. "All right. Now, I need to see where I can place you because"—she looks around the empty room—"you can't stay here. I'll be back soon."

She takes the bowl and puts it in her bag, then she straps the belt around her shoulders and covers her head with her hood again. I think she expects me to say something, but right now I'm processing what had just been said.

"I will come back," she says, then turns around and heads for the door.

"Wait!"

"Yes?"

"What was it that you said, about a Human and a Senthien, that they… loved each other?"

Michelle sighs, looking at the floor. "It happened a long, long time ago. Here, on Zema4. But it's nothing your people would know. It was kept a secret." Then she looks at me. "But it *did* happen. It did. Star-crossed lovers." She smiles dreamily.

"Young don't believe it anymore, but many still do." Then she grins broadly and says, "You hold on tight. I'll be right back." And she walks out.

Josh, who was standing at the door the whole time, nods to me just slightly, then walks out, and the door clicks again.

I lean back in my chair and look up at the ceiling, staring at the crack where the paint is peeling off.

The Human and the Senthien... The Human and the Senthien...

She can't possibly be talking about my mom and dad, can she?

I rub my wrists, happy to have them free, then I stand up and slowly walk toward the door. I enhance my TAEs and close my eyes to focus. I don't hear anything, so I slowly grab the metal handle on the door and push. The lever lets go, but the door doesn't budge.

A loud bang on the door reverberates and shakes it. "It's locked, Senthien!" shouts Matt.

Ouch! I cringe, reducing my TAEs, then rub my ears. I look at the door crossly as if this is its fault.

I turn around and walk to the wall opposite the entrance.

The room has no windows, no other opening but the door. And that seems to be locked.

How am I ever going to escape? Even if I tell them the truth, even if I tell them they should release me so that I can save another Human, they wouldn't believe me. They *didn't* believe me.

I rub my face with my palms, trying to focus, the wound on my cheek still somewhat sore. I lean my back on the wall and look up at the ceiling, fixed on the peeling crack.

But perhaps Michelle would? She seemed a lot less hostile than the rest.

I could tell her that J—no, not J. *Jonathan.* She would know him as Jonathan—I could tell her that Jonathan... Then my shoulders slump. Jonathan what? I don't even know his full name.

Something inside me twists painfully. There is still so much I don't know about him, so much I want to find out. But I never will...

Once again, I am fighting tears, my throat clenched in an aching grip that stops my breathing.

And the tightly sealed chest I locked up inside me opens once more. Without my consent, the sorrow, dark and heavy, seeps out for me to endure, to live through, to grieve over again.

My father standing one IP in front of me as I feel the cold words of Zlathar sink in and my father drops dead at my feet. I'm trembling, shaking, but I can't move.

I am in despair. The gripping loss rises deep in my chest, mingled with an ever-growing icy hate.

My mother hugs me, and it lasts for passes and passes. I want to push her away. I don't understand why she needs to do it for so long. She had hugged me yesterday so long as well. And the day before. I think she is being very Human right now. She did not learn the Senthien way like I did. She still needs to practice.

She finally lets me go. I tell her I will see her after she ports back. She can hug me again then.

She smiles, but her eyes are red, her cheeks wet. This disturbs me. I don't understand. And I don't like when I don't understand. I turn away.

And she is gone.

Heavy liquid sorrow simmers over the dark chest, and I'm not able to close it.

I cry without a sound.

After a long while, my Human feels weak, drenched with emotions, too weak to fight, so my Senthien finally steps up, closes the door, and doubles the lock.

Useless.

This is not helping. Not helping at all.

I wipe my cheeks with the back of my hand.

I take a deep breath and clench my hands into fists.

J is still here. He is still alive. And I can help him. I *can* get him back to Earth!

But I need to focus, focus on my Senthien, pushing my Human aside.

The highest likelihood of success is conversing with Michelle. I will tell her that I have clear data that point out a Human man named Jonathan ported to Zema4 in the past two days.

It is possible that Zema4s don't have the authority for an overview of all the ports that happen on their planet, and she might very well be oblivious that he is here, but—

A sudden thought comes to my mind.

I could ask her to nano-broadcast this information to the general population, or at least the heads of Zema4 and—

Zema4. I cover my face with my hands. *Stupid, Dora. Stupid!* Humans don't have nanoprobes. How could they ever nano-broadcast?

Stupid.

I turn around and walk to the wall again. *Okay. Okay.* Maybe they have another way to communicate. They need to be able to talk to each other. Perhaps—

A metal clicking sound echoes around the room again, and I turn toward the door. Josh enters first, followed by Matt.

They both seem hesitant.

Matt is avoiding my gaze, glancing backward, but Josh's eyes are focused on me, as if he's trying to figure something out just by staring. I don't understand their body language, but then again, I am the last person who can decipher it.

"Here she is," says Josh.

I frown. *Whom are they talking to?*

And only then I see that there is someone else behind them.

I narrow my eyes, stretching my neck to see better, when the two men step aside and the person behind steps forward.

All of my strength leaves me, my muscles give in, and I just slide to the floor.

A painfully yearning grip squeezes my heart from all sides as he stops midstep when he sees me. His breath locks, and for an instant time stops.

No one is breathing.

No one is moving.

All is still.

He breaks out of his stupor and rushes toward me. He slides down on his knees and wraps his arms around me, his hug so strong it feels painful.

I don't have any thoughts.

Nothing.

They are blocked.

All blocked.

But one.

J.

CHAPTER 33

Uni

J keeps hugging me, squeezing me tight against his body. His breathing is strained, long breaks between each breath, while he keeps pressing me toward him more with every gasp.

He leans his head next to mine, and his voice trembles as he whispers, "You're all right... You're safe... You're safe..."

I still can't move. I am just... locked, completely immobile while my muscles ignore all my commands. I feel like a piece of clothing J is clutching to himself.

But I want to hug him back. I want to tell him how happy I am to see him, to see that *he* is safe, that he's not on Fraya or DM38 or any other Descendant world. I'm so happy that Descendants haven't found him first and that—*he's alive.*

I want to tell him he should have stayed on Earth, because he finally had what he wanted for so long. And I want to tell him that it was stupid of him to come to Uni in the first place. It *was* dangerous. Brave, but dangerous. And he needs to go back. Now.

All of this he needs to hear, all of this I need to tell him, but nothing comes out.

I'm silent, barely breathing.

After a long while, J slowly pulls away and looks at my face. His cheeks are wet from tears, but he's smiling.

Then he lifts his hand to my cheek, gently touching the scabs. "What happened?"

I open my mouth to speak, but it takes a moment before I find my voice. "I… I got in the way of the cleaning machine for Senthia's airing shaft systems above one of the portation chambers."

For a second he doesn't move, then his lips spread into a broad smile, dimples appearing on his cheeks, a twinkle in his eyes.

And I melt seeing him like this.

J. My J…

"And what time of the day was that exactly?" he says, lifting his eyebrow.

I quickly scan my nanoprobes to find the time. "According to Senthia local time, it was—"

"I'm just kidding!" He smiles as he strokes my hair, tirelessly gazing at my face. "I'm just… nudging your Senthien."

His dimples slowly disappear as he looks into my eyes, first one, then the other, his gaze intense.

"I'm so glad you're all right, Dora," he finally says.

I try to press a smile on my face, despite the pain in my heart. "I understand," I say. *And I do. It would feel so unfair if the person who saved Monica came to harm.*

But still, his words hurt. He's here only because I brought Monica back. And the only appropriate thing to do now is to save me.

But I wish—I close my eyes, trying to keep the tears inside—I wish he was here because of me. Only me.

J strokes my face, and for an instant, just an instant, I lean into his palm, imagining it *is* only the two of us, just him and me. I feel the rough warmth of his skin. I hear his breathing, now steady and calm. I smell his scent.

Then I feel a warm kiss on my forehead. And I can't hold back the tears. It feels like him and me. It so feels like *us*.

But it's not. And I know it.

Inside, I break.

It would have been easier, so much easier to handle, not seeing him, not feeling his touch, not smelling his skin, not hearing his deep voice… It would have been so much easier. So I pull away and wipe the tears from my cheeks.

"I know it must be a surprise—" he starts.

"I have seen it." I gather the strength to look at him.

"What have you seen?"

I look down, remembering him and Monica together. Close. Like we were, before she came. But I don't tell him that. Instead, I say, "I have seen you decide to come after me."

I clench my fists, feigning courage, then look into his eyes again. "And I am grateful you decided to do that. It is very… brave of you to come to Uni, being a Human. I am deeply honored you decided to do that."

"Deeply honored…" J's shoulders relax and the crooked smile is back. "There's my Senthien. Now let's see the Human. You are on Zema4, you know; it's okay to let it show." He nods at me supportively.

I close my eyes again, unable to look at him.

No, J, it's not all right.

My Human will want you back.

My Human will crave you.

My Human still loves you.

I can't be a Human.

Not in front of you.

I open my eyes and move slightly backward. For an instant he's still holding me. Then he realizes what I'm doing, so he drops his arms, his fingers touching the floor, a trace of confusion unmistakable in his eyes.

"Dora, is everything all right?"

"Of course. I thank you for asking." I don't dare to look at him. I'm afraid he'll see through me.

He tilts his head to the side, all serious now. "No."

I look up at him.

"No, you're not all right," he says. "What's wrong?"

I keep staring at him. *How can he possibly ask me that?*

"It's because I let you go, isn't it?"

"No. It's because you came to Uni. You don't belong here. You need to go back to Earth."

"Yes. I will. And you are coming with me."

I look at him, my eyes wide open. *He can't be serious! Seeing him alone was difficult enough. But seeing him and Monica together will be torture.*

I put on my best Senthien tone and say, "No. Porting to Earth does not correspond with my current plans."

He looks as if I just slapped him. He shakes his head. "But… how can you stay? You are in danger… here… in Uni. Aren't you?"

"No. I've been in Uni for several days now and didn't encounter any difficulties." *He doesn't need to know.*

"But…" His voice is now a whisper. "Don't you… *want*… to go back?"

"No. I belong here." My voice is perfect Senthien: detached and cold.

He stares at me, his lips slightly open. I don't think he's

breathing. It rips my heart in half seeing him like this, because I know he just wants to help me. He said it himself: I did so much for Humans on Earth and for him in particular that I deserve better.

I *deserve* to be saved.

But I don't think he'll let me stay, unless I convince him otherwise. Unless I persuade him I'm in no danger and that he should go back to Earth on his own. "J, I appreciate your concern, but you need to understand that there is nothing for me back on Earth. I *want* to stay here."

"No…," he says, but his voice breaks. "You don't mean that… You *can't*."

"Of course I mean it. Senthiens never say anything untrue. Or unnecessary."

"But I… I thought…" But his words fail. He looks down to the floor, and he looks so weak now, so defeated, that I fight the urge to come closer, to stroke his cheek, to tell him that it will turn out okay for him.

And Monica.

I sigh.

I understand him. He came all this way to save me, to bring me back to Earth, and *this* is how I respond?

"J, it's okay." I smile. "You need to understand that there's no debt you need to feel, there is no obligation toward me. And I'm happy, truly happy that your gratitude was so strong that you came all this way to Uni, in true harm's way just to save me, to bring me back to Earth. I *am* truly grate—"

"What?" He frowns, the skin between his eyebrows in two deep wrinkles.

What is so confusing to him? "Shall I repeat?"

"No, Dora. I heard you… the first time. But—"

"Mr. Farrell?" Josh approaches. "We need to go. The raid's coming. We need to move, now."

But J doesn't move, his face is still in this confused, frowned look.

"Mr. Farrell? Please, come!" Josh is standing next to us now. "Michelle messaged us. We'll take you both to her place." Then he turns to me, and in a voice a lot softer than before, he says, "Dora Dana Dasnan, we need to move you to a safer place. Please, come." And he offers his hand to help me stand up.

I reach up, but then J stands up, slips his hand before Josh and helps me up instead.

We head for the door, J still holding my hand in his, looking at me sideways. "You and I are not done talking. All right?"

"Okay." I nod, somewhat shyly, and let him lead me out the door, trying not to enjoy, too much, the feeling of my hand in his.

CHAPTER 34

Uni

We walk back down the same corridor we used when we came here and within moments reach the transparent sliding doors. Outside, it's already dark. I slow down a bit behind the others, wondering if I miscalculated the time.

"The days here are shorter than on Earth," J says, reading my thoughts, as usual. He then hands me a scarf. "You'll need this."

I put it around my head and shoulders, copying the motions others are doing, then wrap the scarf attachment to cover my face. Josh opens the door, and the wind blows a gush of sand in my face.

I shut my eyes instinctively.

The howling from outside overtakes all the other sounds.

I peek out slightly and see a hand swinging goggles in front of me. "Here." J's voice is loud over the wind. "Take this!"

I glance at J. "Don't you need them?" I shout back.

"I'll be fine. Please, just take it."

I want to decline at first, but then another rush of wind blows more sand in my eyes, and I take the goggles.

"Thank you, J. I appreciate it."

He nods, then covers his face with a scarf, leaving only a

tiny gap for his eyes, and steps forward. I put on the goggles and walk out, following Matt and Josh, their overalls ruffling wildly with the wind. J walks next to me, but he's not holding my hand anymore, and this alone makes my heart sink.

Perhaps it is better like this…

We are finding our way between houses, but the wind makes visibility extremely low, and I can only see a few IPs ahead of me, the path lit by yellowish LED streetlights.

I can't see far, but all the buildings I do see are beige, sand-colored. The architecture is unusual: a combination of straight, smooth-lined Uni buildings, with sliding glass entrances and ID scanners, and mixed in it is old Human architecture, with numbering or writings on the buildings, small black statues hanging next to or above the doors, potted plants on the side of staircases leading to the entrances.

I follow the group, the wind making my advance difficult and uneven. Sometimes I need to strain to walk forward with the wind pushing me backward, and sometimes I stumble forward when the wind slows down.

The three men seem to be handling the force of air around them a lot more triumphantly than I am.

At one instance, I stop. The wind is simply too strong, like an invisible wall I'm leaning on.

J turns to check on me. I think he says something, but since I didn't enhance my TAEs, I don't hear him. Then the next moment, the wind almost disappears and I stumble forward. J jumps in front of me to catch me, but he's quick to take a step back as soon as he does. Still, he's holding me by my shoulders.

"You all right?" he says, then the wind picks up and the defiant howling sound is back.

I nod.

He takes my hand in his and starts heading forward. And I follow, looking down at our laced hands. His hand is warm, and I feel safer just by him holding my hand. I smile behind my scarf, my skin pulling at the rubber edge of the goggles.

Yes, it would be easier if he didn't, but I decide that for at least a few moments, I will not care if he's here for gratitude or obligation or debt. I imagine that he's here for me. And in this finite, limited moment, I find my happiness however short term it is going to be. And I decide this will be enough.

After a few more passes, Matt and Josh stop next to an entrance. Josh climbs a few steps and holds his hand to a scanner, opens up a door, then stands aside. "We will see you later!"

J nods, then guides me in. The door slides closed behind us, the deafening sound vanishing in an instant.

I hear ringing in my ears and wonder for a moment if my TAEs got damaged, but I realize soon enough it is just an aftereffect of the loud noise.

"Why aren't Matt and Josh coming in?" I ask, while the ringing slowly subsides.

"They are going to their homes. We just needed one of their IDs to enter the house," he says and then lets go of my hand.

My temporary bubble of happiness disappears instantly. Though I really disliked the wind, I now wish we were even slower, just so I could have my hand in J's for a little while longer.

J unwraps his scarf and takes off his coat, the sand falling on the floor like a rain shower on Earth, making a small dune next to his feet.

I feel somewhat uncomfortable we brought in all this sand from the outside.

J hangs his coat on the stand and then pushes it into one of the thin slots in the wall. I start taking off my scarf and coat, but then J helps me, taking the protective scarf off and pulling it gently off my neck and shoulders. He's standing close to me, well within an IP distance, and this motion of him taking off my clothes—no matter how innocent it really is—ignites me, raising a unique and unmistakable needy feeling inside me, the one thing only he can do: a sweet yearning of wish and anticipation.

I'm perfectly still, barely breathing as he moves around me. I hope he won't notice, won't realize the fire scorching underneath my skin.

He takes off my coat and shakes it, then slides it into one of the other empty slots.

I breathe out. *I don't think he noticed.*

He gently takes off my goggles and then smiles at me. I don't understand why until he starts brushing sand off my forehead and cheeks.

He's not saying anything, just smiling as he brushes it away, the sandy rough touch slowly replaced by the smooth, warm touch of his fingers as he removes the tiny grains off my face.

I keep looking at him, entranced, as his brushstrokes become slower, and slower, the dimples in his cheeks slowly fading away.

In time, I feel no sand on my face anymore, and the only sensation is his fingers gently stroking my cheeks. All sound is gone, and the lights seem to dim as well. It feels to me that time ceased to exist.

His fingers are on my cheeks now, still and unmoving, and his gaze is intense as he follows the contours of my face, slowly, until he finally lets it rest on my lips.

And just this leaves me breathless, raises my heartbeat to an almost unbearable level, makes my knees weak, my skin tingling in anticipation.

J slides his fingers to my neck, and ever so slowly pulls me closer to him. And—I can't help it. I slowly lean in.

"There you are!"

Both J and I jump backward.

"So sorry, my dears," says Michelle, peeking out from behind a wooden door. "I didn't mean to frighten you!" She walks out into the corridor. "Come in! Come in! J, I have messaged Marco. He'll be here shortly."

J looks at me from the side and smiles, the dimples back in his cheeks.

"Who's Marco?" I ask.

"You'll see!" He winks at me, then takes my hand and leads me forward.

CHAPTER 35

Uni

The room we enter has a soft glow coming from the hidden lamps, reflecting off the yellow wall. Around a low table in the middle of the room, three people sit on flat pillows. The moment we enter, they turn toward us, their faces obviously carrying a strong emotion, yet I cannot decipher what it is. I stop and let go of J's hand.

J turns to look at me. "It's okay, they are expecting us."

Before I take another step, the first one of the group, an elderly man, comes to greet me well within the IP distance. He reaches out with both his hands and takes mine, shaking it for a long time, looking at my eyes.

"Dora Dana Dasnan. I am so, so honored to meet you," he says, smiling broadly. He is not very tall, just about my height, and he's got thinning hair at the top of his head, his deep eye and cheek wrinkles accentuating the enthusiasm of his smile.

I am stunned as I let this man keep shaking my hand.

Michelle steps close to him and puts a hand on his shoulder. "Dora, meet my husband, Gerard."

Gerard is still shaking my hand.

Michelle continues, pointing to a young woman and a man behind Gerard. "My daughter Rebecca, and my son Aaron."

Gerard finally lets go of my hand, and both Rebecca and Aaron shake my hand in turn. Both of them are considerately taller than their father.

"You really do have cold hands," Aaron says as he shakes my hand. Then he looks into my eyes. "And the color of your eyes! I've heard of it, but…"

I feel like I'm back on Earth. Day one.

"She probably feels like a guinea pig right now," says Michelle. "That's enough. Let her go."

Aaron finally lets go of my hand and smiles shyly, shrugging at the same time. "I'm sorry. I'm just so amazed!"

I glance at J, my eyes open in a clear question.

He lifts an eyebrow, shrugging. "What can I tell you. It turns out that you are a celebrity on this planet."

But his explanation doesn't mean anything to me. Before I can query, Michelle pushes us toward the table.

"Come, let's sit down."

We all move slowly to the table and sit down on the pillows on the floor. I sit right next to J.

The pillows are harder than I anticipated, so I adjust.

Michelle and Gerard, who disappeared into another room a moment ago, come back carrying two large metal platters with several deep bowls. They lay it on the table and move bowls around so each person can reach one. Each of them holds food with a different coloring—red, green, beige, black—and the smell they bring into the room is mouthwatering. The two larger bowls with thin slices of bread, Michelle places in the middle.

"Dora," starts Michelle, "this will probably be new to you. You can try different dips and see what you like best. I wish…"

She breathes out, looking around at the dishes. "I wish it was more special. This is such a unique and amazing occasion, and I never expected I would witness it."

Witness what? Even though I don't understand, I say, "Thank you, Michelle. I am looking forward to tasting your food. Why don't you use replicators?" I ask, glancing at the old version of a food replicator in the corner of the room.

"Replicators? Have you tried the food that comes out?"

"Of course. This is all we use on other Uni planets."

"Oh good Lord—poor you!" She scoops red dip with a slice of bread and puts it in her mouth.

Indeed.

I take a slice and use the same dip as Michelle. The taste is fabulous. I close my eyes and enjoy the flavor. Then I feel a cramping pain at the corners of my cheeks as my saliva glands contract from overuse. I rub my cheeks to release it.

"Michelle, when is Marco coming?" asks J, before he takes a bite.

"Soon." She looks at a thin band around her wrist. "Well, he's a bit late. He was supposed to be here at six."

"Do you think the troops stopped him?" asks Aaron.

"I don't know. But even if they did, they shouldn't keep him for long."

"Is this usual, that you have so many troops around?" I ask.

"We've always had Brookonians around, but in the past two weeks things went crazy," says Gerard. "None of our rebellions have ever caused such a response. It's something completely different."

"But Marco has the clearance, doesn't he?" J says. "He should have freedom to move around."

"Yes, he has a medical license. He really should be fine,"

Michelle says and grabs another slice. At that moment, there is a knock on the inner wooden door.

"Oh, he's here." Michelle leaves the slice on her plate and gets up to get the door.

"Who is Marco?" I ask again.

J smiles enigmatically. "You'll see."

I press my lips into a thin line and look back at the door where Michelle disappeared. I find this anticipation somewhat disquieting.

Why won't anyone tell me who he is? What's the big mystery?

My Senthien is silent. There are no Vision imprints, not even the haze around my field of sight. Nothing. I might as well be just one of the normal nonprecognitive people I'm surrounded by.

Michelle and Marco walk in through the door, smiling as they talk to each other. Marco is very tall, and he needs to bow his head to enter through the dining room door.

They both approach me.

"Marco, please meet Dora," Michelle says as she points to me.

I want to get up, but he lifts his hand to stop me, then kneels down next to me. He's got a warm, gentle face despite his height, hazel eyes and a pleasant smile.

"Dora." He takes my hand. "It is an immense pleasure to finally meet you."

Now my heartbeat is up and my senses are intensified automatically. "It is nice to meet you too, Marco." I try to keep my voice flat. "Why did you say *finally*?"

Marko looks at the others. "No one told you?"

"Told me what?"

"We thought it would be a nice surprise if you met him

first," says J, then looks at Marco. "Do you have an image of great-great-great-great"—he's counting with his fingers as he's saying it—"grandaunt?"

Marco smiles. "Always." He swipes the thin band on his wrist, and a 2D holo appears above his hand.

My breath locks up in the middle of an inhale.

On the 2D holo photo is a woman, long brown hair, hazel eyes, and beautiful red lips.

She is smiling.

I press my lips together, trying hard to fight the tears. But I fail, and they slip and roll down my cheeks. I reach with my hand and touch the holo, my fingers making round holes in the photo, breaking the two-dimensional layer.

I feel J's hand around my shoulders.

"She was a very beautiful woman, Dora," J whispers. "And you look just like her."

CHAPTER 36

Uni

I sniff then wipe the tears from my cheeks. "She is your…," I say, looking at Marco, my voice quivering.

"My 5G aunt. And I am her 5G nephew."

I laugh, and a new set of tears roll down. *I thought I lost all my family, but—I didn't. I still do have a family.*

J tightens his hug slightly, our bodies touching. It's a small gesture, but I find it necessary, essential almost.

No one said a word during all this. They let me take it all in my own time. And I do. I need several passes before I am certain I can hold my voice again.

"Can you—?" I clear my throat. "Can you please transfer this photo to my E-band?"

"Of course, Dora." He lifts his wrist up a bit more. "I'm not sure if these are compatible…," he says, but he adjusts the settings, and I see the incoming connection.

He swipes the screen toward my E-band, and I save the image on my device. I project it over my E-band now, the resolution far better as it shimmers above my forearm.

I have many recordings and photos of my mother on my nanoprobes, but this one is different. She is older here, not much, but a few years from the last time I saw her. Thinner than what I remember, a few grays where her hair parts, and a hint of dark purple under her eyes. Although she is smiling a beautiful broad smile, there is sadness in her face, traces at the corners of her eyes, the sides of her lips.

And that same sadness is the one that I kept with me for the past 386 years, since she left us.

"Do you know anything about her?"

But instead of Marco, J says, "You have just tapped into the most narrated story on Zema4."

"I don't... understand."

"As soon as I came here," J explains, "it became clear that there is one story that almost everyone knows. Not that everyone believes it, but everyone knows about it.

"The story is about a forbidden love between a Zema4 Human and a Senthien, and it is the story of your mom and dad, Dora. Do you want to hear it?"

"Can I tell it?" Aaron jumps in.

"No, I want to tell it!" says Rebecca. "I know it best!"

"I think," starts Michelle, "that it would be best if Marco told the story to Dora, don't you agree?"

Rebecca and Aaron reluctantly agree.

Marco turns to me. "Well, the story happened in my family, and I've heard it repeated many times over. A lot more than your usual Zema4 citizen.

"My 4G grandmother, Maria, had the first and the best overview on what was happening, starting from the very first glance your mother and father shared. She was your mother's sister.

"Your father..." Marco shakes his head slowly. "He wasn't like all the other Descendants, distant and vain. He talked to us.

He was what we called Humanitarian, someone who cares for general society, independent of what this society really is. There were not many of those around.

"He participated at our gatherings, joined our meals, and accompanied us during our daytime labor. We always thought he was studying Human behavior and customs, but we recently found out from J that he was, most likely, gathering data for his predictions."

"Didn't my mother tell you what he can do? Didn't she tell you about the Senthien ability?"

"No. It seems that it was important to Fenea that this trait stays hidden. And so it did. Now, because he was close to us, because he talked to us and participated in the gatherings, he at one point met your mother.

"They didn't talk that first time, nor a few times afterward, but Elida told her sister that she noticed him that very first time at the gathering. Not long after, Fenea approached her, asked her if he could interview her for the studies. And she said yes.

"So they spent six hours straight talking at the bench in front of the church. It got so late that the lockdown was already up. They hadn't even noticed until a Brookonian officer stopped them and asked them to continue the interview the next day. Fenea walked her home, which would have been romantic"—he grins—"if only they didn't tow several Brookonians at their back.

"Maria was extremely angry at her sister. And this Senthien as well. Because of him, Elida missed lockdown. And then, when she finally did appear, she had a Senthien, a Descendant, standing next to her. Our official enemy.

"But that same night, Elida told Maria that she was in love. And no matter what Maria said, no matter how she begged her to be reasonable, Elida could not be dissuaded. She said he was the one, that she knew it as a memory come to be.

"I think now," Marco continues, his gaze on the floor, "that Fenea must have told her about his Visions, about what he had seen, about the two of them. And Elida believed him. They kept talking to each other every day until Fenea had to leave because his project was officially over.

"You know..." Marco looks up at me. "We never see a Descendant twice. They all come here because they have to, because they are forced to, and they never come back again.

"Maria tried to convince her sister that this was it and that she would never see Fenea again. In fact, the entire family tried to get Elida out of the clouds, tried to get her interested in someone else, but she would not be persuaded. She was convinced that Fenea would come back. And she apparently even told them when."

"And within a few Zema4 months, he did." Michelle smiles.

"They kept seeing each other for several more months," Marco continues, "but by then, the frequency that Fenea visited a particular Zema4 person became too much even for Descendants, so he left his E-bands at different places while they both went somewhere else, hidden under Zema4 clothing.

"The months went by, and Elida's twenty-sixth birthday was just around the corner."

Corner?

"It means the event will happen soon," says J, reacting to my frown.

"As you might know, every woman who turns twenty-six needs to respond to the calling, the Ascend. Every woman has to teleport to another planet to perform work for Descendants. And that was the moment Fenea decided to take her away."

Everyone in the room is quiet, as if this is the first time they are hearing the story. No one is eating. No one is talking. I can hardly hear them breathing.

"He organized everything for her, told her she should join the group on the first week of the second month, teleporting to Fraya Spark. She was not recruited for this mission, but she went anyway, and the teleportation worked.

"And for six years, no one on Zema4 heard from them. Nothing. Most of our family thought something really terrible happened to her. They thought she died," Marco says.

"And then, six years later, Elida came back, safe and sound. But heartbroken. She had to leave Fenea, and her daughter, behind. We learned only afterward that she was already pregnant by the time she ported to Fraya Spark, and they both knew about it.

"I think this was the reason your father decided to take her out of circulation then, so she never entered the recruitment. You see, many women Ascend and come back to Zema4 after some time. But some, however, never return." He looks down, shaking his head. "And now it's worse than ever."

Worse than ever? I look up at him, my gaze intense, my Senthien intrigued with his remark. But before I can ask, he continues.

"When Elida came back," Marco says, "she was a lot more mature but a lot more pensive, a lot more despondent. She told Maria about you and the short six years she managed to spend with you. And she missed you. Terribly. For the rest of her life…"

My eyes start to sting again, and I press my lips together, trying to fight it, forgetting about my curious Senthien.

"Did my father ever come back?" I ask after a while.

"Your mother said it was too dangerous to come again. She wasn't expecting him to either."

"But he did," jumps in Aaron.

"Yes. Only one more time, when your mother was in her late nineties. Just before her health began to deteriorate, your father came to her unannounced, out of the blue. Now that I think about it, I think he must have known. I think he came to say goodbye, even though it was dangerous.

"There are no pictures of them taken at that time," he continues. "Elida would not allow it. But she told her family afterward that it was the most difficult time for her. Fenea looking the same as he did when they parted, and her old, gray and wrinkly.

"Fenea told her all about you. He showed her your holos. She cried a lot that day. And many days after." Marco lowers his gaze. "It must have been extremely difficult for her."

I lower my gaze too, my throat getting tighter again. "He never told me he went to visit."

Marco nods.

"What happened afterward?" I ask.

"Your mother… died a few weeks after. And we never saw your father again. We never knew if you were still alive or what became of you. But the stories got told, by now outside of my family as well. And within two generations, everyone knew about this forbidden love story."

Marco takes a deep breath, then takes a slice of bread and dips it into the soft green paste. With this, everyone else starts moving again.

"So," Michelle continues. "You can imagine our surprise when we heard a story from J. He told us about a woman who is five Zema4 generations old and has the unique mixed heritage, her father Senthien, her mother Human."

"So as soon as J recognized you, the word spread across Zema4 like wildfire," explains Aaron. "You are the most famous person on this planet right now." He grins.

"Everyone will want to meet you!" Rebecca says.

"A real celebrity!" Gerard nods.

And I look at them all in turn, but the only thing I want to do is shrink, to disappear.

This is not me, *so* not me.

For all my life, I've tried to blend in. I've tried to make myself as invisible as I could, to pass through masses of people without anyone taking a second glance.

That was the only way I could survive.

This here?

This is exactly the opposite of where I want to be.

J looks at me from the side and says, "Perhaps it's not important to meet *everyone*?"

"You don't need to meet others if you don't want to, of course," says Marco.

"But I am sure everyone would love to meet you," points out Rebecca.

"Yes, dear, of course they would," says Michelle, raising an eyebrow at her daughter, "but it's not possible anyway. She can't meet four million people." Then she glances at me. "Maybe just a few?"

I look at the floor, feeling self-conscious. "Maybe… a few."

"Perhaps we could gather city principals," says Marco. "That would make sense anyway. They would then spread the word in their cities."

"But I want to be there!" says Rebecca.

"Me too," Aaron adds.

Michelle and Gerard look at each other, then at me.

"Okay, maybe city principals and… a few others," I say.

"Yes!" Rebecca and Aaron turn to each other and clap their hands.

I turn to Marco. "Did my mother have anyone else, after my father?"

"No, she never remarried. I think she—"

"Did you say—remarried? Were they married?"

"Yes. They were married. You didn't know?"

"No. When did they get married? Where?"

"Here, on Zema4. A few months before they went to Fraya Spark. It was all hidden, of course. No one but our family knew about it."

"Do you have any images of that time?"

He shakes his head. "No. I'm quite certain none were taken. I'm sorry you are not able to see it. It would have been special."

I nod.

"After Fenea, Elida never fell in love again," Michelle says.

I look down, sensing a sad smile on my lips. *Just like my father.*

Then I remember there was something I wanted to ask Marco. "When you told me about my mom and dad—"

"Yes?"

"You also talked about *Ascend*?"

"Yes. This is the time when Zema4s get their projects and they need to teleport to different locations."

"You said that many women leave and come back, but that some don't. Where do they go?"

Marco shrugs, looking at the others, then back at me. "I don't know. I'm sorry."

"What about the women who come back? Where were they?"

He shakes his head. "I'm sorry. I don't know that either."

I look at Michelle. "Do you?"

"No, it's not that they wouldn't tell me," Marco explains. "It's just that they themselves don't remember."

Julie and Andrea for sure remembered seeing me at the Boolean Institute.

Before I manage to voice the thought, a double tone sounds from the bands of all Zema4 people, their thin electronic bracelets flashing yellow.

"*Merde!*" says Gerard, looking at his wrist.

They all start placing their plates back to the table and standing up.

"What's going on?" I ask.

"It's a domicile raid!" explains Aaron.

Michelle nudges me to stand up.

"I-I don't understand."

"They are screening the houses," she explains. "This is unusual, but in the past two weeks, they've increased the recurrence dramatically. Now, come! You need to disappear, quickly."

"Where should we go?"

"I have just the place for you," she says and heads for the door.

CHAPTER 37

Uni

At the corridor of Michelle's house, we say goodbye to the others.

Rebecca hugs me, which takes me by surprise, but I don't recoil. In truth, I enjoy it. It's honest, pure and emotionally charging, even though it's done quickly while we all try to rush.

"I will see you tomorrow," says Michelle. "Please follow Marco, all right?"

"We will. Thank you, Michelle," J says, then takes my hand and walks out a few steps behind Marco.

It's dark, the windy streaks of grainy sand twist in the air against the black background. But I don't feel the wind or the cold. I am blissfully suspended in happiness as I watch my hand in J's. He took it spontaneously, without thinking. Perhaps he anticipated the strong wind? Or maybe, just maybe, he *wanted* to hold my hand?

I look away. *Don't be so naive, Dora.*

J notices when I slightly release my grip. He looks at me, but I can't decipher his expression, then looks forward, keeping pace with Marco.

After a few more passes, we reach a square, and Marco leads us to a large unattached building.

Underneath patches of brown sand, the house is clearly white.

I look up.

It is also higher than other buildings, topped with a tower.

Marco pushes the door open and it squeaks, audible even over the deafening sound of the wind. J and I climb up the few entrance stairs, and the door closes behind us with a thud. The sound of the wind immediately subsides, the clothes that were ruffling around me a moment ago now hang lifelessly at my feet.

We all take off our hoods, scarves, and goggles.

There are many slots for clothes on the wall, but when I want to use it, Marco stops me. "No. This place should appear empty. You need to keep your coat on."

I look down at my sandy clothes. "But… I'll leave sand all over. Won't the owner be unhappy?"

J and Marco look at each other, then grin.

"I don't think God will mind." J winks at me.

Why not? My Senthien resents being clueless, and I don't think my Human likes it either.

"We just need to make sure not to leave any traces," Marco adds as he jumps a few times, shaking the sand off his clothes. "Just in case troops decide to search the church."

J and I do the same, and the sand gets sucked into the thin grid at our feet.

Marco heads toward a glass door at the end of the corridor, but just before he swings it open, he stops. He dips his fingers into a small basin next to the door, then he makes unusual movements around his head and whispers something.

By the time I remember to enhance my TAEs so I can hear

him, he stops talking and enters through the swinging door, leaving it open for us.

Inside is a large hall, fairly dim with occasional LED lights on the wall. I enhance my ONCs and see many wooden benches aligned one after another. At the end, there is a stage, raised half an IP off the ground, with a simple dark wooden table and two plants on each side.

Behind are several images and statues.

And all of this space—is completely empty.

I frown, my Senthien full of questions. *Shouldn't God be here when the troops come so she's accounted for? And why does she need such large living quarters when there is no one around?*

But I decide to ask later. I assume my Senthien curiosity wouldn't be quite welcome at this particular point in time.

"This is the musalla nave," says J, pointing to the large hall, his quiet voice echoing. "A place where people congregate for prayers, masses, weddings, funerals…"

"Come!" Marco waves at us, standing next to the open dark wooden door of the cupboard in the side wall of the building.

We head his way and stop in front of the cupboard.

"Quickly," he insists. "Go in!"

I frown, staring at the empty cupboard. *Go where?*

"Raids don't normally happen in churches or places of prayers," Marco explains, "but recently they have been sweeping everything, so you need to hide, just in case."

J nods, then takes my hand and enters the cupboard.

I expect Marco will close the door behind us and our hiding place will be this old wooden construction, but J moves even farther into the cupboard and then starts climbing down.

I realize at that moment that the dark wooden planks hold an optical illusion: they seem like a small finite space of an inside of the cupboard but are actually double doors and a staircase into the basement.

"I'll close these doors," Marco shouts from up above. "You need to close the inner doors as well, all right?"

"Got it, Marco! Thanks!" says J. "We will see you later!"

Next moment, I hear the thud of the cupboard door closing.

I touch the cold stone walls of the narrow spiral staircase, using my enhanced ONCs to see where I'm going. "Will Marco be all right? What if the troops stop him before he's back at his home?"

"It's possible, yes. But he should be all right. He's got more freedom to move around because of his medical profession. He can say he was checking on one of his patients."

We might have descended about two stories when we finally pass through another narrow door.

The place we enter is dark, but then J turns on the light.

The room is small. The walls look just like the walls outside—white, rough, with just a bit of sand in their grooves.

In the corner there is a basin and a partially separated toilet. In the other side of the room, a mattress is lying on the floor and a small wooden case stands next to it.

J closes the doors behind us, then leaves his coat on the hanger next to the door.

He walks to the other side of the room, then bends to pick up a pillow that's lying on the floor. He taps it a few times and throws it on the mattress.

His back is toward me, and I realize at that moment that we are alone. J and I. Just as I would have wanted.

But now I feel uptight and downright anxious.

I rub my hands against my thighs, feeling the drumming in my chest.

I glance at the door.

Perhaps I could wait at the staircase?

I shake my head. *Stupid. And utterly unreasonable.*

I slowly look back at J.

But why am I so afraid to be here? With him?

"I'm sorry," J says, still looking at the wall.

I want to ask why, but my throat is clenched shut and nothing comes out.

I close my eyes and breathe in, then focus on the task, on the question at hand. Not my emotions, not my feelings, just facts.

"There is no need to be." I look at him. "You've just brought us to a safe place." My voice is Senthien-flat, just as I wanted it to be.

He turns around, a wrinkle of confusion between his eyebrows. Then he shakes his head, looking at the floor, and starts walking toward me. "No… No… That's not what I mean."

He stops just at the IP limit, then looks into my eyes. "What I mean is that I am sorry I let you go. It all came so fast, so sudden, and I didn't know what to do. I—"

"No, J, I understand. Really, I do. And you don't need to be sorry for anything. My leaving was solely my decision. And you need to know—you really need to understand—that there is absolutely no need for you to feel any kind of obligation toward me in any—"

"You keep saying obligation. What do you mean by *obligation*?" The wrinkle between his eyebrows grows into a deep frown.

"Look, it's very clear to me what you feel. In fact, if I were in your place, I would feel the same. For such a long time, you have been unhappy, because you thought Monica was dead, and then, after nine years, you realize she's alive and that what you wished for so long came true. And, of course, I understand how happy that makes you feel, and… and…" *Oh, the Moons of Senthia, I am losing my smooth Senthien didactic.*

I exhale somewhat impatiently and continue. "What I'm trying to say is that I understand that you feel obliged to a person who quite literally brought your wife back from the dead. But you really don't need to feel any obligation to help me.

"Now, don't misunderstand me! This really is the most decent, the most selfless thing to do, and I'm happy that you felt the need to save me from possible dangers that might arise for me in Uni. But I can assure you, J, that I am fine. Just consider that whatever debt you think you might have toward me is paid in full. I completely understand."

His confusion wrinkles smooth out; his eyes are now wide open as he listens to me.

I find that utterly distracting, so I look away. "I will be fine. Really. You should have the life you wish." I take a heaved breath. "The life you deserve." And I exhale. *A great finish to my not-so-smooth Senthien speech.*

"Are you done?" J says, the side of his lip tipped into a half smile.

I blink. "I… guess…"

"Good." He takes one step toward me, closing the IP distance, then cups my face with his hands, leans in, and kisses me.

And my thoughts are gone. Blank. My mouth is glued to his, a few grains of sand trapped between our warm lips.

Then J pulls away slightly so he can look at me. "You don't."

I can barely take a breath. "I don't… *what?*"

"You *don't* understand," he says, his gaze alternating between my eyes and my lips. "I said I shouldn't have let you go but not because of an obligation. Or gratitude. Or a debt that I feel toward you. It's because… I'm in love with you."

He gently leans his forehead on mine. "I love you, Dora. And I never want to lose you again. Ever."

Then he sighs and says quietly, "The only real question"—he looks into my eyes—"is what do *you* want?"

I can barely keep myself up. His hands on my shoulders are the only thing keeping me balanced.

I look into his eyes, and I can't believe what I'm hearing. *How could I have been so* wrong?

I've seen it! It was… clear.

"Dora?" He leans closer, looking into my eyes. "Talk to me. Please."

I swallow hard. "But…"

"What?" His voice loses confidence a bit.

"I've seen it."

He lifts up his head just slightly. "You've seen what… exactly?"

I close my eyes, the memory of the Vision tearing at my heart. I swallow hard, then clench my fists and look at him again, hoping my face won't reveal how terribly weak I feel right now. "I have seen Monica. And you. Together."

J closes his eyes and lets go of my shoulders.

So it really is true…

My heart gets pierced once again.

And I hate it! I've been through that before. I've grieved before. *Why does it hurt again so much?*

"I'm sorry, Dora. I needed time to realize what I really wanted. What I really needed. I wish I had known it from the start. So you'd never have left Earth in the first place. But I didn't. And I'm sorry." He swallows hard. "I hope you can forgive me, because I know what I want now, what I've wanted ever since I met you. It's *my* life with *you*."

Then, so unexpectedly, he kneels in front of me and hugs me around my waist so I'm wrapped in his arms. He leans his cheek to my belly and closes his eyes. "Please, forgive me."

My arms are hanging next to my body, passive, and I don't know what to do.

I'm terribly hurt, and part of me wants to push him away, jealous stitches crisscrossing my heart. But on the other hand, I understand him. I know—no, *I feel*—what he has been through.

He lifts his head up to look at me, but he doesn't say anything. He keeps holding me in this tight embrace, his beautiful dark eyes fixed on me. And he waits.

I ever so slowly lift my hand and place my palm on his cheek, the tips of my fingers touching his hair.

And I realize at that moment how much I missed this. How much I missed touching him, feeling his skin underneath my palm, feeling his arms around me, seeing his messed-up hair, his deep, dark eyes so close to mine. And without warning, tears roll down my cheeks, but I smile. "I have missed you." I slide down to my knees as well.

We hug each other, and it feels like two matching pieces of a puzzle sliding back into place, a form where you can't tell where the borders are, where one piece ends and the other one begins.

"I have missed you too." He whispers next to my ear. "So badly you can't imagine…"

We stay like this for a long while, taking in the closeness, stretching ourselves onto and into one another, ignoring the borders our skin makes.

I feel alive again.

I feel like this is the only way my life can exist.

It's hours after midnight, and we are still talking quietly, lying on the bed with our backs against the wall, softened by a pillow, our fingers tangled together between our laps.

J tells me about my Earth friends, about Old Mike, Tania and Peter, how they all helped him when he was down, how Patrick stood by him every step of the way, including the last moment when he ported.

He doesn't tell me a lot about Monica, and I don't know if this is because he wants to save me from a difficult topic or because it is easier for him not to relive that part.

I tell him about everything that happened to me up until now. About the Boolean Institute, about the lab and the women I saw there. About coming back to Senthia and finding out that things have been drastically changed. About the Seekers.

And then I open up the lock on my buried feelings, and I tell him about my father.

I need to stop in the middle, my clenched throat blocking me from talking.

He hugs me close, and I lean in toward him, my head on his chest, my tears making wet spots on his shirt. I feel his strong embrace, his lips pressing kisses on the top of my head, like warm seals of empathy and love.

"I'm so sorry," he whispers against my hair. "I wish I was there to help you."

I know he couldn't have. And I know that if he was there, he would be dead too.

So I'm glad he wasn't.

After a while, I force myself to tell him more, to forcefully move my thoughts elsewhere.

I tell him about nanoprobes. And how Zlathars control the Descendants this way.

I tell him about Lesya, and BD308, and how I barely escaped Lorea.

I also tell him about all the strange and illogical events that I could not explain that happened along the way and that in more cases than not saved my life.

And I tell him about my long porting sessions and about the strange Void experiences while I was *nothing*.

"Oh, Dora, you've been through so much." He presses another kiss on the top of my head. "You really are a fighter. You don't give up." Then he pulls away from me a bit so that he can look into my eyes.

He smiles and shakes his head in disbelief. "Truly, I'm in awe. You're so amazingly brave."

I smile, then lean back on his chest, his steady heartbeat calming me down. I don't tell him that I did.

I did give up.

And that I am not brave. Not at all.

In fact, the only skill I am amazing at is hiding and not being noticed. And that's who I was, right up until the moment I had a Vision of him, a Vision where he decided to leave Earth and port to Uni.

I sigh. "No, J, I am not."

"What?" It's been several passes, so he doesn't immediately link my answer to what he said before.

"I am not brave. Quite the opposite."

He moves away from me, two deep lines between his eyebrows. "Well, everything I've seen so far falls under the encyclopedic description of one adjective: brave." He shakes his head. "Why do you say you're not brave?"

"When I left Earth, it was because I *wasn't* brave. If I was, I would have stayed."

J sighs, then pulls me back to him, leaning his cheek gently on the top of my head. "I understand. Not many people are brave in that way." Then he squeezes me to him even more. "But it's all right now. Now it's time to come back home, where you really belong."

He moves his head away, and I lift mine up to look at him.

"You will come back with me, back to Earth, won't you, Dora?"

I smile. Then nod. "Yes," I say as I lean my head back on his chest as a blanket of calm covers me, my mind finally at peace. I'm certain of what I want. Even if I know I'll need to face Monica and ladies with pitchforks standing behind her, probably.

I will.

Because it's worth it.

This life, a life with J, is worth saving.

CHAPTER 38

Uni

Tania frowns, then wraps her fingers around the thin silvery pendant around her neck. "I... I don't understand."

"I think it will become clear."

She nods, the expression on her face wary. She takes the necklace off and gives it to me.

"Thank you," I say and turn over the pendant on my palm. The bottom surface has an intricate pattern of thin indentations along the shiny metal surface.

I look at her. "I am not sure if it will work, Tania, and I'm not sure what should actually happen once I do this." I look at the machine in front of me. "But I have seen this device before. And I have seen myself doing this." I slide the pendant into an empty slot in the device in front of me, and the machine buzzes to life.

I wake up with a start. I'm lying on J's chest, the slow rise and fall over a steady heartbeat. I sigh and close my eyes.

Tania. I remember the pendant on her necklace. *Was that just a dream? Or was it a Vision?*

If it was Vision—my heartbeat speeds up—this might mean that we'll go back, go back home, to Earth. *If* it was a Visi—

There is a knock on the door.

I realize then that this was what woke me up in the first place.

I lift my head, remembering what Tania once told me. "Yes, come in."

In pokes a head. "Hello...," Rebecca says quietly. "Good morning."

"Good morning, Rebecca," I say in a quiet voice not to wake J up.

"I didn't mean to wake you, but the principals are gathering already."

I sit up and rub my eyes. "Come in, Rebecca, come in. I'm sorry, I didn't realize it was so late."

She enters, holding a pile of clothing folded over her forearms. "My mom arranged some clothes for you, so you can change, if you want to." She puts them down on the case next to the mattress.

"I'm sorry, the church doesn't have showers, but you can use ours in the afternoon. We have two credits for today."

"Thank you. We will be right up," I say, then glance at J. His eyes are closed, lips just lightly parted, his mind dwelling deep in the subconscious spheres.

"Well, perhaps in a few passes." I smile at her.

"Okay, I'll tell them." At the door, she turns around. "Afterward there'll be a ceremony and a banquet. In case you are hungry."

"Thank you, Rebecca."

She closes the door behind her, and I look back at J. He looks so calm and peaceful, and I hate that I need to wake him up. I lean in next to his cheek and whisper, "J… J, wake up…"

His breathing pattern changes just slightly for a few breaths, but then he goes back to the steady, calm rhythm.

I look down at his lips. They are pale red and very smooth and so incredibly, immensely attractive that I sometimes wonder how any woman can pass him by without automatically gluing her lips to his.

I swallow, my breathing getting heavier, feeling the fire within me breaking through the cracks of a hardened lava crust, spilling into the meshwork of dense riverbeds, the glowing ember pulsating through my body.

My heart is drumming, the craving tangible underneath my skin. So I lean in and very slowly, savoring this anticipation, I press my lips onto his.

Before he's consciously aware, his lips respond, shifting, molding perfectly to mine. And I can't believe how I ever managed to live through a day without him.

He doesn't open his eyes, but I can tell he's now clearly awake. He slides his arms around me and hugs me closer, a content "mmm" rumbling in his throat.

The moment our lips part, we look at each other, his eyes drawing lines on my face with his gaze. Then he lifts his head and kisses me once again, this kiss firmer, a seal confirming his thoughts. "I'm so glad I found you. I don't know what I'd do otherwise," he whispers.

I smile, still astounded that I actually get to hear him say that.

Then J frowns as he hears the thumping sounds above us. With every moment, it's getting louder and louder.

"What's happening?"

"Rebecca came around," I say. "She got us some new clothes, and also, she said the gathering is starting now."

"Wow, they don't waste any time. It for sure sounds like there are a lot of people," he says as he looks at the ceiling.

I swallow a lump in my throat, anxiety creeping up at facing such a large group.

"Hey!" J says. "Don't worry about it. Just remember, you are a star."

I manage to smile. He really does guess my thoughts very well.

"Well, we shouldn't keep them waiting," he says and stands up, then picks up the pieces of clothing Rebecca brought to separate the one for him. "I think this is for you." He turns and hands me a smaller beige skinsuit.

I stand up to pick it up but then stop, frozen, realizing something.

And I think he just realized it too.

His dark eyes bore into mine. Then, slowly, still holding the skinsuit between us, he steps closer, his breathing getting heavier.

"Do you... want me to"—his voice is deep—"turn around while you change?"

My heart goes wild as he says these words.

"Do you want to?" I whisper.

He swallows and steps even closer, the thin skinsuit the only thing between our bodies.

"No." It's a husky, incredibly seductive whisper that makes my insides flutter with anticipation. "I want to look at you." He leans in and kisses my temple. "I want to touch you." He kisses my other cheek as I close my eyes, feeling his warm breath across my face. "I want to *feel* you."

I moan involuntarily, sparkling heat pooling inside me. I crave his body, eager to feel him too.

I let go of the skinsuit, then rise on my toes and kiss him, wrapping my arms around his neck.

He opens my lips with his, and we kiss, deep and long, and this perfect interplay between our tongues ignites me; my patience to wait for him is gone. I want to have him—I *need* to have him—right now.

We somewhat awkwardly stumble back toward the mattress, J unzipping my old skinsuit at the same time I'm taking off his clothes, my nails leaving marks on his skin.

Our breaths are loud and loaded with emotion, his lips on my neck half kissing, half biting as we both fall onto the low bed.

Within moments we are completely naked. But then he stops. He moves an inch away and looks at me while still breathing heavy, entrapped in my arms and legs. I can feel his wish, his need, his lust, hard, touching me just barely.

I need him, I want him, I am crazy for him. I squeeze my legs around his waist and want to pull him closer to me, but he resists.

"J…," I moan. *I need you. I want you.*

"Promise me something," he whispers, his fingers gently touching my cheek.

I breathe heavily, my eyes half-open as I try to comprehend his words, trying to bring back logic to my wild, passionate body. "Yes?"

"Don't ever leave me again."

I blink, looking at him, dazed. "I won't."

He looks down at my lips and leans in to kiss me. The pressure of my legs around him is gone, and the next moment, he enters, releasing the trapped joy in the center of my body, satiating my thirst a thousand times over.

Our bodies blend, arms and legs woven together in a sweaty, rhythmic motion, where I kiss him so deeply I can't get enough, where his hands touch me in the most exasperating way, bringing me to the peak of my pleasure within moments.

I cry from the intensity, my whole body spasming, lost from this reality while I hold on to the most thrilling, earth-shattering sensation my body has experienced.

For many passes, we are silent, the room filled only with our heavy breaths, enhanced by the empty white walls.

I keep holding him tightly, completely wrapped around him, his head next to mine, feeling warm breaths on the side of my neck.

"That was," he says between breaths, "very much… the Uni speed… Sorry about that."

I laugh but then turn to look into his eyes. "This was not even vaguely comparable. It was *amazing*." And I squeeze him tight again.

He grins, returning my body hug. "Oh, better than amazing!"

We stay like this for a few more passes, and I wish we could stay like this for hours. But I know we can't: we are already late.

As usual, he knows exactly where my thoughts are going. "I'd love to stay here forever," he whispers, "but we probably need to appear at the gathering. We don't want them peeking through the doors right now." He winks at me.

"Yes." My lips spread into a smile. "That would be most unfortunate."

CHAPTER 39

Uni

We walk into a crowded hall. It's loud and buzzing; voices reverberate off the walls and the hum sounds like music.

J heads toward the center of the hall, holding my hand, making a tunnel through jam-packed people. As soon as they realize who we are, they stop talking, and within a pass or so, the entire hall is silent.

I have an urgent need to turn around and go back to the secret room. If J wasn't holding my hand, I would have already done that. But J is confident in his steps, his hand holding mine securely as he guides me to the center.

As I walk, I feel a soft hand on my shoulder, a fleeting touch at my elbow, my hair brushing against someone's fingers; one woman even reaches out and touches my cheek as I pass.

I cringe, bowing my head low. My Senthien is curled up in a ball inside me, and even my Human finds it extremely unsettling.

Why are they touching me?

J notices, then slows down a step and hugs me with one arm, shielding me from the curious strangers while my eyes are glued to the stone floor. Only once we stop do I dare to look up. I see

Michelle, Marco, and several other people gathered around a low elongated table.

"I don't think they doubt she is real now," says J under his breath, looking at Michelle. "Dora, where do you want to sit?" he says more quietly.

I choose a place where we can sit next to each other, still not wanting to let go of his hand.

"Please welcome Dora Dana Dasnan," Michelle announces loudly, standing so everyone can hear her. "The daughter of Elida Demasio and Fenea Maswan Denk, a Human and a Senthien, that with their love, defied the laws of Uni."

There is loud applause with shouts and whistles, cries and laughs.

I look at the floor again, leaning into J as much as possible, shying away from them all and trying to hide, disappear, vanish.

Michelle sits down and whispers, "I apologize, Dora. I realize this must be difficult for a Senthien."

"It would be difficult for a Human too," says J.

"Yes, I suppose it would," she says after a few moments pause.

The loud noise slowly subsides into a high murmur, though I can still feel eyes boring into me from all sides.

I ask Michelle, feeling uncomfortable under so much scrutiny, "Why are there so many people here? Are they all city principals?"

"No, not only city principals. You see, the problem is that we can't gather in such large numbers for no specific reason. It's being tracked. But we do have a few exceptions, and weddings are one of those." She points to a group around us. "So most of these people are here for a wedding celebration that comes afterward. I'm sorry you don't feel comfortable, but this is the only way we can pull it off without attracting attention."

I nod. "Yes, Michelle. I understand."

"Good. Now, we don't have a lot of time, so let me introduce you to some of our principals. Zameret heads 03."

Zameret, a gray-haired broad man with a dull nose and thin lips, smiles at me. "I am very happy to meet you, Dora."

"I am pleased to meet you, Zameret."

"I am here for the principals of 01 and 02," he continues. "It was too far for them to come to the gathering, but if you stay here for a few more days, I am sure you will meet them."

"Pierre is leading 16 and Enrique city 17," Michelle continues.

They are both very thin and tall, darker-skinned than others sitting around the table.

"We are glad you are here," Pierre says.

"And we are eager to find out more," adds Enrique.

Michelle turns to the other side of the table and introduces Anirbana and Haruki, leading 28 and 33, Dragana leading 52, and Runa 76.

"And this"—she points to the last one—"is Father Vincent."

I frown as I look at the person on the other side of J. *Father? I don't understand.*

"Father Vincent," says J, "is responsible for the church of 53. He's their priest."

I take a sharp breath. *Priest? Like the high Zlathar priest?*

Vincent smiles gently and explains, "The name Zlathars took for their main leader differs by a great margin from what priest means here, child."

It stings just a bit when he calls me child. I swallow. "Yes?"

"The name is part of the religion Humans had for many thousands of years, and for the most part, a priest is a person who helps people raise their souls to a higher, more profound level, using prayers and meditations so that they can communicate with God."

"I don't understand." I look around. "Isn't she here?"

Vincent smiles. "God is everywhere."

I am really confused now.

J winks at me. "I think I need to give you some background since it seems you are lacking the nano knowledge on the most common topic in history. And it seems that the high Zlathar priest has nothing to do with religion or belief, despite the grandiose name he chose for himself."

Just as J said, my nanoprobes are empty, and I am curious to find out more. But much more than that, I am curious to understand why all these people are here, and why they are so incredibly focused on *me*.

"Michelle, I have an inquiry. Why is my presence inducing such a strong reaction? Many people were trying to touch me."

"You are the daughter of a Human and a Descendant," she says as if this is the answer.

"Yes. But why is that important to them?"

"Your existence was a myth, a legend. Many people believed in it. But many didn't because there was no proof that you actually existed or that the story, the love story between a Senthien and a Human, actually happened.

"The fact that you are here, the reason some of them—and again I do apologize for that—wanted to touch you, means that it *did* happen."

"Yes, but I still don't understand why is this important for Zema4s. It's just something two people felt for each other five centuries ago."

Michelle shakes her head, but she's smiling. "No. It's not just two people falling in love, because this love was not meant to happen in the first place. Not between a Human and a Descendant. Not between enemies. But it did, you see. It did! And that means that it is possible.

"It means that no matter how bleak our life looks, how hopeless we feel, it's not all lost."

She opens her arms, pointing at the people in the hall. "This is why we are all here, because your existence means hope."

"The timing of your appearance," says Anirbana, "is special as well."

I turn to look at her. She is small in build, with long, curly black hair and black eyes. At the bridge of her nose, she has a small red circle, a coloring that must have a meaning, but of course, it is nowhere to be found on my nanoprobes.

"What do you mean?" I ask.

"In the past two weeks, we've had more Brookonian legions coming to Zema4 than at any other time before. They are performing daily raids of the cities, public houses, and recently our homes as well. We feel that something really big happened that made them do this. And of course none of us has the slightest idea of what it is."

"Also, in the past six months," Haruki adds, "we've had many more women targeted for Ascend than before, and many of them didn't come back as they usually do."

"Jonathan just told us that some of them ported to Earth," Pierre says, and his voice is echoed by an excited murmur spreading around the hall.

I look around, not understanding the excitement.

"Earth," says J, with a nod. "They, just as Descendants, had no idea it exists. Or that there's life."

"So we know some of them are alive," says Pierre. "But there were thousands of women who left to Ascend, and we are still waiting for them to come back."

Automatically, I think of the women I saw at the Boolean Institute, immobile and unconscious in their med pods.

I glance at J, wondering if I should tell them what I saw.

He's looking at me. He knows what I'm thinking. But if I do tell them, will that make it better? Or will it make it even worse?

Will they ask me why I didn't help them when I was there?

Should I have helped them?

Could I have?

Did I make a terrible mistake by not getting them out?

I shiver involuntarily, but my thoughts remain hidden.

"And naturally, many of us are afraid that our wives, our daughters, our sisters, will be taken away at the next Ascend," Zameret says, motioning to the rest of the people with his hands. "And that this will be the last time we will ever see them."

Anirbana continues, "When J teleported to us, Dora, and told us about Jumpers, about Earth, and about *you*—that had such a big impact, not only because of what it meant, but because we found out about it *now*, with everything that has been happening in the past few weeks."

A soft murmur rises through the hall.

"And this means," Zameret continues, responding to the murmur around us, "there is a reason you came to us now. It means that you can save us."

"A Descendant is finally on our side!" someone else shouts.

"The time for change has come!" A shout in the back.

"She is the one!" A woman's voice to my right, changing the murmur into a loud uproar endorsing her statement.

The sound is intense but not because it's loud. It's because it carries such a strong emotional charge that my Senthien needs to shrink away, afraid to be in the center of their needs and wants.

I feel J's arm around my shoulders, pressing me closer to him as Michelle stands up and raises her arms, her palms flat as if stopping the sound waves coming from the crowd. "Calm down! Calm. Down."

Although she's not yelling, her voice is strong. The crowd grows silent for a moment, but within a half pass, the murmur returns.

Michelle's eyes are narrow as she scans the group. "Is she your savior?"

Loud yeses echo around the room.

"Is she the one you have been waiting for?"

Yeses yet again.

"Do you want her to take your little hand and guide you through the horrible gates of Uni to the other side where the honey flows in riverbeds?"

The murmur dies out.

Then a man several rows behind stands and shouts, "She has to help us!"

"No, Sandro, she does not! She doesn't have to do anything for you or anyone else. She already did more than enough for Humans on Earth."

"Why can't she help Humans on Zema4 then?" someone behind Michelle shouts.

"She did," Michelle says as she turns around. "She gave you hope. She gave you opportunity, a possibility that there is another way. And for that"—she fixes the man with her gaze—"you will remain grateful."

The man sits down again, and the murmur continues louder, but no one is raising questions anymore.

My heart is still drumming from all the emotions clashing in this large hall, so fierce one can hear sparks flying.

They don't agree with Michelle. The hesitation, anger, and despair are palpable in the air.

Michelle loudly breathes out, then sits back down and whispers to me, "I am sorry, Dora. I know this is difficult to understand, but we have been under a lot of pressure lately and it takes a toll." She shakes her head. "This here… don't take it to heart. When you feel there's nowhere to go, you grab at straws."

"A drowning man catching a straw to stay afloat," explains J.

"But… a straw would not be useful."

"Precisely."

"Oh… I understand." I nod.

I really do. I know they want out, away from this place they did not choose for themselves, away from being used by Descendants for a host of tasks I only know half of, away from being subservient to anyone else but themselves.

I understand.

But I am not the one, as one person claimed. I am not their savior. I cannot lead them anywhere.

I am exactly the opposite.

I am someone who hides, who stays invisible just to stay alive. *In truth, I am a coward.*

I bow my head low.

"Hey." J squeezes me closer to him. "Don't let this get to you, all right?"

I don't dare look at him.

"Michelle is right," he continues. "No one can force you to do anything. And no one should."

He sighs and hugs me with both arms, kissing my hair. "You

have been through so much. The only thing you need to do is come home, with me, back to safety."

Back to safety…

Back to—

"So, who is the happy couple?" J asks Michelle.

"Ayshea and Mars," she says, then turns to me. "You haven't met them yet, but Ayshea is twenty-six and she will for sure be called to Ascend in the next round."

"They are getting married?" I ask, my eyes wide.

"Yes."

"Even though she will be going away?"

"Precisely because of it," explains Vincent. "They don't know if she will come back, so their marriage will mean commitment and love for eternity. This is what they want to give to each other. Even if their bodies are not together anymore, their souls always will be."

Wiry metal strings wrap around my heart.

And me?

I am going to safety, to a safe place, leaving them all behind.

I shake my head.

"Dora, what's wrong?" asks J.

"It's not fair," I say, my voice thin.

"No. It's not. But it's not up to you to make it right."

I look at him and whisper, "But what if it is?"

"No." He moves in front of me so he can look straight into my eyes. "Don't let them manipulate you into this. Just trust me. We have our plan, and this is to go back to Earth. And they will devise their own."

"Your plan might not work," Zameret says.

J turns to him. His body posture and the fine lines on his

face tell me he is extremely uptight, such a contradiction to the flat voice that comes out. "And why would that be?"

"All the teleporting chambers are heavily guarded by Brookonians. I don't see how you will be able to teleport out of Zema4. You might need to spend your *happily-ever-after* on our prison planet." His sweet words come through an acidic voice.

"They might not need to go the teleporting chamber," says Rebecca.

Everyone turns to look at her.

"What do you mean?" Michelle asks.

"Well…" She's unsure as her eyes switch from one person to another. "Both Miss Dasnan and Mr. Farrell teleported in the middle of Musk Street. Perhaps they could use the same place to teleport out?"

Of course! "You're right! It's the same as the porting spot on Earth!" I look at J. "There must be a porting chamber somewhere very close by. Probably underground."

"No, there is nothing," Haruki says.

"Perhaps not for passengers," I say, a hidden enthusiasm lighting up inside me. "But for supplies or automation, there might be. And you wouldn't have access or the awareness of their location."

J looks at me and nods. "This is a really good idea. We need to give it a shot. And we shouldn't waste too much time either." He turns to Michelle. "I understand it's important for you to have Dora here to get all the information. But Brookonians are searching for Dora. We need to get her out of Uni as soon as possible."

"But you can't just leave!" someone shouts.

"She's only been here for a day."

"We need more information!"

"What will happen with the Brookonians when she leaves?"

"You can certainly spare a few more days!"

Michelle nods, raising her palms up. "Yes… Yes… It would be nice, useful even, for us to have her here for a little bit longer. But Jonathan is right. They need to leave."

I shake my head.

"What?" J looks at me, an eyebrow raised. "Don't you want to leave? Don't you want to go back to Earth?"

"Yes, I do! Of course I do." I look into Michelle's eyes. "But not alone."

The hum in the hall is loud, but the group around me that heard what I just said grows quiet.

"If it worked for two people"—I look at J, a broad smile on my lips—"it will work for twenty, fifty, one hundred!"

I feel so ecstatic I can barely keep my voice calm. "Ayshea, Rebecca, all women turning twenty-six soon that are about to Ascend. We'll take them away."

Michelle holds her breath, then looks back at Rebecca.

"Mama?" Rebecca says weakly.

Then Michelle turns to me. "Can you do that?"

"I don't know with certainty. But I will try."

"Mama, I don't want to—"

"Stop!" She raises a finger at Rebecca, not looking at her, then she looks at the others. "Spread the word. We need"—she glances at me—"fifty…"

"One hundred," I say.

"One hundred. Gather the people who are most likely to Ascend in the next round. And people who are most likely not to come back."

Haruki looks at her. "Which would be…?"

"Healthy young women."

CHAPTER 40

Uni

I stand close to J, touching his arm with mine, almost leaning on him. I glance at my E-band, Earth coordinates already entered. When I copied the data to my E-band, I had originally planned to send only J back, but now it's a lot more than just J.

I turn to look behind us. Clumped together, a lot closer than necessary, are a hundred people, mainly women who will most probably get recruited to Ascend in the next round. About fifteen children, a few strong Zema4 men, resistance soldiers who are supposed to defend us should our port lead us anywhere other than Earth, and Father Vincent.

I turn around, taking a heavy breath, my heart pounding. *I hope this works.*

On both ends of Musk Street stand several resistance soldiers carrying confiscated weapons and safeguarding the area, protecting us until we port, because such a dense population of ID wristbands in one area might cause an alarm.

Probably will cause an alarm.

Michelle and Aaron are standing in front of us. She gives Aaron a backpack and gently pushes him toward his sister, then she looks at me. "I hope your next stop is Earth. If not, here is something for the next two or three days. Josh and a few of the women have extra supplies, just in case."

I nod while J takes the backpack from Aaron and swings it over his shoulder.

"Thank you, Michelle," he says. "For everything you did."

She smiles. "Of course, Jonathan. You are welcome." Then she looks at me. "It was an honor and a privilege to meet you, Dora. I will never forget it."

I swallow. I am not comfortable with the hidden-between-the-lines feeling I get as she says that. It sounds very final. And it crunches my stomach in a tiny ball.

"We will meet again."

She nods, but the emotions on her face are clear, even for an untrained Descendant: she doesn't believe it.

And somewhere inside, it hurts. It feels like I have abandoned them. All of them. Like I should have done something different, something bigger to protect them, but I don't know what. And I don't know how. The only thing I ever learned was how to hide, how to blend in.

But right now I feel that I should do more.

Then, quite unexpectedly, Michelle steps toward me and hugs me. "Thank you for saving Rebecca and Aaron," she whispers for only my ears.

In that moment a realization hits me. Michelle is the 53 city principal, one of the leaders of Zema4. She wants to do good for her people, help them as much as possible. But underneath that is something else as well. A hidden drive, deeper and far more self-absorbed, and that is saving her own children. Saving Rebecca, who will be assigned to Ascend and who might never come back if she goes to Uni.

"You are welcome." I hug her back.

Then a sound on my E-band alerts me that the time is nearing.

"Good luck!" She steps back, but then Rebecca, standing next to me, runs to her and hugs her. "Mama, come with us!"

After hugging for a little while, Michelle gently peels her off. "I can't. I'm not in danger, Becca. You are. And as a principal, I need to stay. We have talked about it."

"But Mama!"

"Now, Becca, please."

"But—"

"No!" Michelle's face changes. Not a mom, not a nice lady who brought food to a prisoner, but a principal, a leader of city 53 and of Zema4.

Rebecca steps back.

Then Michelle's face softens, and she mouths without a sound, looking at her children, "I love you."

Aaron bows his head low, and tears start streaming down Rebecca's face. I feel for them, all of them, so much that my throat clenches and tears congregate at the rim of my eyelids.

I take a quick breath, then quickly wipe the tears away and look down at my E-band.

I use the same sequence I used every time I was outside the chamber, but this time I set the broadest area, connecting to all the wristbands our group has.

Somewhere in my mind, I expect to hear a countdown, but of course, there is nothing. We are not in a chamber.

We are just standing in an open space, our feet on the sand, and I have no idea when it will happen. Or *if* it will.

So I just wait.

Michelle and the rest move back farther still. Many of them

are crying, moms for their young daughters, some for their wives or their husbands, a few resistance men that are coming along.

One hundred...

I glance back.

One hundred is not enough!

We should have taken more. Many more! Why did we take only one hundred?

I glance down again to see if I can pause the port, when I realize I don't feel J next to me anymore.

I turn to look at him but don't see him.

I don't see anyone.

ALL IS GONE.

I KEEP TURNING, OR AT LEAST I'M TRYING TO TURN, BUT ALL AROUND ME IS EMPTY.

AND I FEEL SORROW. AND SADNESS.

WHERE IS EVERYONE?

WHY AM I ALONE?

AGAIN...

THEN THE BINARY PATTERN STARTS AGAIN.

ZERO ZERO, ONE ONE, ZERO ZERO, ONE, ZERO ZERO ZERO ZERO, ONE ONE ONE...

BUT NOW I KNOW WHAT TO DO: I DON'T WAIT TO PORT LIKE LAST TIME. I START THE TRANSLATION RIGHT AWAY.

AND—HE IS HERE. A SMALL DARK—EYED BOY, CURLY DARK HAIR IN TOO—LOOSE LINEN CLOTHING.

I KNEEL SO THAT I CAN LOOK AT HIM FACE-TO-FACE.

HE SMILES AT ME, AND IT'S THE MOST WONDERFUL THING I HAVE EVER SEEN. HIS SMILE, HIS HAPPINESS, MAKES ME HAPPY TOO.

I DON'T UNDERSTAND, BUT I JUST SMILE BACK.

"WHO ARE YOU?" I SAY WITH NO WORDS.

HE DOESN'T OPEN HIS LIPS, BUT I HEAR THE ANSWER ANYWAY. "YOU KNOW."

DO I? I TRY TO FOCUS HARD NOW, STRAINING MY MIND. "I AM SORRY. I-I DON'T. I'VE NEVER MET YOU BEFORE."

HE STEPS TOWARD ME, AND HE'S NOW REALLY CLOSE, DEEP WITHIN AN IP DISTANCE. BUT I DON'T MIND. NOT AT ALL. MOREOVER, I HAVE THIS URGE, THIS IRRESISTIBLE NEED TO HUG HIM.

AND SO I DO.

AND HE HUGS ME BACK. "IT. FEELS. LIKE I THOUGHT. IT WOULD," HE THINKS.

"YOU HAVE NEVER HUGGED ANYONE BEFORE?" I ASK.

HE RELEASES THE HUG BUT STAYS WHERE HE IS, STILL CLOSE TO ME. "NO."

HE LIFTS UP HIS HAND AND TOUCHES A LOCK OF MY HAIR. "IT IS SOFTER THAN I EXPECTED. IT LOOKED SHARPER. HARDER. IT FEELS DIFFERENT TO THE TOUCH." HE LOOKS AT MY HAIR WHILE TOUCHING IT, AND I CAN'T EVEN BEGIN TO EXPLAIN HOW NICE THIS FEELS, THIS LITTLE BOY TOUCHING MY HAIR, TALKING TO ME.

My nonexistent breaths are getting heavy though. I know I can't stay here for very long. But I want to.

"Who are you?" I ask again.

He lets go of my hair, his face suddenly serious. "We don't have much time."

"Of course we do. I can—"

"No." Though his thought-voice is childish, the thoughts themselves are not. "I have tried to stretch it to the limit. Every time. A little bit more. But the last time was the furthest that was possible. More than that, and I would not be able to restore you."

I feel the need to frown. "I don't understand…" I'm heaving for breath now.

"Next time. I will see you again. Now go. We need to part."

I shake my head. "No!"

But I can feel the pull, the reality of existence reshaping again. "No. I don't want to. I want to stay."

My lungs are empty. No air.

"I need to know…" I try without a voice. "Who are you?"

I'm moving away, fast. And faster again. Away from him.

He's smiling at me. And waves at me from far,

FAR AWAY. BUT HIS VOICE IS NEXT TO MY EARS.
"THE FIRST THAW. WAS MINE."

AND HE'S GONE.

I'm on my knees, just as I was when I talked to the boy, but on the soft surface of the soil.

I take a deep, wheezing breath, the oxygen filling my lungs, making my eyes teary, my mind dizzy.

Did we make it?

I look up but get blinded by the white brightness.

I close my eyes, then shield them and look again. I'm at the top of a small hill, and—I know this place. Underneath me, the ancient porting chamber lies buried.

At the base of the hill, in the shadows of the forest, some standing, some sitting down, are a hundred people we took from Zema4. They are gathered in many small groups, talking excitedly, loudly. Their words mingle over each other, blocking all the natural forest sounds.

We made it!

I breathe out in relief.

We are back on Earth.

"Dora!" J runs toward me.

The crowd goes quiet within moments, their faces turning toward me.

J kneels next to me and grabs me in a tight hug. "Oh, you're here! Thank God!"

God? No... No, it wasn't God, it was the Mind that ported me here.

But before I manage to voice this, he pulls away, still holding my shoulders. "*Where* have you been? It's been more than half an hour!"

More than…?

He hugs me again. "Oh, I'm so glad you're safe. I was going crazy!"

"I'm sorry." My voice is rough, so I cough to clear it. "I guess we talked for too long."

He looks at me again. "You… spoke to someone? Who?"

I blink a few times, thinking. "I talked to…" And then the answer appears as if it was there all along, an unmistakable certainty in the midst of all the speculations.

I look up into J's eyes. "I talked to the Mind."

CHAPTER 41

Earth

J stands up and offers a hand to help me.

I take it and slowly get up, still feeling my muscle fibers stretching and aligning in discomfort as I once again begin to exist outside the Void.

I close my eyes, feeling the warmth of the sun on my eyelids, and take another deep breath.

I'm back.

A smile escapes my lips.

I am back.

I take another breath. It smells of Earth; wood, wind through the green leaves, and fresh soil.

I shield my eyes with my hand and glance at J. "I'm sorry you had to wait."

He smiles sideways and points at me. "Damn right! And you better not do that again, you hear me?"

What an unusual request. "I don't think I have the ability to control this particular aspect."

He laughs and takes me in a hug. "I'm just kidding with you. I know you can't control it."

Then he looks down at the base of the small hill. The people who were sitting up until a moment ago, chattering away, are now standing still, their eyes fixed on me.

I swallow and look away, avoiding the stares. As always, it makes me feel uncomfortable.

"Thanks for your patience," J says in a louder voice so everyone in the group can hear him. "We can head home now."

There is a loud cheer all around.

J laughs.

"We have a bit of a hike to do and not a lot of food, so we'll need to keep our pace." Then he takes my hand and leads me to the base of the hill. The newly ported Jumpers are waiting as we pass, a hum of hushed, excited voices around me as their stares bore into me.

I feel self-conscious and extremely uncomfortable. The way they look at me, the expression on their faces, is nothing I have seen before, and it's nothing I can decipher.

Once we are in the lead, the people follow our every step, like shadows on a bright morning.

"J," I whisper. "Why are they looking at us like that?"

J glances backward, then smiles at me. "Well, first of all," he says quietly, "they are not looking at us. They are looking at *you*."

Well, that makes me feel all better.

"And second, you need to understand that for the first time ever, they are free. Their imprisonment is over. And it's all because of you."

I shake my head. "No. It's because of the Mind."

"Ah, yes, the Mind." He now remembers. "You said you *talked* to the Mind?"

I nod, still astonished by my last port experience, bewildered to find out that the rules I've taken for granted, the rules I thought abiding, are wrong. "I always thought... No, everybody in Uni thought and still thinks that the Mind is an extremely well built, amazingly accurate portation AI system. And nothing more than that. I also thought that the Mind was fully controlled by Zlathars, obedient to Zlathars if you like. And everyone else thinks the same, but…" I shake my head. "That's simply wrong!"

"And you are sure about that?"

I bite my lip, thinking. "No. I'm not sure. But I am 98.2 percent positive."

He laughs, then leans toward me and hugs me with one arm, squeezing me toward him while still walking. "Ah, the Senthien part." He kisses the side of my hair. "I love it."

I look at him, smiling shyly. "Really?"

"Yes, I do. As long as it comes in a package with a Human part. Because that makes it *you.*"

This makes me feel good. *He* makes me feel good. My self-consciousness and inadequacy drift into the background, aided by the soft but excited murmur I hear behind us: happy—and free—people.

"So if you say 98.2 percent certain, then I'd say that's very certain in my eyes. So what did the Mind do to make you think that?"

"I should have seen it from the beginning. It was there all along." I keep shaking my head, thinking about the past few days. "Remember when I ported to Boolean and all the rooms were closed?"

"Yes, I remember, except one."

"Yes, and it opened based on my ID! I don't have any authority in the Boolean Institute, yet a door opened for me. I would have been seen by Booleans if I didn't manage to hide in one of those labs."

"Could it be just be a bug?"

I blink to the image from my nanoprobe search. "A *bug?*"

"I mean, a mistake in programming code, something like that."

"Possible, yes, but there were so many other things. For example, when I needed to find a porting chamber on Boolea, I got a DR path over my ONCs. And on Senthia the path was inside the aeration system. *Inside.* Those were not saved maps that I could get access to. They were made just for me and my particular need, my particular request."

"And are you sure that all these things *were* because of the Mind?"

I take a moment to think about it, but the answer appears before I even run it through any logic checks, and I feel like I've known it from the start. "Yes. It's the Mind. Every time I barely escaped, every time I managed to avoid Brookonians, every time I got access to things I should not have had access to—all of that was the Mind. I wouldn't have survived if it wasn't for the Mind!"

J nods. "I see what you mean."

"And then the ports. All the ports I've had since I left Earth were so different than before."

"Yes, you said that it felt like *communication...?*"

"Yes, it really did feel like it, and I was right. The Mind did want to communicate with me, but... I think it just didn't know how. Up until now."

"So what was different?"

"It gave me the information in binary code. A simple computer processing instruction. At first I didn't understand it, but then I realized I needed to translate the sequence. And the translation gave me an image."

"An image? Of what?"

I shake my head and smile. "Of whom."

"All right, of whom then?"

I look at J intently. "A boy. A small, dark-haired boy."

"A boy?" He narrows his eyes. "Hmm, all right. So, were you talking to this… boy?"

"Yes, but without using words. We just *thought* our sentences, and we could understand each other."

"Wow, that's something different! So what did he tell you?"

I'm silent for a moment, wondering how I am going to communicate this best.

"Nine years ago, when your batch de-froze…," I start.

"Yes…?"

"And everyone thought it was because of the lack of electricity?"

He looks at me speculatively. "Something tells me that wasn't the case at all."

I shake my head and smile. "No, it wasn't. It was the Mind. *It* thawed the very first batch."

J stops walking. "Really? Are you sure about that?"

"One hundred percent."

J sighs heavily and starts walking again, but the deep frown is still on his face.

He doesn't believe it. Yet.

"But why would the Mind do that?"

"I'm not sure. My time was insufficient for a proper interrogation."

J's face relaxes into a smile, and he repeats after me, mimicking my tone. "*Proper interrogation.*"

"Are you making fun of me?"

"No, no!" he says through the laughter. "I just think you're in desperate need of some Human influence again."

"What do you mean?"

He hugs me closer. "I just think you need to be surrounded by Humans, that's all. Get some normal terminology back."

We keep walking, still hugging. Our pace is a little difficult like this, but I so immensely enjoy being this close to him that I don't mind.

"So, do you know if anything similar happened before, to someone else? With the Mind, I mean."

I shake my head slowly. "Not that I am aware of. The Mind has always been important to control the portation, but it had no obvious communication interface. It was never needed.

"The possibility always exists that the Mind tried to reach someone else, but perhaps they didn't—"

Then I stop.

A sound, far away.

I enhance my TAEs and close my eyes to focus.

"What is it?" J asks, as all the people behind us halt as well.

"Do you hear it?" I say with my eyes still closed.

"Um… no."

An engine. Several of them. Coming closer.

Behind me, I hear worried voices.

"What's happening?" asks Aaron a few IPs behind us.

"Wait!" J says.

I open my eyes, my heartbeat accelerating.

It can't be. Descendants couldn't possibly be here.

Could they?

"I think we have a problem," I say.

"All right, everyone under the trees. Get out of the path! Now!" shouts J, then he leans toward me. "What is it? What do you hear?"

Hidden under tree crowns, I look into the sky. "I hear… machine engines."

J looks up as well, but the sky is clear. "I can't hear any—Hold on! I hear something!"

A few moments later, a large dark gray drone appears above us.

"An A-drone?" J says and starts walking to the clearing.

"J, wait!" I quickly lift my hand to stop him, but he's already out of my reach.

He looks up, then lifts both arms in the air and waves.

The Moons of Senthia! What's he doing?

The drone turns around and starts descending above the clearing.

J looks at me, a broad smile on his face. "These are A-drones."

I frown but slowly walk out as well. "What are A-drones?"

"Auto-drones. This is how we used to get around. The old version of portation." He looks at the vehicle just touching the ground. "I just didn't think we had them."

The A-drone slowly settles on the meadow about a hundred IPs from us, with a little wave and a shake just before touchdown. Zema4's people huddle behind us, some curious but most fearful. *They haven't seen anything like that either.*

For a few moments nothing happens. The curiosity, anxiety, thrill, and fear make my heartbeat race. Then the door opens upward, and I feel like my heart just stopped. But my fear is gone the instant I see Rick climbing out.

"Dora!" He runs toward me. He's so fast I expect him to hug me, but at the last moment, he stops, probably thinking of my IP border.

I, however, lean in and hug him.

"Oh, I thought that would have been too close," he says, hugging me back.

"I got used to it." I smile and take a small step back, still within an IP.

"Good to have you back, J!" says Rick, offering his hand to J, and for some reason I have the feeling he's grown up immensely since the last time I saw him.

"Good to be back, Rick. So…" J glances at the A-drone behind him. "Want to tell me what that was all about?"

"Oh, two days ago, we found several drones in the Underground facility! All in great condition."

"And you can pilot the auto-drone?" I ask.

His lips spread into a broad grin. "Yes, isn't that cool!"

"It truly is. But why *auto*? Shouldn't it fly on its own?"

"Yup, it should," says Rick. "But we can't recover the sky-road maps, and without a map, the drone is as good as lost, so back to manual."

"So how come *you* can pilot it?" asks J. "When did you learn, when you were seven?" He grins.

"Actually, yes! I did quite a lot of drone driving when I was a kid. You know, small stuff." He shows the dimensions with his hands. "Just for fun, you know. But the basics are the same, even when you drive this." He points with his thumb backward. "It took me one or two hours to get the hang of it. But I got it now. I'm a *pro!*" He nods slowly to stress that last point.

"And this, Rick, we truly appreciate," says J, tapping Rick on his back. "So, why don't you give us a lift?"

"That's why I'm here," he says. "We saw the teleportation beam an hour ago, so I headed straight here to pick you up, though"—he glances behind us—"we might need to do a few rounds. How many of you are here?"

"One hundred and two."

"Good." He lifts a wrist to his face, and looking all serious, he talks into a small device on his wrist.

I check the image of the device and scan it against my database. "Isn't that a watch?" I ask J quietly.

"That too. But you can also use it for chat, games, and many other tasks. Nothing like Zema4 wristbands or E-bands, of course, but during our time, it was quite a hit. And I guess it was a prototype for all the fancy stuff that happened next."

"Rick?" I hear Peter's muddled voice from Rick's wristwatch. "Did you find the Jumpers?"

"Yes, I did. And you will not believe who's here, Dad."

"Who?"

"Dora and J!"

Peter's voice breaks. "Thank Heaven! Bring them here, son!"

"Well, there's a bit of a problem."

A small break.

I have to smile within. I can imagine Peter's thoughts rumbling with possibilities. Finally he says a bit more quietly. "What problem?"

"Dora and J are not the only ones. We have about a hundred more people to move."

"Jesus, Mary, and Joseph! What?" Peter yells. "One hundred?"

"Yes."

I hear Peter breathing into the device. "Okay, okay, okay... Listen, boy, take as many as you can. I'll send another one your way. Can you send me the coordinates, son?"

"Already on it!"

Peter gives a rumbling laugh on the other side of the watch-line. "Well done, boy!"

"Thanks, Dad."

Rick drops his hand and looks at us. "Care for a ride?"

I smile. "Why don't you start with Zema4 people first." I glance backward. "I don't think they would feel comfortable left on their own here."

There is a fleeting look of disappointment, but Rick nods. "Sure thing, Dora."

"How many can you take in one go?"

"Nineteen."

I turn to the expectant crowd. "Rebecca, why don't you go with the first group? Aaron, can you take the second?"

They both nod boldly and start calling names.

The group divides seamlessly, and the first round is ready to go.

Rick, leading the first group to the A-drone, turns toward us, lifts his arm in a wave, and shouts, "Wait for my ride, guys! I want to be the one who takes you home!"

"We will!" J shouts back.

Rick lifts off the ground somewhat shakily but then finds his groove. He continues upward until he's well above the treetop level, and then he zooms away in the direction of the tree village.

J breathes out a content sigh, then looks at me, smiling, dimples in his cheeks emphasizing his smile even more. He hugs me and leans to kiss me. "Welcome home, Dora!"

I smile back.

I am home. Finally.

But a thought appears in my mind, a thought I try to push away, a thought I don't want to bring to the surface.

I am home.

And I am safe.

But four million Humans in Uni are not.

And I feel guilty. Guilty for leaving them there while I found my happiness.

CHAPTER 42

Earth

The ride is rougher than I had expected.

On several occasions there are air vacuums above the forest and the drone drops ten or more IPs, leaving my stomach a bit closer to my mouth than I want it to be.

When we finally touch the ground, Rick turns to us. "Sorry, guys. It's usually a lot smoother. It's season change, and we've got air pockets. Can't do much about it."

"Excuses, excuses," says J, winking at Rick.

"Why don't you try to fly it!"

"You are the master of the sky. I couldn't lift a meter. And if I did, I would crash."

"There you go!" Rick says and stands up to open the hatch door.

J smiles and whispers to me, "I don't think he got the joke."

"I think he did, but he didn't find it funny."

"Yes, most likely. Now, let's get on firm ground."

As soon as J and I exit, I need to close my eyes. I am blinded by the sunlight again.

Then I hear someone calling my name. And my nanoprobes identify the voice at the same time as I do. *Lemony.*

I open my eyes and see her running in front of everyone else.

She runs into me, almost knocking me over, then hugs me around my waist.

And it happens so fast that my emotional response comes out without restraint, without a second thought, and I hug her back, a smile from ear to ear I can't erase, tears streaming down my cheeks.

"Talk about a proper welcome," says J.

Then Tania comes, followed by Peter, Patrick, and Simon.

Tania stops an IP away from me, a broad smile on her face as well, her eyes watery too, while Peter's beard is masking a grin of his own.

I reach out to greet her in what I've learned is the classic Human way, but instead she steps in and hugs me over Lemony. Then Peter comes, and Patrick and Simon too, all of them hugging me over one another. In the end, J hugs me from behind, closing the circle of this amazing, breathtaking bubble of pure emotion, joy, and happiness this group of people has made around me.

For some unexplainable reason, this seems like a once-in-a-lifetime moment, when my emotions are so strong, so overwhelmingly powerful, that I feel like my body can't handle the pressure and I'm going to burst.

But I don't.

My skin seems impenetrable.

Or perhaps it's my Descendant skinsuit?

We stay like this for a very long time while I'm half-aware of the many people around us: just-ported Zema4s, Earth natives, and Jumpers. There are shouts and cries, laughter and tears all around as family and friends are reunited.

I close my eyes and enjoy this crescendo of emotion, so thick you can reach out and touch it.

All of a sudden, I realize something. Something amazing.

When I came to Zema4, I was so happy to have found out I still have a family. My 5G cousin. But I realize now that my family is a lot larger than I had imagined.

These people here… They are my family.

And unmistakably, the tears appear. Happy tears, running down my cheeks, sliding sideways into the grooves of my smile, salting my lips and the tip of my tongue. After a long while, everyone moves back, and I wipe my cheeks with the back of my hand. Then my gaze falls on the flat pendant Tania has around her neck.

The Vision. I have to tell her about my Vision.

"Welcome home, Dora," says Peter, distracting my thoughts.

I smile, looking at everyone. "It's—" My voice breaks. "It's so nice to see you again. All of you."

"We've missed you," says Patrick, then he looks at J. "And you? I didn't even get a chance to miss *you*." Then he hugs J, tapping his back. "Glad you're all right, mate!"

Then Lemony looks up, a frown on her face. "I was angry. I thought you would never come back!"

The whole group laughs.

"Aye, so was I!" Peter lifts a finger.

"Me too," jokes Simon.

"I'm sorry I left," I say, then glance at J.

Lemony hugs me again. "I'm happy you're back."

"Hey, can I get some credit here?" says J, grinning.

"Well done for bringing her home," says Simon.

"There." J nods. "Thank you."

"So, you managed to find her?" asks Patrick.

"Well…" J rubs the back of his neck, glancing at me. "If I'm to be quite honest, she found *me*."

For a moment there's silence, and then they all burst out laughing.

"I told you!" says Patrick, pointing a finger at Peter.

"Aye, that's not a surprise! She probably saw him coming." Then he looks at me. "Didn'ya?"

I nod. "I did. But I only managed to find him because I had a little help."

"Oh yeah?" Simon raises his eyebrows in question. "From whom if we may know?"

I let the question sit for a bit before I answer, looking at them intently with a smile on my face. "The Mind."

"Huh?" Peter scratches his head.

"You mean the computer? The AI?" asks Simon.

I look at all of them, slowly scanning their faces, caressing them as I gaze over them. "I guess I need to give you a small update."

"A large one would be even better!" Peter laughs.

"Let's do that *after* we have something to eat," says Tania. "Come, I arranged a new cottage for you, Dora, just next to Avila's place. It's a bit bigger—"

"I-I'm sorry?"

"The new cottage," she says again. "It's a bit bigger than the last one you had, and I thought—"

"Cottage?" I interrupt again. "For me? But how did you know I would come back?"

She wipes her palms over her skirt, looking at the ground for a moment. "I didn't. I just hoped."

And the tears come again without warning, and I simply have to hug her. "Thank you," I whisper.

After a moment, she sniffs, then pulls away. "Anyway, I

thought you two might need more space." She wipes her cheeks, then looks at me.

J hugs me. "Thank you, Tania. That's… very special."

"Since we're talking about the cottages," Rick says, "we will need a lot more than we originally planned for."

"Aye, we can see that!" says Peter. "Didn' know ye could hitchhike so many at one time. Where did ye pick 'em up?"

"Zema4," I say.

And there are many more.

A thought appears again at the back of my mind. And it's clear, very clear. But I turn away. I don't want to look at it. I don't want to acknowledge it. So I deliberately push my thoughts elsewhere. "I understand we might not have enough space for everyone."

Tania waves her hand once. "Don't worry about it. We'll just need to squeeze in a bit until we build more."

I turn to the group of Zema4s and clear my throat.

The talking dies out and they focus on me.

"This is Tania," I say. "She will show you to your living quarters—I mean your cottages. There won't be a lot of space at first, but with time, the village will spread, so please have patience, it won't stay like this for long."

Then one of the soldiers says, "Even if it does, that's fine."

There is a round of yeses among the people.

"It doesn't matter if there's no physical space," another woman says. "We now have more space than we'd ever imagined."

"That's right, Carola," a young dark-haired woman says, then looks at me. "You brought us to freedom!"

And there is a loud, almost deafening cheer from all Zema4s.

Tania glances at me. "I see you brought your fans."

So I have been told.

I turn to the last person speaking. "Thank you, but this wasn't me. It was the Mind."

"The Mind was there all the time," someone shouts. "We are here only because you came to Zema4."

J takes my hand and squeezes it. *He understands.* Then he turns to the people and says, "Please, follow Tania and Peter. They will show you where you need to go. We will see you later."

As the people leave, I feel relieved.

Once J gets directions for our cottage, he turns to me and takes my hand. "Come, let's find our place." His smile is enchanting, boyish and sexy at the same time.

He starts walking, but then suddenly stops. I look as well, checking what caught his attention.

A dozen or so IPs away, I see Monica.

A spiky grip clenches at my heart, and I let go of J's hand.

I knew that sooner or later I would have to deal with this, but—I silently breathe out—I was hoping it would be later.

Monica is looking at us. Wild red hair like an aura around a beautiful pale face. Her expression—blank. I can't read anything.

I don't know what to do. I quickly glance at J.

He slowly inhales, then steps in front of me, turning his back to Monica. He leans his head toward me so that he's almost touching my forehead.

"Dora…" His voice is quiet, his gaze intent, looking deeply into my eyes. "When I left Earth, I didn't know what would happen. I didn't know if I would survive. And even if I did, I had no way of knowing if I would ever be able to find you. But one thing became crystal clear: I didn't want to live on Earth—or anywhere else—if it was without you." He takes both my hands in his, the faint pressure of his fingers oddly encouraging. "We are in this together."

I take a deep breath. "Okay."

He turns forward again, still holding my hand, but Monica is not there anymore.

I unintentionally sigh with relief.

We slowly start walking again.

"I feel very uncomfortable."

"I know, Dora. It's not an easy situation. For any of us. But there is this, or there is nothing at all. So you see"—he smiles at me—"it's not like we have a choice." And he leans toward me and kisses my hair.

For a while we walk without talking, hugged, but each in our own thoughts.

Then suddenly I feel a change. I glance at him: slight movements of the fine muscles of his face, the set of his brow, the pupil contractions of his eyes. He's been—I narrow my eyes— thinking about something—my heartbeat accelerates—and the decision is now here, firm and set.

And I feel it, a decision that changes the future.

"So… I've been thinking," he starts.

The sides of my vision get blurry, and then darkness cloaks the real life before me as a new Vision opens in front of my—

"Hey!" He points a finger at me. "Don't cheat!"

And just like that, the Vision is gone, the real world around me as sharp and crisp as before.

"Okay, okay! You know, I'm not doing this on purpose."

"I know, but you should really try to *not* see this one. I would really like it to be a surprise. Are you in agreement with me?" He uses the classic Senthien wording.

I smile broadly. "Yes, J. I am in agreement with you."

"Very good! So, do you… have plans tomorrow evening?" he asks nonchalantly.

I have to laugh. *I guess I do.* "No. Nothing in particular. Why do you ask?" I play the role.

"Well, I was wondering if, um, we could spend some time together?"

My heartbeat accelerates again, precognition of what's coming. It's exciting. I can feel it, even my Senthien is jumping on her feet. The oncoming Vision starts again, but I stop it.

Black. Black floor, black walls, black ceiling. All black.

And it dissolves, dissipates into another random thought.

I sigh and look at him again. "It will take some effort, you know."

"Just try, okay?"

I nod. "I will. Try."

He squeezes me closer to him as we walk while I keep blocking the future-reshaping, heart-racing Vision that wants to push through.

My Senthien feels blindfolded while my Human jumps on her tiptoes, her curiosity excruciating.

I sigh inwardly. *It's only one day. I'll manage that long. I have to. For him. And for me.*

CHAPTER 43

Earth

I thought I'd be on my own for most of today, waiting for J as he finishes some things as he mentioned in the morning, but my day has been packed full with visits from Jumpers, old and new ones, original tree village Humans, looking for advice, as if I can turn my precognition power on and tell them exactly what they want to hear.

I sigh with a smile. *It's not magic. It's just science.*

Then I hear footsteps coming into the cottage. *J. Finally.* I turn around. "J, perhaps we can—"

I stop.

It's Monica.

My nanoprobes immediately alert me to my higher heart rate, my chest getting tight. I engage my Senthien and let the monotonous tone into my voice. "Hello, Monica. How can I help you?"

She's standing still, her head tilted slightly, looking at me. The last rays of sunshine cast a halo around her red curls.

She is beautiful.

And I hate myself for thinking it.

"Is there something I can help you with?" I ask again.

She's looking at my hair, my face, my body, down to my legs and then back. She seems confused. She blinks a few times, then slowly walks around me and keeps looking at me, her eyes locked.

She's not saying anything. And it unsettles me in a deep, gut-crunching way, raising the hairs on my body. She makes a full turn around me and finally stops, standing in front of me again. She is breaching the IP border. She is too close.

I have the urge to step back, but I sense that in some primal, unconscious way, this would make me look weak. So I don't.

"What… is it?" she whispers.

"Excuse me?"

At first she doesn't answer. She slowly shakes her head and gives another full-body scan, and as she does, I become more aware of my features, and I involuntarily compare mine, quite plain, with hers, fiery red hair haloing her flawless face.

"What is it?" she repeats in the same voice. "There is… *nothing*… in you. I kept thinking, wondering, questioning, what it is. No breasts, no hips, no curves at all for that matter. Without this long gray hair, I could mistake you for a man. *A small man.*" At the last bit she pitches her voice an octave higher, and that too I find unsettling. Still, nothing of what she said I can defend against. She is right. I can hardly compete against her.

And I hate myself for thinking this too.

"I've heard that women," she starts, looking at me with an icy stare. "Can I even call you that? That Descendant women are all barren. None of you can get pregnant. How then—*how then*—can he find you attractive? Are you at all different to a man, I wonder."

I clench my jaw. My Senthien pushes my Human aside, and

I say, "There are some subtle differences, yes. But I regret to observe, it seems we are quite similar in that way."

She continues, however, as if she didn't hear me at all. "And this little person," she says, looking down at me, "stole my husband."

Her voice is soft, frightfully calm, opposing the meaning of her words even more, like the brewing of the sea underneath its dark, apparently flat surface.

"So…" She looks back up into my eyes. "The real question is, what am I going to do with you?"

And with this, my heart kicks into a higher gear. I clench my hands into fists, my Human loud. "Stole your husband? You make it sound like J is a skinsuit I took from your closet without asking for permission. Amazingly enough, he does think for himself."

She laughs, closing her eyes, arching back, as if I just told the best joke.

I'm staring at her, my eyes wide.

I could not understand her less.

Then she abruptly calms down and says, "No. Apparently he *can't* think for himself. But I still can't quite grasp it," she says and scans me once again. "It's like he's blind." She says this so quietly as if it's meant for only her to hear.

Then her face changes dramatically and there is no smile, not even a fake one. "We have been together for seven years, child." She leans into me, her head tilted forward, fists tight, and my nanoprobes alert me of a possible incoming physical impact.

"And then you come… For just a few days. And he loses his marbles. Completely. It's beyond me." She takes a breath. "But do you know what, little person? This will not last long. It's shallow. It's weak. And it's just an infatuation. You can't compare the seven years we have been together with a handful of days since you appeared. You will lose."

"I will lose?"

"Yes, and sooner than you think."

It dawns on me: she is completely failing to see the obvious. "Monica, this is not about me. Or about you. It's about J and what he has chosen for himself. You've been away from him longer than you have been together. And what he went through made an immense impact on his life.

"He mourned you, Monica. He mourned you, thinking, no—*knowing*—you were dead. And after nine years, you appear out of nowhere, and you think it's the same as day one? Even if I wasn't here, even if he didn't find anyone, he is nine years older than the last time you saw him, he lived through a tragedy that one cannot easily erase, and after all that, you think things will be back to normal, as if nothing happened? They won't. In whatever way you turn them—they won't."

"You don't know what we had!"

I take a step toward her. Anger bubbles up in my steady Senthien and boils over the rim. "Well, if you want him, you will need to play something other than your history card."

Her eyes are wide. She's taken aback.

I want to dismiss her, but then I stop. There's a subtle change in her expression, a vague smile she's trying to hide.

Oh, the Moons of Senthia, the Human body language! What does this mean?

"You are right, Senthien," she says softly. "I guess I *do* need to think of something else."

And she turns around and leaves, her hair swinging around her in a large arc, almost touching me.

I keep staring at the place where she stood, transfixed, my

heart beating wildly, my fists clenched. My throat is dry, and my tensed stomach feels like I'm digesting stones.

What did she mean by that?

I shiver again.

What could she possibly do?

CHAPTER 44

Earth

The sun has just set, but the sky is still bright and warm above the vibrant village thick with the sounds of the birds, people talking, children shouting in play. But I hear all of it as though through a thick glass wall, muffled and dull, while my mind spins in the circle.

I sit on the bed, my back straight, my eyes fixed on a dark brown knot on the wooden floor.

The Vision keeps coming, blurring the sides of my field of sight, constantly. And I keep fighting it, constantly. But it's so much more difficult than before. Whatever J has been planning, it's taking a strong hold and I won't be able to keep fighting it off for much longer.

And with all of this, I still keep hearing Monica's voice inside my head.

I'll think of something else.

I'll think of something else.

I clench my palms into tight fists. *What does she mean?*

And the Vision creeps in again.

Stop.

Stop!

…And it's gone.

I breathe out, my shoulders relax.

I stand up and walk to the window. *J, where are you?* I will *see* it if you don't come soon…

And just then I feel a slight shake of the floor.

"Hello, beautiful!" J comes in.

I run to him and hug him so strongly it takes him off guard.

"Hey, are you okay?"

I don't answer. I only nod firmly.

I sense he wants to move away, he wants to look at me, but I don't let him. I just need him to hold me.

"Hey, what's wrong?" His arms close tightly around me.

Should I tell him about Monica?

"Dora, what happened?" he whispers.

My eyes are closed and my body's finally relaxing in his arms.

I won't tell him now. It would spoil whatever he has planned.

"I just…"

"What?"

"I just had to fight the Vision. It was… difficult." I pull away to look at him.

Dimples slowly appear on his cheeks as his lips spread into a smile. "Well, you won't need to wait for long. Are you ready?"

"Ready as I'll ever be," I say, using the words he said to me a while back.

"Let's go!" He takes my hand and squeezes it gently into his rough palm.

We climb down the exit tree and head for the fields, but within a few passes we encounter cottages, four of them aligned next to the road, each standing on several thick pillars, wooden stairs leading to their porches. The last two are still in the making, their roofs looking like the rib cage of a large animal, but the first two are finished and very much inhabited.

J guides me to the second in the row, which is the largest of the four. It has a large wooden terrace, five tables scattered around, filled with loud, bantering villagers. The ceiling is decorated with hanging colorful bulbs, giving beautiful prismatic patterns to the wooden floor.

We climb the stairs onto the terrace, and several people notice us right away, lifting a hand in greeting. A few of them actually stand up and approach us. I assume they want to talk to J, but they come to me instead. They shake my hand, nodding their head as they say their thanks.

Thanks for bringing my brother.

Thanks for saving my sister-in-law.

Thanks for "lighting up the bulb," which I learned meant thanks for bringing back the tech.

Thanks…

Thanks…

Thanks…

I listen to all of them, smile and nod. But I don't say anything. Their presence, their close contact, is just too much. I have opened up to being a Human in many ways, but my Senthien is still in there, still in me, and now she is cowering, hoping I can disappear. J notices it, so he politely excuses us and guides me toward the door of the cottage.

At the same time, Rafael appears at the door, wiping his hands on his apron. "Dora, J, welcome, welcome! Please, come in." He guides us in, and as soon as I enter, the smells of the kitchen hug me.

I take a deep breath.

Meat, roasted potatoes, thyme and basil, and—I take another breath—something else.

Four other people are busy cutting, chopping, stirring, grinding, as we pass them.

One of the cooks lifts a hand to greet us while holding a long, sharp silvery knife. With a smile, I wave back.

"I've reserved the back terrace for you," Rafael says. "Nice and quiet."

"Thanks, Raf." J winks at him appreciatively.

We enter a small terrace on the other side of the cottage. This one has only one table and two chairs. There is a red flower—I quickly search—a rose in a transparent glass in the middle of an off-white tablecloth.

"I've reserved this especially for you, away from your fans," Rafael says. "Please, have a seat. I'll be back with the menu."

"Dora?" J is holding the backrest of the chair away from the table. "Would you like to sit down?"

I nod and sit, still smiling broadly as I look around.

"Thank you, J. This is just beautiful."

"Yes. It is." He keeps looking at me with a smile on his face, but his eyes are intent. He licks his lips, then opens his mouth to say something, but his voice breaks.

I narrow my eyes slightly.

But this is not all, is it?

J closes his eyes and rubs his palms on his trousers.

And the Vision starts creeping in from the side. This evening, this restaurant, our dinner and—something else. Yes, there *is* something else!

He takes a deep breath, then opens his eyes, and says, still not looking at me, "I thought… I wanted to do it later…" Then he looks into my eyes. "After dessert, maybe. But..." He laughs nervously. "I can't wait. I just don't have the patience."

"Wait for what, J?"

He swallows hard.

With all the body language I am receiving, I would almost think that... that he's afraid!

My heartbeat instinctively accelerates.

What is it, J?

He digs a small wooden box out of his pocket and places it on the table between us.

I look at the box, then back at him. He's incredibly uptight and anxious.

I frown and look back, expecting him to tell me what this is about, but he doesn't. Instead, he opens the box.

Inside is a small circular metallic band.

I do a quick image search on my nanoprobes, but the results come back empty.

I look back at him, and his smile is starting to fade, his eyebrows fold over his eyes, and his face darkens.

By now I'm getting seriously worried.

I look at box again, now trying a search based on the description. But once again, I get no results.

I look at him again and raise my shoulders in question.

Then his expression changes, and his lips spread into a smile. "You have no idea what this is."

"No... Should I?"

He smiles even broader, dimples appearing on his cheeks. "No. No, Dora. You shouldn't."

Then he stands up, takes the little box, and kneels next to my chair.

My eyes are wide as I look at his broad smile—the same one I saw as the Vision pushed in—lifting the open box toward me.

"Dora," he says softly.

My heart is beating so wildly I think it will jump out of my rib cage.

"Will you marry me?"

CHAPTER 45

Earth

I'm smiling.

I think I have been smiling the whole day. In fact, I know I have, because my cheeks hurt, and I know I should relax them.

But I can't.

I lift my left hand again and look at what I now know is called a ring.

It's beautiful, a plait of four different metallic threads, each a different color, braiding intricately around each other, holding a small yellow stone in its cage.

The stone, J tells me, is not a stone at all but a fossilized tree resin thousands of years old. It's called amber, and it looks beautiful.

Frances made it, J tells me. Most of the time, she's making cutlery, cups, and plates, an unrewarding set of tasks for a goldsmith. But every now and then she makes something—she creates something—extraordinary, with no blueprint, no plan, no manual, only pure ideas seeping from her mind.

I look at it again, then let my hand drop. *I could never do something like that.*

I come out of the forest into the clearing and look up. There's not a cloud in the sky, just a dark canvas with an uncountable number of stars, like on the very first night I ported to Earth.

It seems like eons ago.

A soft breeze from the warm night forest stirs the dress around my legs in rhythm with my steps, tingling my skin. *I missed Earth clothes.* J steps next to me, hugging me with one arm. I can feel the warmth of his fingers on my shoulder, the slight pressure through the soft fabric.

I missed him touching me too.

I look at him and smile, then slide my arm around his waist.

"Welcome home, Dora," he says again and kisses the side of my head, a soft imprint I feel through my hair.

Home... I am home... The thought I keep trying to push away resurfaces unexpectedly.

But four million people aren't.

"Come, let's join the others," J says, and I push the thought away once more.

Hugging, we find our space on the other side of the bonfire where Tania and Peter already sit.

"Did you enjoy the bath?" Tania asks.

J and I glance at each other and smile.

Tania grins. "Okay, I assume you did..."

Peter raises an eyebrow, looking at Tania. "If only *I* had that expression when we go and take our baths, *dear.*"

Tania rolls her eyes, and J and I sit down next to her.

J is just about to say something when a small Zema4 woman comes to us. I don't remember her, but my nanoprobes confirm that she was in our last batch of the hundred people we took from Zema4.

She kneels in front of me and reaches toward me with both her arms stretched out.

At first I'm not sure what to do. *Is this another type of greeting?*

But before I query, I realize that on her open palm lies a necklace, dark and beige leather threads interwoven in various complicated designs.

She keeps it in front of me without saying a word.

"It looks… nice," I say.

"It is yours," she says quietly.

"Thank you, but it doesn't belong to me. Perhaps it's from one of your companions? I'm sure—"

"Dora, I think this is a gift," J whispers in my ear. "I think you should take it."

I look back at the young woman. "Is this a gift?"

"Yes. I made it for you."

I slowly pick it up from her palm. "It looks beautiful. Thank you. I don't have anything I can give to you in return."

For a moment she stares at me. Then she smiles. "You already gave me your gift, Dora Dana Dasnan. You saved me. And my sister."

Then she smiles broader, pushes off the ground, and goes back to the group of Jumpers.

Throughout dinner, as I'm talking to my Earth friends, explaining what had happened, Zema4s keep coming over to me, keep thanking me or giving me handmade gifts or asking if they can do something for me—a massage, a hairstyle, a tattoo—I cringe after my nanoprobes give me a definition of what this actually is—and by the end of dinner, I am surrounded with various items, widgets, and gizmos, lying on the ground around me.

At some point, Mike joins us as well though his bones, he says, feel the change of weather and it's not easy for him to walk.

Peter helps him to sit down and arranges a folded blanked behind his back so he can rest.

By now, my mouth is completely dry from so much talking, and I'm happy J picks up the story once I get to the part where I ported to Zema4.

Old Mike shakes his head, once J is finished. "That was quite an adventure," he says in his rumbly voice. "I am… very sorry about your father, Dora. We could hold a ceremony for him? Would you like that?"

"Like we had for Stevanion?"

"Yes."

I nod. "Thank you, Mike. I would…" But I stop, feeling my throat getting tighter.

"I think that would be really nice," J says instead.

"Good. Now, it's been a long evening for me, can't stay up so long anymore like you youngsters." Mike chuckles and tries to push himself off the log, but then his face distorts in pain and he drops back.

"Let me help you!" J says, and both he and Peter help Mike up.

"I'll be right back."

The three of them slowly leave the bonfire.

"Hmm, maybe not right away," says Tania quietly to me. "Mike's gotten quite fragile in the past few days."

"How old is he?" I ask.

She shakes her head, still looking at Mike's thin figure as he leaves the bonfire. "I never asked, but I reckon over ninety."

If only we had the equipment Anas have, it might help him.

Tania looks at the gift collection at my feet. "Do you want me to give you a hand with those?"

I focus on the gifts now too. "Oh yes, I would—" I look at her, then stop, my eyes on her pendant.

"Where did you get that necklace?" I ask, remembering the Vision.

She lifts her hand and closes the pendant inside her fist as if hiding it. "That's... That was from Harry, my first husband. Why?"

"Can I see it?"

She hesitates a bit, but then she takes the necklace off and gives it to me. I turn the thin metal pendant around. The backside is engraved with numerous lines and dots.

"It is...," she starts. "It's a memory key. We had pictures and videos of our family saved there. I... can't use it anymore, but I keep it... as a memory."

I frown. "And you had this from before the cryo?"

"Yes. Both Harry and I had a copy for years. Why?"

"I just... I had a Vision of using this memory key. You and I looked at it together, but..." I shake my head. "Why would that be important if it holds only family videos?"

Unless it holds something else. "Do you mind if we check it out in the next few days?"

CHAPTER 46

Earth

We enter the dark Underground storage, the heavy metal door squeaking on rusty hinges, as the yellowish lights flicker for a moment and then turn on. I follow Tania one floor down and step onto the metal grid floor, tightly holding on to the railing as I look down.

A grid lines up the massive concave wall of the deep concrete tube, like a gallery, each floor opening to numerous doors on the sides, but I can only see four floors underneath us. The rest is hidden in the dark, and I can't really tell how deep this cylinder is.

"After you powered up the Underground, the guys discovered quite a lot of tech storage down here," Tania says, her voice echoing off the smooth gray walls many stories down.

"Like A-drones?"

"Yes." She smiles. "Like A-drones, though I wish they hadn't. Rick's in the air all the time now."

Three stories down she stops next to a large metal door with a massive handle. As she turns the lever, an electronic buzz sounds and the door opens inward. Automatic lights flicker on.

The room is packed full of desks, each stacked with different devices.

"Do you know what you're looking for?"

"Yes. I have seen it."

As I walk between the desks, glancing around, I ask, "Tania, was this key with you in your crèche during cryo?"

"No." She is one step behind me. "We had to leave all our jewelry outside. In a safe box."

I stop and look at her. "Could anyone have gotten hold of the safe box while you were asleep?"

She shakes her head. "It was password protected. And nothing was missing in the box, so I don't think so."

I nod and continue searching.

In the second to the last row of desks I find a device that looks very much like the one I saw in my Vision. It looks very similar to an old CAD 3D printer, with a solid base and transparent box on the top, only it's lacking the extruder, and there's no sign of filament storage either.

I find the entry slot and then push the pendant key inside. The machine, however, doesn't take it. A third of the chip sticks out of the slot, and I can't push it any farther.

The Moons of Senthia, it doesn't work!

I'm about to take it out, but then Tania leans toward the back of the machine, clicks a button, and the machine buzzes to life. The chip is pulled away from my fingertips and swallowed somewhere inside the device.

After a moment, blue flowing letters appear in the transparent box, floating in the air.

Tell me about a maze run.

Maze run? I glance at Tania then back to the floating letters. "Does that mean anything to you?"

As I say this, a series of spikes appear underneath the blue letters, the red peaks corresponding to the tonality of my voice.

"What is a maze run?" I ask again, my tone lower, but the system picks it up, transforming it into red spikes again.

She doesn't answer but instead crosses her arms on her chest, placing two shaky fingers on her mouth while still looking at the blue words glowing over squiggly lines.

"Tania?"

She takes a deep breath. "It's… it's how Harry and I met, but I don't understand…"

On the screen, her voice transforms into a series of spikes, but these are blue. The moment she stops talking, the spikes stop as well, the blue question still floating in the air.

"Go on…," I whisper.

"I used to be able to just see the files with photos. I don't understand this *thing*. What is this?"

Blue spikes.

"It's voice recognition," I whisper on. "Just talk."

She turns back to the blue glowing words floating in front of her. "Maze run… It was a virtual reality party Brian, a friend of mine, organized. He had just turned twenty-one, and he invited about fifty of his friends, some from his classes, like me, some from his dorm."

Blue spikes dance to the tone of her voice. "Everybody had goggles on, so we didn't really see each other, but we all interacted in the virtual world, each of us with an avatar we chose.

"In reality, it was only a large empty hall, but what we saw in VR was a six-foot-high hedge maze.

"There was a lot of laughter, we could all hear each other and talk to each other, but we couldn't see each other if it didn't correspond to the program. But then, and I think Brian planned it, that was so much like him"—she laughs—"the program changed and it showed a different floor plan of the maze to different people. So you can very well imagine, from one moment to another, we started bumping into one another."

She sighs then.

"That's how I met Harry. We… bumped into one other. We took off our goggles, apologizing until we saw each other for real. And then we stopped talking."

For almost a pass she stays silent.

"It was love at first sight." She turns to me and smiles. "From then on, we always celebrated our maze-run anniversary."

"Hello, my dear." A deep voice sounds from the device.

Tania slowly turns her head to the glass cube, and then she takes a sharp breath, pressing her fingers to her lips.

Instead of the blue floating letters, in the glass cube is a crude recording of a man. He's wearing a white coat and has a silvery beard and hair, deep, dark rings settled under his eyes.

"Harry?" Her voice is a squeaky whisper coming between her fingers. "Can he… can he hear me?" she asks without looking at me.

"I'm afraid not. This is a recording."

She takes another tight breath. "He looks so much older… How is this… possible?" She presses her lips with her fingers again, as if stopping herself from talking.

And I vividly remember the Vision I had when I'd just come to Earth and met Tania the first time. It was the very first Vision of the past I ever had, and it was of the laboratory in the University of Nanotechnology and Innovation, where Harry worked. In that Vision, Harry's lab exploded, only no one was in the lab at the time.

I take a deep breath as the realization slowly surfaces.

Everyone thought that he and his team died then and there, and Tania being heartbroken decided to cryo for one hundred years together with her children.

But, as I assumed, he survived, and it seems he left a message for her to find when she woke up.

I wonder if I should have told her about my Vision in the first place...

"How can this be?" Tania talks through her fingers, the shape of her eyes contorted as she fights tears.

No... I don't think it would have helped...

"I am so happy to talk to you again," Harry says. "I wish we could really talk. A real long conversation like we used to. But this is just for you to hear a long time in the future. I can't even imagine how long." He laughs half-heartedly, looking at the ground.

Tania's lips are trembling and tears stream down her face.

"Tania, shall I... leave?" I ask quietly.

"No!" She lifts her hand. "No, please stay. I need..."

"Of course." And I move an IP behind her, my eyes on Harry.

"You need to believe me, Tania," he starts. "It was the hardest thing I ever did, but I don't think I had any choice."

He takes a breath, then rubs his hands over his face. "Let me start from the beginning; you don't even know what I'm talking about. If you're not sitting, take a seat. It's going to be a while." As he says that, he moves as well, the camera following his motion. He sits on a chair, a desk and a computer screen visible in the projection.

Tania, however, stays standing, even though there are several chairs around. I stay standing too.

"There must be two thousand people on Earth now, if all

the batches went off cryo. I hope you already found the storage of seeds."

"Cryo?" Her hands drop from her mouth. "How does he know about the cryo?" She looks at me but then turns to Harry when he continues.

"I need to tell you about my research. I think it's important, or more precisely, it *will* be important in the future. Your time. Your *now*.

"But before I tell you that, I need to tell you why I am alive." It looks as if he's really looking into Tania's eyes. "Everything is linked to my research, from when the accident happened."

Tania is not moving. She is still as a statue.

"You might remember that I was working on something intriguing. I couldn't tell you then. It was dangerous. Dangerous for you, and our family. But I can tell you now, because"—he shakes his head in thought—"because I believe this is more important than I ever could have imagined.

"In our lab, we have been trying to develop a computer chip that has the same characteristics as the neurological network in the brain. A lot has been done synthetically, networks that work amazingly well, on the verge of true artificial intelligence, learning on their own. But there was one problem. The electrical networks, like any electrical system connected to the grid, is vulnerable to electromagnetic interference. We have been fearing a NEMP might bring the country down, terrorists, state enemies…" He waves his hand in front of his face, a dismissive motion.

"Nuclear electromagnetic pulse! What a bunch of crap!" He puffs and waves his hand once again. "What we should have been afraid of was something larger, something scarier, and also something we had no control of. Our beautiful life-giving star.

"At any rate, our goal was to create a system that would be resistant to NEMPs. Many other groups tried different techniques, like Faraday shielding or force fields around their system. All the groups were in the institute when the accident happened. Accident! I keep calling it an accident." He shakes his head, then looks at Tania. "This wasn't an accident, you understand that, don't you?

"It was a setup, sabotage. They did it on purpose. The Uni committee. The people in power. They hijacked the whole team, transferred us to a new secure location and kept us working so our families would stay safe. I… I had no choice, Tania… I had to obey to keep you safe." He raises his eyes to the camera, looking into Tania's eyes. "But I never expected you would do this."

His voice starts trembling and tears start running down his cheeks, disappearing into his gray beard. "I know how difficult it must have been for all of you to accept my death, but I never expected you would make such a decision. I never thought"—his breath hitches—"that you would decide to stop living! For goodness' sake, Tania. And our children too?" He says this as if he expects her to answer.

But Tania only bows her head in response.

I know she feels the same way as Harry. She told me about it herself.

"I understand it was hard for you, dear, but I knew it would just take time. And it would have! It would have taken time. But you jump-started! You cut the grieving process and went cryo!"

A long break.

"Maybe it worked. But I doubt it. Cryo is like a dream; it passes by with no concept of time.

"In the beginning, I didn't think it was all that bad, you see. I was sad that I could not see you—observe you, if you want to be precise—because I did. I figured in one hundred years, things would continue as normal.

"But then in 2232 the News came. And I knew that meant trouble. I knew there would be no way for two thousand cryo sleepers to be chosen for the Evacuation. You would never make the Voyage.

"And I knew that when you woke up in a hundred years, the Earth, or at least the surface of it, would be dead. So I decided to wait. I decided to stay living as long as I could, until most of the chosen ones were evacuated, so that in the end, I could transfer you—all two thousand of you—to a secure facility where you hopefully could survive the storm and then continue living when Earth was habitable again."

Tania staggers backward at the same time I make the link too.

The mysterious well-meaning transfer manager who saved the cryo people... is Harry.

CHAPTER 47

Earth

"Oh my God!" She looks at me. "It was Harry!" Tania's face is wet with tears, eyelashes clumped together, rimming her dark eyes.

I hug her with one arm, and she leans into me.

There is so much to say, yet no words can do justice. So I just keep her close, hoping this contact will help her, will somehow support her, like it helped me when I needed it.

"If you are listening to me now," Harry continues, "then I know you are alive, and I know it worked. I know that I managed to save you. And it was worth it. All of it.

"I told you that everything is linked to my research," Harry continues, but he strangely avoids looking into the camera. "So, I need to tell you about it because I think this is still a secret, and not many people know about it." He looks at her. "This information will be extremely, extremely valuable, and I hope you can use it for a good cause.

"As I said, many groups in the institute tried to build a system that would mimic a neural network, but my group had a different trajectory altogether. We had something that no EMP could destroy, something that has no silicon, no copper, in fact no metal component at all, and we were extremely successful. We surpassed all the systems made before."

My Senthien curiosity awakens and I am superattentive, eager to receive this new information. *What a source of Visions this would be!*

"At the time, I was ecstatic!" He smiles, looking at the floor, shaking his head. "It was so difficult to keep this from you. But I managed. And that was good." He looks into Tania's eyes and sighs while combing his gray hair. "That probably saved your life. Rick's and Melissa's too."

Oh, this has to be big. *What is it?*

He stands up and starts walking around the room, the camera automatically focusing in the direction of his movement.

All my senses are intent as I look at the back of the white lab coat hanging over Harry's somewhat hunched shoulders.

He turns toward us, rubbing the back of his neck. "Lukasz, you remember him?" Harry swallows hard. "He didn't manage to keep it a secret. It was just too big. He told his girlfriend about it."

Harry looks away, his voice quieter than before. "They told him it was a complication during the birth. But…" Another heavy sigh. "I don't believe it. At the time, I thought it was the truth, but now…" He shakes his head. "Now, looking back, knowing everything that I know… I think they killed her. Because she knew things she shouldn't have. Magda and their newborn baby died."

Tania swallows and presses her lips with her palm, forcefully, trying to fight the tears but failing, and her tears flow freely.

"It was because of this project, Tania. They died because they knew about it."

He looks away. "I think Lukasz figured it out as well. He

never actually told me, but I think he did, otherwise he wouldn't have stayed. He wouldn't have helped me like he did… I guess since he couldn't save his own family, he tried to help mine."

Harry sits down again, his fingers touching each other as if surrounding a transparent sphere, the recording zooming and refocusing on him again.

He's silent for a while, then he continues, his voice different, more authoritative. "Did you know that neurons live for decades, centuries even, unlike any other cell in the body?"

I frown, unable to make an immediate connection.

"I'm sure I told you that many times. It's a unique characteristic. Every cell in the Human body is replaced, skin cells fall off after six weeks, erythrocytes die after four months, all the cells get replaced, but not neurons. Neurons die *only* because the body dies.

"And I was always amazed by that. It's what drove me to the research in the first place."

He stops for a few moments, as if juggling some hidden thoughts.

"People are born with a set of neurons, and many still grow in the first one and a half years of life. But then, with a hundred billion neurons, we continue throughout our lives, and the only thing that happens is that we keep on losing them, more quickly if there is a specific disease, slower if we are healthy. There are no new neurons. But those that are there, those that keep the highway of memories, capabilities and sensitivity, they are there from the start. And most of them live until our death.

"You realize that it makes the neuron the best cell to study. It's not eternal, but with a bit of chemistry, one can use it for research for a very, very long time."

He takes a breath, opens his hands, and looks at his palms as if he's seeing something in them he doesn't want to see. Then he clenches both hands into fists.

"I keep telling myself it wasn't my fault," he says quietly. "I keep saying that I couldn't have done anything. That I was only the chip builder." He's fiddling with something in his fingers. I step closer, hoping to see what it is.

"And I was afraid they would… do something to you if I didn't continue with my work. So I did. And I built something amazing, but… I'm afraid to tell you how because…" He lifts his head up to the camera. "Because I'm afraid you won't see me the same way after I do."

Tania slowly steps forward. "Harry?" she says weakly.

Harry is silent for a long moment, then he stands and walks toward the camera. Automatically, both Tania and I take a step back.

"Our neurological AI system worked so well because"—he sighs heavily—"it was made from neurons themselves."

Neurons?

Harry takes something from his hand and holds up a small, thin chip pulsating slowly from purple to pink.

Oh, the Moons of Senthia!

It's not a chip. It's *the* chip! The APC chip!

Harry *is the one who developed the Mind prototype!*

"When we started the project, we used new neurons from mice and rats. It functioned fairly well but not well enough. The Uni committee wanted more. So… I used a different source."

The next words fall hard as if every breath is a chunk of rock he needs to swallow. "To make our Axon Porting Chip supremely better, we needed a Human." Then he looks into the camera, his eyes on Tania. "I used embryo neurons from abortion clinics."

I stagger backward, my eyes wide. I can't take a breath.

The Mind is made of Human embryo neurons?
The very next moment I am embraced in a purple wind, the Vision and the Void combined, as I watch the past unfold, dreading to see it but unable to turn my gaze away.

A sterile white room. Five people wearing white coats move around, preparing something. In the middle of the room is a strangely shaped chair, and on it sits a young woman.

She is wearing a green shirt that only comes down to her navel, and the chair makes her spread her naked legs uncomfortably wide.

I shiver internally, anxiety crawling up my back.

The young woman is looking at the people walking around her, and she is trembling.

This makes her look even younger.

She keeps looking, hoping to meet their gaze, but they are all focused on their task. Then a woman, an assistant wearing all white, stops next to her and places a hand on the young woman's shoulder. "It will be all right." She smiles.

"I'm afraid," the young woman says.

"The doctor used a local anesthetic. You won't feel a thing."

The young woman's lips tremble, and she looks at the doctor now leaning between her legs.

"Stay with me," the young woman pleads.

"Everything will be done in a few minutes." The assistant's voice is gentle as she takes the young woman's hand and squeezes it softly.

"What is happening?" the young woman asks as she feels movement at her hips.

"Do you feel any pain?" the assistant asks.

The young woman shakes her head, but tears fall down her face nevertheless.

"What is happening?" she asks again.

The assistant looks at the doctor, then at the young woman. "The doctor is performing the procedure. It will only take a minute, sweetheart. Just relax."

Between the girl's legs, blood gushes out, spilling on the white tiled floor. The doctor retracts a bloody metal tool, then drops it next to him into a prepared metal cup, the metallic sound echoes in the room.

"It's finished," the assistant says and smiles, tapping the young woman's hand.

She tries to smile as well.

In the metal cup, in a bloody puddle with bubbles on the edges of the metal tool is a sixty-two-day-old embryo.

Another assistant, a man wearing all white, takes the metal cup and rushes out of the room.

The scene changes in a swing of purple wind, and now I am back in my memory.

I am looking at the hundreds of Zema4 women in their med pods, sleeping peacefully. My gaze falls on their vital signs' screens, and I read the large number at the base: sixty-two.

I look up at the other screens, and the numbers on the bottom that I couldn't figure out when I was there flash large, zooming into my face, their meaning now clear. The number of days of pregnancy.

I am back in the past.

An assistant is carrying the metal cup, hurrying along the corridor. A few drops of blood splatter on the floor as he turns a corner.

He enters a lab and heads straight to a laminator with a scientist already sitting there ready to take the sample.

The assistant leaves, wiping his hands on his lab coat, making a remark about a rugby game.

The scientist turns to the laminar desk and starts her work. She washes the bloody blob with a saline liquid, and as the dark red disappears, the tiny wormlike structure appears, with a large head, miniature arms and legs, and two black dots that would have become eyes.

The person takes a scalpel and cuts away the head. Then using the pincers, she peels off the thin soft tissue of a future skull, revealing the pink brain.

She transfers it to a petri dish and walks to the other side of the lab with the laser slicer.

My legs are shaking and my stomach is crumpling into a tight, rigid ball, but I still stand, held upright by the purple wind, which transfers me to one of my previous Visions.

Dr. Zamnan stares at the holo screen data in front of him. He turns to TA-002 and says, "This will make our production unyielding. Do we have any reserves?"

"No, distinguished Dr. Zamnan. We already used them."

"We need to notify the High Priest. The seeding needs to be increased dramatically if we are to obtain the same level of production. Place all our remaining yield into the Mind."

The scene changes yet again and I am in Boolea. The large dark hall is cold. I am standing behind one of the oval robots, hovering on AG tracks. It's working at the lab bench, delivering round pink samples to the laser slicer. Then it leaves as fast as it came.

I slowly approach the desk as the excruciating realization hits me. I now know what these samples were.

Young embryo brains of the artificially impregnated unconscious Zema4 women, there to provide a yield to a ruling Descendant species, a necessary building block of their supreme AI.

Acid rises up my stomach, pushing through my crumpled throat. I fall on my knees and vomit through my mouth and nose at the same time.

Then all strength leaves me at once, and I fall on the floor.

CHAPTER 48

Earth

It's late evening, and the village is asleep, the forest quiet.

Even the crickets' chirping is gone.

I'm sitting on Tania's bed, my legs pulled up to my body, and I'm holding a bag of ice on the side of my head that met the floor, resting my elbow on my knee.

The cold feels good. I'm glad Earth is back on some technological trajectory. Or at least enough for basic electric appliances, such as an ice maker.

"Here, drink!" says Peter, handing me a cup of steaming liquid.

I put the ice pack on the side table and take the cup. "Thank you, Peter."

"It looks a wee bit better than half an hour ago," he says, then sits next to Tania again.

I nod. "I'll be—" I stop.

Nodding makes me nauseous.

"I will be fine."

I take a careful sip. It's hot and a bit bitter, with some strong herbal flavor. I like it. I take another sip, then look up.

Tania is clutching a steaming cup of her own, sitting at the table, her gaze empty, her face blank. Rick and Melissa are sitting next to her.

J is leaning on the doorframe, looking outside, a mesh of shadow patterns playing on his clothes, warm orange light from within mixing with the cool blue light of the moon.

And Patrick is here as well, sitting on the floor with his knees pulled up with his arms crossed over them. He's leaning his forehead on his crossed forearms, and I can't see his face. At first glance, they all seem calm and composed, but underneath, I read tension.

I look down, my gaze unfocused on the steaming cup.

I already know what I will say.

The decision was there, simmering in the background of my mind despite my wants and needs and egoistic wishes.

I saw it in the white world of Boolea, trapped in the dim lab, watching the little pink tissue samples being sliced and handled.

I heard it in the humming world of tall computer racks in the dark halls of Lorea, with cold metal floors and green blinking lights.

I sensed it as chills crept up my body when I came down the stairs of the 3D algae lake room.

I could almost taste it at Zema4, as the wind whipped my skin, the sand grinding between my teeth.

I felt it. I knew it was there. And yet… I fought it. I didn't want to see it. I closed my eyes, diving back into the transparent little Senthien, blending in and molding with the rest of the blind Uni Descendants, pretending that the world didn't need me, pretending that things would get solved while I looked the other way.

I sigh.

Not anymore.

Not after all that I've seen.

Not after knowing what—no, not after knowing who—the Mind is...

I know what it wanted to tell me. I know why it so desperately tried to communicate while I nonexisted in the Void of the infinite frequencies.

Uni was never perfect and I, of all people, knew that.

But never, until now, did I realize how weak and undignified the basis of the Uni worlds are, how false the reality Zlathars put forth is, and how vicious and malign the path to control the space port has become.

I know what I need to do. I don't know *how* yet... but I know what.

I close my eyes and put the ice pack on my head again. "I have to go back."

"No!" J snaps, his face intense. Even the warm colors of the room can't diminish the visible tension, the fine shadowing around his eyes. "Dora, we just got here. Barely!"

"I know... I know we did, but..." I sigh again. "This is the only way." I look at him, and our eyes lock onto each other.

I know what he's thinking. He *does* see it the same way as I do. I can feel it. But he doesn't want to admit it.

J shakes his head and looks away, crossing his arms on his chest. "No. No, I'm not buying it. There's got to be another way!"

I glance at the others, looking for some feedback—for approval really—but there is none. Worry and confusion are written all over their faces.

"Dora, why do you want to go back?" asks Patrick. "You can't help them. It's too big."

Everyone looks at me. Patrick asked the question everyone wants to hear the answer to.

"Because if I don't, no one else will."

Patrick exhales and looks away.

"Patrick, I'm the only one who has seen it. I know what is happening; no one else does! And I somehow think I was meant to do it. Zema4's people think the same."

"Bullshit!"

I look up at J.

"They made up this story like it's a prophecy, like you *have* to be the one to save them, like you are the special chosen one. And then if you do go back and you die somewhere along the way, no one knowing where your body lies, *they* are going to make yet another story, yet another prophecy, and this time it will be a different chosen one, and they'll pull someone else into their bridle and request salvation." He's louder with every sentence, his emotions getting the better of him. "Why don't they try to save themselves?"

My breath is slow and calm as I answer. "They did try."

"Well, they should try again. And again, and again if it doesn't work!" He's breathing heavily, his chest rising and falling almost uncontrollably.

I understand him. I do. And there is nothing I can tell him that he doesn't already know. He's talked to these people, he knows what they have been through.

But he's rejecting the only solution I see possible.

"I'm sorry you see it that way, J, but my mind is made up."

He looks at me and his face changes. "Don't *we* mean anything to you? Don't *I* mean anything to you?"

I put my feet on the floor and remove the pressure of the

ice pack as I answer, "Of course you do! You mean everything to me!"

"Then show me!"

Silence. Everyone is frozen in this moment of emotional friction, no one is daring to move.

"Because I don't see it…"

He shakes his head, then turns around and leaves, the leaf curtain twirling outward and then slowly settling back down.

For a moment no one talks, then Peter exhales loudly, and the rest unlock from their frozen positions, moving and adjusting in their seats.

I'm not sure what to say. I just know what I need to do. And I don't even know how, but the urge, the certainty is here, as unmistakable as the oxygen we are all breathing.

"Dora, what do you plan to do?" Patrick glances at me sideways. "You realize it only makes sense to go if there is a solid plan."

I nod.

"Otherwise," he continues, "it's a suicide mission."

"I understand."

"So?" Peter shrugs. "Ye better have a plan."

After a few moments of silence, Rick asks, "So do you?"

"No."

A series of exasperated breaths around the room.

"But I know someone I can ask."

They all look at me, and for the first time this evening, I smile. "The Mind."

CHAPTER 49

Earth

My fingers are wrapped around the smooth green bark of the intricately twisted tree making its way around the large brown trunk.

My gaze follows the strangler plant, looking up to the lush crown of the inner tree, where they lace their branches together, then spread as they radiate into the sky, wearing millions of dancing leaves.

And just like the first time I saw it, I think of J.

And me.

This time, however, I see something else, something I didn't notice before. The crown, the lush green foliage, is so dense, so full I can barely see the sky through it. This tree is alive, fully and completely. And the green strangling plant doesn't seem to disturb it at all, despite the many times it wraps around it. Perhaps, then, the green is not the strangler, despite its name. Perhaps they can live together. Or better yet, they can complement each other.

I place my other hand on the brown bark, my amber ring even more beautiful with this dark background. I close my eyes and bow my head slightly, leaning my forehead on the rough but warm brown wood.

Behind me, I hear the sound of twigs crunching under weight.

I quickly turn around, then smile. "How did you find me?"

J doesn't answer my question. Instead, he looks up the tree and says, "This was the place where I finally realized what I needed to do." He looks into my eyes. "When I realized I needed to go to Uni to find you."

"For me, it was the place where I decided to leave Earth… the first time around."

"Hmm…" He touches the smooth green bark. "It seems to be a place people come when they decide to leave Earth."

I look at him, unsure I understand what he means.

"I am sorry I reacted like that yesterday," he says.

I smile and nod, then come closer to him. He takes a lock of my hair to put it behind my shoulder, but then he stops, keeping it between his fingers, looking at it, brushing his thumb along it. "I want to spend time with you, here, in this beautiful, free place. I want to enjoy being with you, just existing together, breathing the same air together, feeling your skin against mine, with no concept of time. I want *us*." He releases the lock of hair and looks at me. "It is selfish. I know it is, I realize that, but… I still wish for it." He smiles, then sighs, gently leaning his forehead onto mine. "I so wish for it, Dora," he whispers, and I feel his words more than he can imagine, because I wish for the same thing too.

I close my eyes, feeling the rising pressure in my throat. *But I know it can't be, because I have seen it. I have seen the truth.*

He moves away and places his warm, rough palms on my cheeks. "So… I'm coming with you."

My eyes are wide open, my lungs suddenly lack air, and I can't seem to take another breath.

"It won't be the life on Earth I want. And probably not as

long as I want either." He coughs out a laugh. "But I will go with you. Because I simply don't want to live my life without you."

I breathe in.

I'm so happy you'll come.

I'm afraid for you.

We'll be able to do more if we are together.

I want you to stay here where you are safe.

I'm so glad I won't lose you again.

I don't want you to go to a world where you might die.

But despite all the thoughts, words fail me, and I only manage to whisper, "J…"

"I know…" He smiles softly, as if he understood my unspoken thoughts. "Wherever you go, I will go too… But hey!" He points a finger at me. "You just need to promise me one thing."

"Yes… anything…"

"We need to have a solid, working plan before we leave. Not just flying off and hoping for good luck, all right?"

I nod, smiling. "Yes, of course. I wouldn't leave without one."

He sighs contentedly, then leans in for a kiss. I melt yet again as my lips touch his, fitting perfectly, molding completely to each other.

We part, then slowly walk back toward the village, still hugging.

"So, about your brilliant plan—"

I need to grin.

"You said you want to… communicate with the Mind, right?"

"Yes. I think I might get some good ideas on how to approach the whole issue."

"I was also thinking," J goes on, "that perhaps some of our

guys might give some interesting thoughts as well. We should do some brainstorming."

Brainstorming. I like that term. "I'm in agreem—" Then I shake my head and smile. "I agree with you."

J squeezes me to him, and we head back to the village.

CHAPTER 50

Earth

I look through the window at the sun setting on the village, golden rays spreading like a fan above the crowns of the trees while the air is filled with a myriad of sounds. People talking, children shouting and playing, birds chirping close by though invisible to the eye.

I fill my lungs with air, savoring it.

It is wonderful here. And not just this life with nature. It's the way people are. The way Jumpers are learning to be as well.

They lost it, or they almost lost it. And then by some miraculous series of events, the chance was given to them once again.

And they learn to treasure it, living with joy in every day, every moment, in peace with the planet they live on, inwardly grateful for their amazing second chance.

I got my second chance too, despite all odds. But now I'm throwing it away.

Is there any other way though? Now that I know what I know?

I close my eyes.

It would be so easy to postpone. To procrastinate. To prolong.

And I would enjoy my beautiful moments on Earth with J,

having everything—I remember my father—*almost* everything I wished for.

Yes. It would be easy to postpone. To prolong.

But what after that? How would I live afterward, knowing I decided to place my happiness before millions of others, deciding my life was more important, more valuable than theirs?

How would I live through hundreds of years knowing I was selfish, knowing I was a coward, knowing I hid away?

I bow my head low.

The part that cracks my heart open in a freezing, bone-numbing way is the fear. The fear that we won't come back. That something will happen to us.

That something will happen to J.

And it instantly raises my heartbeat, accelerates my breathing, pierces a sharp pain through the middle of my body, tensing my muscles.

I close my eyes and breathe out.

Breathe in.

And out.

In.

And out.

I'm not going to get anywhere if just the thought affects me like this. How am I going to go through with it for real?

But I'm afraid.

I am so afraid…

Another breath.

In.

And out.

In. And out.

I bring back my years of training: the dark room, no sounds, the comfortable air of body temperature.

No thoughts.

No judgment.

No regrets.

Just sensing. And existing.

Gradually my heartbeat slows down, the tightened muscles relax, my stomach unknots, my shoulders loosen.

Could I convince him to stay here on Earth?

Is there a way?

I slowly breathe out, then head back to the table.

He won't let me go on my own…

In front of me are pages and pages of handwritten notes from different villagers, thoughts and ideas, anything that could be valuable when planning the trip back to Zema4.

I collect all the papers in one pile, bind the sheets together, and then lock them under my arm and head to the meeting.

I enter the cottage, ducking under the curtain, and step inside the room full of people.

Old Mike wanted to do it in his cottage, but it was way too small for the number of people here, so the newly built gathering hut, the first of the ground huts, serves the purpose.

J is already here.

He's been working during the day, and he said he'd come directly since it was on his way back from the fields. He's talking animatedly to Old Mike and Peter, but as soon as he sees me, he smiles, then stands up and walks toward me.

He kisses me, his lips still in a smile, just like mine, and then takes the pile of papers from my hands.

"Come. Everyone is eager to start."

We walk to an empty spot next to Old Mike. He looks up

at me and smiles; his face withers into a hundred more wrinkles. "Are you ready?"

"Yes, Mike, thank you."

But he shakes his head and says, his voice even more rumbly than before, "No, Dora. Thank *you.*"

He returns to his seat, his face contorting with pain as he sits down.

For a moment I stay focused on Old Mike, but as he relaxes, I refocus and think about what I want to say.

I want to tell them about the options I see. I want to get their thoughts and opinions, find out about the capacity of the tree village, ask about the porting chambers on Zema4…

But I don't.

There is something that has been brewing inside me, boiling on a low fire, something that for a long time went unnoticed. But with everything that has happened in the past few days, these somewhat hidden, inner thoughts got unveiled and are now sitting here on a pedestal in the middle of my consciousness, too obvious for me to ignore anymore, too clear for me not to see it.

I begin. "I never could figure out what was it that made Descendants hate Humans so much. They were outnumbered. They were imprisoned on an inhospitable planet. They couldn't go anywhere. They couldn't fight back. They were, for all intents and purposes, conquered. And after everything, Descendants always kept them. They fed them. They dressed them. After all the hate they apparently had for them, they never obliterated them." I lift my gaze to the group. "They could have. They were certainly capable of doing it. But they didn't. And I never understood that. Until now."

I look down to the freshly sanded wooden floor.

"Zema4 Humans were never a work force. They were never

an aggressor that got defeated and needed to serve its sentence. Zema4 was never a prison."

I take a heavy breath.

"It was a farm."

The room is quiet. I can barely hear people breathing.

I look down at my ring, then I roll it around with my thumb, the amber switching sides to the palm, then the back, then palm again, then back.

I look up at the group. "I want to evacuate Zema4. I want to reach as many Humans in Uni as I can. And bring them here, because Earth is their true home."

A choir of the intake of breaths, all eyes fixed on me. Then they start looking at each other, nodding at the same time.

One person says, "Dora Dana Dasnan."

Someone else repeats it. Within moments, everyone is saying my name, and though I don't understand why, it feels like an impenetrable wall, a support, a backup, a pillar for my cause, from a group of like-minded people.

And for the first time, the fear I always felt—the fear of standing out, of being noticed, of being discovered—is now facing a new opposing emotion: rebellion.

It's been three hours, and I'm still answering questions about my experiences with the Mind, about the Boolean Institute, about Harry's message. They have all heard it before—the news spread as fast as portation between two neighboring planets—but they wanted to hear it from me.

I'm getting tired now. It's not just the talking, it's the emotional drain this has caused me. Yet I'm careful none of my emotional exhaustion is obvious.

"How many porting chambers are there?" I ask the Zema4 soldier in the front row.

"In D53?"

"No, on Zema4 in general."

"Five to six in each city, so I'd say between five and six hundred. These are for passengers. I don't know how many were hidden from us though, the chambers for food, merchandise and robotics."

"That's fine. I can find that out. The Mind can use any chamber, independent of what it was designed for. In fact, we would aim for freight chambers. We could port a lot more than a hundred people in one load, maybe even a thousand."

"How many people are on Zema4?" asks Tony.

"About four million," answers Rebecca.

"And how many should we expect and when?" Tony asks, looking at me.

"How many can you handle per day?"

Tony shrugs, but before he answers, Mike jumps in. "You just keep sending, we'll… find a solution on our end."

"So, how *will* you send them back?" asks Frank. "How do you know the Mind will do what you want it to do? You can't control it."

"You are correct, Frank. I can't control it. But from the experience I have had with it, there is a very high probability the Mind will continue porting Humans to Old Earth. I also want to have several sessions into the Void. I will use them to communicate with the Mind, get some of our questions answered, and ask for suggestions. I also want to check if—"

At that moment, a wind blows into the room, moving the fabric around my feet. I look at the door.

Monica is standing there, her hand holding the curtain open.

Her eyes are fixed on me; she's not seeing anyone else. She lets go of the curtain, creating another gush of air, and then walks toward me, her steps quick and deliberate.

J stands up and positions himself in front of me. "Monica? Do you want to contribute to the discussion?"

She stops in front of him, puzzled, as if he just materialized in front of her.

Next moment, she quickly loops around him, and before he manages to react, she grabs my hand.

"So it's true," she whispers to herself, looking at my ring.

A nauseous Vision creeps from the sides, and it's not the first time it appeared. I sensed it before. I fought it before. And I can feel it, the slight sense of an oncoming future that brings chaos, disaster, and despair.

I fight it again.

I need to stay here.

I need to be focused.

I can't lose myself in the Vision now.

"Monica," says Mike, his voice soft but authoritative. "Why are you doing this? This is not good for you."

She turns her head toward Mike, but it's as if she's looking through him. "You don't know me, old man. You don't know anything about me," she whispers.

She drops my hand and looks at J. "You've broken many promises, stepped over many vows, including our marriage. But let me tell you one thing, Jonathan, one thing you will not be able to do. One thing you won't be able to break. One thing I know will keep you here."

She puts her hands on her lower belly. "You will never be able to leave your child. I am pregnant with your baby."

As she says that, the Vision sweeps over me, my eyes black

out, and I see the terrible yet at the same time beautiful scene unfolding in front of me.

A hairless, wet, and slippery baby, its face wrinkled and red. It wails and shakes as it's handed over to Monica.

She is covered in sweat. Her red hair hangs down in wet ropes, her face exhausted, lips colorless, eyes teary. She reaches out and smiles the most beautiful, blissful smile as she cradles the baby in her arms.

She looks up. "It's a boy..." Her voice is broken and weak.

Then J kneels next to her, tears in his eyes as well, as he hugs them, one arm over Monica's shoulder, the other over the wrapped-up baby.

"He is beautiful," he says, then closes his eyes, leaning his forehead on the top of her hair. "Thank you, Monica. It's the most precious gift you could have given us."

She closes her eyes. "It was... worth it..."

EPILOGUE

J and I are sitting next to a small fire.

A few people wanted to join us, but J asked them to leave.

Our shoulders are touching, and he keeps my hands in his, stroking them.

"Are you sure, Dora?"

I nod. "I saw it, J."

He sighs, then hugs me and squeezes me close to him. "I'm so sorry, Dora… I am so sorry."

I lean my head onto his chest, feeling surprisingly peaceful. *He will stay here. He will stay safe.*

"Don't be sorry, J. You wanted a child for so long. It is"—I need to swallow—"it is wonderful news."

"But I wish"—his voice breaks—"I wish it was with you."

I close my eyes. *Me too.*

We are hugging, cuddled next to the fire, sparks cracking every now and then, spurting outside the large metal bowl.

"I don't want you to go alone." He pulls away from me so that he can look at me. "I need to be with you. I don't ever want to lose you again."

I lift up my ring hand and stroke his cheek. "I know."

"But you won't let me come with you, will you?"

I sit up straight, moving a bit away from him. "My father

told me that there is not one thing he would not do for me. He said that what it brings—having a child of your own—is something no one can contemplate, and no one can be told what it really means until the child comes. The first time you see it, feel it, truly understand it, is once you hold your baby in your arms. And it is an experience he would never want to change, no matter the cost."

I look into J's eyes. "I know what's behind your thoughts, J. I understand you completely. But I love you. And if this is really like my father says, then it's something I never want to take away from you. It's"—I remember J's words from my Vision—"the most precious gift there is."

He looks down at the ground.

He knows.

He understands.

And he will stay here.

"Promise me something," he says, looking at the fire, the orange flames licking the black of his irises.

"Anything."

He looks at me, his eyes intense on mine. "You need to promise me that you will come back."

"I promise," I say without pause.

So he wouldn't know I was lying.

GLOSSARY

APC chips: Axon Porting Chips. Building blocks of the Mind.

Airing channels: The shafts and tubes for oxygen transport from oxygen-producing plants.

AP rooms: Access Point rooms/station in Lorea—coding, developing, and data access stations for Loreans; limited to Lorea only.

Ascent: Zlathar-proclaimed annual event for Zema4 citizens where roles and tasks for young men and women turning twenty-six are decided.

AirTran: A monorail around Senthien cities.

Anas: Descendant species designed and specialized in medical care and intervention.

Boolean Institute: A large research construction built on M639 where Booleans live and perform their research.

BD75: A BD robot used for repetitive tasks on Lorea's servers.

BD308: A BD used for combat, surveillance, and joined work with Brookonians.

Belthomians: Descendant species designed and specialized in building and maintaining mechanical groundwork of Uni planets.

Brookonians: Descendant species designed and trained for military operations, conflict, and surveilling Zema4 Human citizens.

Booleans: Descendant species designed and specialized in performing biological scientific research and genetic experiments.

Cryo crèches: Pre-ev def. stations for cryopreservation.

DC Hall: Data Center Hall. Centers for specific data research, mainly used by Senthiens.

DRP: Direction Route Path. Map overlaid on ONC view to provide guidance.

Ev: Evacuation. Several decades of evacuating people from Earth after the News.

E-fitness Hall: Station with a large number tech devices aimed to strengthen the muscle mass of Descendants living on low-gravity planets and moons.

Flexile IP skin protectors: Skin shields Descendants use when engaged in interactive coupling to diminish any physical sensation.

Food recycling machine: Machines producing food bars consisting of necessary nutrients.

General classes: Zlathar audited information on current economic, social, and technological state of Uni worlds for all new Descendant students.

History Re-cap classes: Zlathar audited information on pre-ev time given to all new Descendant students.

IPS: Information Point Station. At public areas, a station point to access general types of information.

IP: Interpersonal space. Allowed distance between two Descendant individuals.

IC Hall: Interactive Coupling Hall. Stations where Descendants engage in intercourse, usually shortly after a Rejuvenation cycle.

Interpersonal coupling: Intercourse between Descendant people using flexile IP protectors; usually, between the same species.

ID scan: Identity scan, can be based on palm skin recognition, DNA, voice pattern, iris color, or spectrometry of breath molecules.

Jacobsons: Descendant species designed and specialized for data, transportation, and logistics.

KCFC: Krebs Cycle Fuel Cell. A microscopical device to produce energy based on biological principles of Krebs Cycle in living cells.

Lorea: The home planet of Loreans.

Loreans: Descendant species designed and specialized for building and maintaining the Mind, robotics, information technology, and overall Uni AI systems.

Med pods: Medical pods. Stationary crèches for health and medical purposes.

Mag-tracks: A transport path using magnetism for propelling the vehicle.

Mag Rail (Hub): Transportation for Belthomians.

Musalla nave: A large hall in general religion church buildings of Zema4.

M34: A garbage disposal and storage planet; an uninhabitable planet, M34 was purposefully not terraformed to be able to support life.

Nuclear micro generators: A small device using a nuclear chain reaction to produce power.

Nanoprobes: Nano-size devices integrated in the bodies of all Descendant species, enhancing their health and memory, enabling communication and other functions.

The News: 2232—The year when scientists discovered that Earth will change her magnetic poles within a few decades, coinciding with the violent solar storms periods; in effect, end of life on Earth.

NEMP: Nuclear electromagnetic pulse. Electromagnetic disturbance as a result of a nuclear explosion; a variant is the high altitude nuclear EMP (HEMP), which produces a secondary pulse due to particle interactions with Earth's atmosphere and magnetic field.

ONC: Optic Nerve Cam. A miniature camera installed and connected to optic nerves of all Descendants, it can zoom, record, and augment images perceived at the optic nerve; it can project any kind of visual graphic information from nanoprobes.

OC power plants: Oxygen Combustion power plant. Industrial facility to produce oxygen on some of the Uni planets and moons.

Office of Progeny: A governmental structure trusted to control the number of new Descendants based on the current need.

Porting field resonator: Technology to enable teleportation.

Pre-ev: Pre-evacuation. Events that happened before Evacuation.

Principle: Elected or appointed executive head of cities and districts on Zema4.

Rec-hibe stage: Enhanced brain recovery and recuperation after the mind has received a large amount of data, trained to and used mainly by Senthiens.

RT on Mind: Repetitive tasks for maintaining the Mind.

Skinsuit: A full-body suit for citizens of Uni.

Skinsuit Recycling Hall: Hall for recycling the used skinsuits.

Sol-LED: Solar light LED torch, pre-ev time.

Seedships: Spaceships built to transport Voyagers, people who were recruited to leave Earth and save Humanity.

Seekers: A group of Descendants, mainly Senthiens, who are looking for the truth.

Senthia: The home planet of Senthiens.

Sky-road maps: Pre-ev def. sky roads for A-drones.

Scramblers: Pre-ev def. Diseased people affected by a strong debilitating disease caused by a newly developed drug.

Stadtrat: A house of a municipal body having legislative and administrative powers on Zema4.

Senthiens: Descendant species gen-designed for precognition of future events that they are obliged to report to high Zlathar council.

TAE: Tympanic Audio Enhancers. Miniature device installed in the middle ear to enhance audio signals.

UNI: Descendants planets and moons spanning several neighboring galaxies, connected with portation; pre-Ev def: University of Nanotechnology and Innovation.

Voyage: Travel of Seedships to other planets and moons that can be terraformed and colonized.

Void: Place of infinite frequencies where Mind coexists.

VR-08: High-carb food bar produced by food replicators; diff. A code word between Dora and Maswan for high alert.

Vev-3: A low-carb, high-protein meal produced by a food replicator.

Watch-line: Pre-ev def. Thin, wearable computer in form of a bracelet, devised for communication, data access, biomonitoring, and global-positioning system.

Zlatharing: The home planet of Zlathars.

Zlathars: Leading Descendant species. Official roles: leading Descendants to obtain the most efficient, productive, and peaceful society. Effective role: controlling thoughts, memory, and behavior of all Descendant species.

ACKNOWLEDGMENTS

I am eternally grateful to my family. They are my stronghold, my harbor, a place I can let my creativity fly free. I would never be able to write as I do without my three wonderful boys.

Additionally, to my husband, thank you for being my in-house editor, for noticing my plot errors and for finding my embarrassing typos. I still think this could be one of your future careers :)

To my mom and dad, for constant support and love. I promise I will translate my books for you soon. I love you!

An enormous Thank You to my sister IL, Karin Brown, my loyal beta reader who gave me invaluable comments and first-draft feedback. It helped me shape up the story as you see it now.

To my darling friend on the other side of the world, Jade Phipps, for being my beta reader and a fan of *The Mind* long before it had its final shape. I would write books even if you were my only reader :)

To Deranged Doctor Design team for making the most awesome cover ever. I love it!

To Streetlight Graphics, thank you so much! You did such a wonderful job formatting my book!

To my editors Lisa Gilliam for copy-editing, and Victory Editing team for proof-reading *The Mind*.

And finally, to my readers, thank you! I write books because I love it, but I am truly grateful to be able to share my imagination world with you.

ABOUT THE AUTHOR

Tara Jade Brown lives in Switzerland with her husband, two sons, two cats, and a dog. Before becoming a full-time writer, she worked as a neuroscientist, an entrepreneur, and a marketing manager. Her works include her debut novel *The Senthien* (the first book in the Descendants of Earth trilogy), *Swift Escape*, *The Mind,* and a few short stories: *Dante's 9*, *Forbidden*, and *Far Away.* To find out more, please go to www.tarajadebrown.com.

9 783952 494639